WITH FRIENDS LIKE THESE

WITH FRIENDS LIKE THESE

A Novel

ALISSA LEE

EMILY BESTLER BOOKS

ATRIA

New York Amsterdam/Antwerp London
Toronto Sydney/Melbourne New Delhi

EMILY BESTLER BOOKS

ATRIA

An Imprint of Simon & Schuster, LLC
1230 Avenue of the Americas
New York, NY 10020

For more than 100 years, Simon & Schuster has championed authors and the stories they create. By respecting the copyright of an author's intellectual property, you enable Simon & Schuster and the author to continue publishing exceptional books for years to come. We thank you for supporting the author's copyright by purchasing an authorized edition of this book.

No amount of this book may be reproduced or stored in any format, nor may it be uploaded to any website, database, language-learning model, or other repository, retrieval, or artificial intelligence system without express permission. All rights reserved. Inquiries may be directed to Simon & Schuster, 1230 Avenue of the Americas, New York, NY 10020 or permissions@simonandschuster.com.

This book is a work of fiction. Any references to historical events, real people, or real places are used fictitiously. Other names, characters, places, and events are products of the author's imagination, and any resemblance to actual events or places or persons, living or dead, is entirely coincidental.

Copyright © 2025 by Alissa Lee

All rights reserved, including the right to reproduce this book or portions thereof in any form whatsoever. For information, address Atria Books Subsidiary Rights Department, 1230 Avenue of the Americas, New York, NY 10020.

First Emily Bestler Books/Atria Books hardcover edition November 2025

EMILY BESTLER BOOKS/ATRIA BOOKS and colophon are trademarks of Simon & Schuster, LLC

Simon & Schuster strongly believes in freedom of expression and stands against censorship in all its forms. For more information, visit BooksBelong.com.

For information about special discounts for bulk purchases, please contact Simon & Schuster Special Sales at 1-866-506-1949 or business@simonandschuster.com.

The Simon & Schuster Speakers Bureau can bring authors to your live event. For more information or to book an event, contact the Simon & Schuster Speakers Bureau at 1-866-248-3049 or visit our website at www.simonspeakers.com.

Manufactured in the United States of America

1 3 5 7 9 10 8 6 4 2

Library of Congress Cataloging-in-Publication Data has been applied for.

ISBN 978-1-6680-9400-6
ISBN 978-1-6680-9402-0 (ebook)

To my mother, the fiercest warrior I know

1

NOTHING interesting ever happens in January, which is why January makes sense for killing. I can't remember now who came up with that haunting sentiment—most likely it was Wesley, whom I can still picture teetering barefoot on the back of the threadbare sofa in our fifth-floor common room, practicing her Latin oration with such campy enthusiasm we would be rolling on the floor—but memory's funny that way. The line between what's real and what we want to be real becomes more porous with age. The truth is that any of us could've said it—that was how my college roommates Allie, Bee, Dina, Wesley, Claudine, and I saw the world back then, when January in Cambridge was cold and dead, two weeks of reading period and long days spent pretending not to care that our worth was so easily summed up in a handful of letter grades.

I always assumed the eccentric Harvard tradition we carried with us after graduation would peter out in the years that followed, a casualty of frenetic schedules, geography, or common sense. None of us imagined we'd drag it with us for two decades, across states and countries, through marriages, births, and deaths—especially when we grew into jobs, families, and reputations that couldn't be put on hold for a game. But it makes a certain sense now. We made a pact on the eve of graduation to live unconditionally, and the Circus, as we affectionately called it, was how we made good on that promise. It made us feel powerful in ways our everyday lives didn't. It was a secret that reminded us of who we were and the history we shared. And it was the tether that helped us find our way back to one another year after year, when the rough seas of circumstance might have otherwise scattered us apart.

In the three years since that last round of the Circus, I've come to view life as a series of tiny, seemingly unimportant decisions. The catch is that you never really know, even in hindsight, which ones matter in the end. Don't get me wrong—I still beat myself up over the choices we made and rummage through memories of that time in a desperate search for a single fatal decision. On sunnier days, I think it could've been greed or just bad luck that sank us. But I suspect our fundamental misstep was simple: we were told at an early age we were special, and somewhere along the way we began to believe it.

The place to start, I suppose, is the night of Fabby's gallery opening, which was the first indication that something was very wrong. It was a week before Christmas and I was intent on arriving early as a show of gratitude to Fabby, an older photographer who had been good to me. She had thrown me part-time work as one of her assistants and insisted I keep shooting, even though my photo series on women in invisible jobs was going nowhere. I was always grateful to have Coulter by my side at these arty parties, as he called them— he was a clever conversationalist, equally at ease with celebrities and art history students—but he still hadn't come home and wasn't answering my texts when we were due to leave. He was inundated at work after his front-of-house manager quit three weeks before; the stress had driven him to smoking again. But his prolonged funk was understandable, really. Neither of us imagined he would take over his family's restaurant when his uncle passed or that his detour from travel writing would stretch into a six-year odyssey.

Thirty minutes later, I found myself clopping down Tenth Avenue in too-tall heels, a cold drizzle undoing my hasty blow-dry. I had just turned onto the side street where the gallery lived when I welled up with dread at the prospect of facing a den of art-world insiders alone.

Under the thin protection of a restaurant awning, I yanked off my gloves to text my college roommate Dina, imploring her to save me. She taught at Harvard four days a week and spent her weekends in Manhattan. I figured she would be riding the train back to the city after wrapping up her classes for the week, and the promise of free champagne wouldn't hurt. I was about to slip my phone back in my hip pocket when a cab shot out of nowhere, honking obnoxiously at a man crossing diagonally up ahead.

That's when I saw her.

A woman stood beneath the steel-pipe scaffolding across the street. Her figure was slight, her gray belted coat almost baggy. Blond hair tumbled past her shoulders. I sensed a skittishness—like a doe that would dart away the second I moved—but there was something familiar in the way she was standing. The hand in her pocket, the sharp bend at her elbow, the dropped hip. She was staring at me like she knew me.

I stood perfectly still. As a photographer in a city where the wildlife is temperamental, I had my phone ready, but I managed only one shot before she bolted toward Tenth, leaving me dumbfounded on the sidewalk.

When my fog dissipated, I zoomed in on the hazy image.

It was Claudine, the roommate who shattered our lives all those years ago.

The light in her eyes was undimmed by the years that had faded the rest of us. Incredibly, she looked the same as she had the day I first met her in the freshman dining hall. Tiny—barely size two, which made her easy to underestimate—but one of the most remarkable people I'd ever known. A free spirit, an artist, and a romantic for whom ancient Greek legends were as real as whatever was on the news that day. The perfect foil for the rest of us, who were too concerned with where we were headed and how fast we could get there. How many times would we be walking somewhere, only to discover Claudine had disappeared? We'd turn back to find her crouching down, entranced by a daffodil or a chubby-cheeked squirrel, or craning up to take in a night sky crammed with stars, and all we could do was stop and marvel beside her.

She still haunted my dreams, a queen parading around the Winthrop House courtyard on the shoulders of two senior boys, her flaxen hair glinting in the winter sun and her face lit up with a beatific smile.

I should've been thrilled to see her, but the sight of Claudine that night on the street was both electrifying and unnerving. My imagination had to be acting up; the stress of my uncertain livelihood and the strain of a mortgage Coulter and I could barely cover were catching up with me. Or perhaps it was the guilt that still plagued me over what happened all those years ago.

I remember thinking of the Fitzgerald quote Dina liked to throw around: the test of intelligence is the ability to hold two opposing ideas in your head and still function, or something like that, but the thought only added to my alarm. The woman I had seen was my college roommate Claudine. I was sure of it. And yet that was impossible because I also knew with absolute certainty—for I was with her on that terrible day twenty-three years ago—that Claudine was dead.

2

I WAS slinking around the edges of Fabby's reception, pretending to contemplate the photographs lining the stark white space, but I was more than a little spooked by the sight of Claudine. Why would she haunt me now, years after her death? Was this a warning, administered on the eve of another round of the Circus—our twentieth—that my roommates and I had been tempting fate for too long? To keep Claudine's memory alive was one of the primary reasons why we played on, but seeing her now—with that hollow-eyed look—was a searing reminder of her death and the part we had played in it. I'd grown increasingly uneasy with the Circus in recent years, but now I felt like our good intentions in honoring her or even atoning for our mistakes were misplaced, and instead something dangerous lay in store if we continued down this path.

I was in line at the bar, swimming in utter confusion, when Dina appeared so suddenly I jumped back, knocking into the fashionable couple behind me. After offering up a harried apology, I turned back to Dina, her presence filling me with warm relief. Her flat-ironed-straight black hair was pushed behind her ears, flattering her dark eyes, and she was unapologetically herself in a neon pink plaid blazer with matching pants. Dina always understood. She would help me make sense of what I'd seen.

We wended our way around the gallery, taking in Fabby's pieces in their prescribed order. Dina could tell I was distracted; she was watching me with curious interest. Claudine's name was stuck in my throat, but I didn't know how to broach a subject we had locked away, an unspoken agreement that old wounds were better left alone. So I rambled on nervously and asked about the freshman philosophy seminar she was teaching. We talked about the *Times* article naming Bee, the Manhattan DA, as a real contender in what was shaping up to be an expensive mayoral race, then moved on to Wesley and her father's ongoing threats to claw back her trust fund unless she could convince him she had finally jettisoned her less healthy habits.

We were standing in front of Fabby's shot of a spectral jungle at night, overlaid with the words *nothing is what it seems* in a pink neon scrawl, when I couldn't hold my tongue any longer. I still couldn't summon the courage to tell her what I'd seen, so I opted for a lateral approach.

"I can't play," I said more loudly than intended, and we both glanced around to make sure we weren't being overheard. We weren't in the habit of trotting out the Circus in public—we were careful to cordon off its messiness from real life.

"Coulter finally put his foot down?" Dina whispered with genuine surprise as we steered through the crowd toward the next photograph. It would've been easy to let her think my husband was the catalyst, given how much he loathed the Circus, and my roommates because of it. But there was enough bad blood between Coulter and Dina, so I found myself in the unexpected position of arguing his side.

"No, it's common sense," I whispered back. "The world is completely different from when we started. We can't justify what we do when there's a mass shooting every other day."

Dina refused to look at me as we drifted onward—her way of saying she didn't agree.

"And we're not exactly young anymore," I added.

We found ourselves standing shoulder to shoulder in front of Fabby's signature piece: a vast, empty desert at dusk with the words *what if this is all there is* blazing brightly over the dry, cracked earth. I'd seen smaller versions of these pieces in the studio, but I still didn't like the way this one was trying to provoke me, playing the denuded earth off the urgent desire we all feel to live more fully.

"We've been lucky to get by with a few scrapes," I whispered. I didn't need to remind her how Bee had broken her leg three years ago after leaping off the roof of Wesley's summerhouse, or how hard we'd worked to get Dina's charge for breaking and entering dropped a few years before that. "You know it's only a matter of time before our luck runs out."

"Sara, we've been at this for almost twenty years," she said, then leaned in. "Have you said anything to Wesley?"

After Claudine, Wesley had always been the most zealous about the Circus. She was the most daring of us, at times bordering on cavalier, and Dina insisted this was because Wesley was the heir to a seed fortune on her mother's side and could afford to be this way. I knew she was more complicated than that. Wesley had followed her father into the brotherhood of orthopedics, but abhorred exercise, drank too much, and did a little blow on the side. She was exceptionally generous with her resources and time—her guest bedroom was perpetually occupied by old friends and new, and I think all of us owed our first jobs out of college to the introductions Wesley made for us. At the same time, she despised liars and cheats and could be evasive and hard to pin down. She ran with an artsy crowd and had friends everywhere, but I'd be surprised if more than one or two people outside our college roommate group knew the real Wesley: the girl who despite (or because of) her name and money was still a kid determined to prove her worth.

"No, not yet," I said.

"You know she's planned some big surprise to commemorate our twentieth."

"A surprise? What kind?"

"She wouldn't say." Dina shrugged. "But what's this really about? What's changed?"

I knew I wasn't making sense; I figured Dina could handle the truth.

"I saw Claudine."

She didn't answer, but I felt the hitch in her breath.

"I did. I swear."

"We both know that's impossible."

"She was outside. On the corner of Twenty-First and Tenth."

"I know you still feel like her death was your fault. It wasn't."

"It was her."

"Or a figment of your subconscious."

Dina had always been in my corner, but as a tenure-track philosopher, logic was her profession.

"Should I talk to Allie or Bee first? I mean, before I tell Wesley."

Dina shook her head.

"It won't matter," she said. "They're all in. Bee can't resist a chance to prove herself, even with the mayor's race heating up. And we both know Allie's a pleaser—if Wesley or Bee even look at her the wrong way, she'll move mountains to justify playing."

Dina was right about Allie, who was our peacemaker, but I wasn't so sure about Bee. She was our Golden Girl, a nickname Wesley gave her senior year after Bee was crowned captain of the varsity soccer team and a finalist for the Rhodes in the same week. She'd always had an uncanny ability to forge real connections with people of all stripes and had fought tougher odds than most, becoming the first in her family to go not only to college but to law school too. Now she was the Manhattan DA with her sights trained on Gracie Mansion. I couldn't imagine her risking her current role or her shot at being mayor to indulge in a college tradition that wasn't aging well.

"But rules are rules," Dina said. "If this is really what you want, then we're done. Game over."

The five of us had agreed after graduation: the game only worked if we were all in. We'd taken turns wobbling over the years, but this would be the first full-blown mutiny.

Dina crossed her arms over her chest, pretending to study Fabby's work, but I caught a glimmer of disappointment beneath her coolheaded veneer. Was she actually hoping to play? It didn't make sense.

Dina had been chasing tenure at our alma mater for as long as I'd known her, and this was her year. The committee would be reviewing her file any day. Still, I could tell she was struggling with my decision, even if she was doing her best to hide it.

When we finished our champagne and found ourselves on the sidewalk, Dina asked, "What if this is all there is?"

I'd had too much free booze on an empty stomach, so I assumed she was making fun of the artifice of parties like this one or pressuring me into playing. But the question grated on me. I'd hoped by now I would have found my footing in the photography world, not just because the women I'd photographed deserved a voice, but because I was dying to live up to Fabby's charge of creating work that mattered. And perhaps I still believed that there was a certain selflessness, or at least a decency, in making art—an idea that Claudine had impressed upon me sophomore year when she dragged me to a photography exhibit in Boston a few days before finals. We walked through ten stunning black and whites that captured Americans of Japanese descent closing up shops, crammed together in lines, standing in the doorways of horse stalls where they were imprisoned. My anger bloomed as I took in each photo, but what mesmerized me was the range captured in each image: the distress, the bewilderment, the struggle to maintain dignity. I'd had no idea a photograph could make me feel so much.

Despite having little formal training in art, Claudine was a star in the Visual Studies department even then, and I was impressed by how much she intuited about technique and composition. As we left the exhibit, I asked her how the photographer had accomplished so much with each shot, and she looked at me as if the answer was the most obvious thing in the world. To this day, I still remember her exact words: "If there's an equality on both sides of the frame, the artist and viewer can meet and be drawn in to help each other make the world a better place."

Dina stifled a yawn. It was too late to explain these tangled-up hopes, and I was about to tell Dina this when I realized she was quoting Fabby's work. *What if this is all there is?*

"I'm thinking of taking the commercial job," I said instead.

She looked at me like I'd lost it.

"You can't."

"Why not?"

"Your photographic talent is wasted on pink razors and Cheez Whiz."

"Their dental is pretty comprehensive."

"You know I'm all for good hygiene," she said. "Just not at the cost of your sanity."

"Who needs sanity when you have a steady paycheck?"

Dina frowned. She knew I wasn't good with conflict, but she refused to let me hide.

"Sara, what's going on?" she asked.

How could I tell her about the rumor Bee had shared a few weeks earlier? The one about the Middlesex County DA reopening cold cases and taking a special interest in Claudine's death. Neither Bee nor I had the faintest idea why he would revisit something that happened two decades ago, but the prospect that old accusations could resurface tormented me. It was bad enough that the press might catch wind of our game, but some overachieving reporter might dig up our history and uncover the circumstances of how Claudine died—a combination that none of us would survive.

The day after that conversation, I found a listing for a commercial photography job. Defense lawyers didn't come cheap.

"No, nothing," I said. "I've been feeling a little lost, I guess. Maybe it's a good time to switch things up. Get a real job."

"This is because you saw Claudine."

"No. Maybe. I don't know."

"Seeing her wasn't a portent of impending doom or anything."

"You don't know that."

She tilted her head, acknowledging but not conceding.

"Sara, nothing bad is going to happen," she said with such conviction that I believed her.

"Thanks for rescuing me," I said.

"Not hard when there's free Veuve," Dina said and stiffened as usual when I hugged her tightly.

"See you on the twenty-seventh," she called over her shoulder as she trotted off. "Unless you're dropping the bomb before that?"

I held my hands up as she disappeared around the corner. Our annual dinner—the night my college roommates and I always got together to plan the next round of the Circus—was ten days away and as good a time as any to deliver the news, since we'd all be together. But I dreaded the firing line, especially if Dina wasn't going to back me up.

I stood in front of the gallery, Fabby's signature work drawing me in.

What if this is all there is?

The words reminded me of a passionate promise my college roommates and I made decades ago on a Montauk beach to live our lives unconditionally. How I envied the idealism of our younger selves, when our futures were a blank canvas, undefined and infinite, when we thought there was nobility in living according to our own priorities, ignorant of the compromises we would make.

I had assumed Fabby was exhorting us to embrace life in full, which would be in line with the good energy she exuded and her frequent admonitions that every day should be filled with joy, but seeing Claudine had rattled me. I was reminded of the questions Claudine had put to me as part of another game she liked to play when we were tucked into bed late at night as roommates sophomore year. We would take turns posing either/or questions to each other. It would start out innocently—desert or forest, ketchup or mayo, morning or late afternoon—but the choices soon grew more demanding, the stakes escalating. Mine were always too vanilla, but hers hit hard. Money or passion? Career or friendship? A short, bright life or a long, humble one? I'd been impressed that she had spent time thinking about such weighty considerations when I was still preoccupied with shallower pursuits like grades and crushes and what I was going to wear. But her either/or game was how we came to know each other so well in a short period of time; it was a way of rooting around in the other's mind and peering into her soul.

    I still didn't have a good answer to Fabby's question, but the evening had made me more attuned to the fragility of our existence. Maybe I'd been wrong about Fabby's intention. Maybe her work wasn't encouraging us, but sounding an alarm. The thought troubled me, filling me with an overwhelming sense of foreboding that everything I had, everything that mattered—the good history, the people I leaned on, the comfort I took in knowing I wasn't alone—could vanish in a second.

3

I PANTED up the stairs to our fifth-floor apartment, blaming my wobbly state less on free-flowing champagne and too-tall heels and more on the evening's strange turns. Dina had shaken my confidence. Was Claudine a product of my imagination running wild? It was only as I was climbing the last flight that I remembered the picture on my phone. Proof of what I had seen.

Unlocking the apartment door, I jumped back.

"God, you scared me," I said with a hand on my chest.

My barefoot husband stood in the entryway, wearing the wild-eyed look of someone who hadn't slept in weeks, which wasn't far from the truth due to the hours he'd been working at Sempre, the family restaurant he took over when his Uncle Chuck died. His gray T-shirt and jeans were dusted white, evidence he'd been mucking around in the kitchen. Coulter claimed cooking calmed him, but I knew to keep my distance when the santoku and whetstone came out.

"Why didn't you call?" he asked, running a hand through his shaggy brown hair. I'd left home in a hurry, annoyed that he'd made me late for Fabby's party. Once I found Dina, I'd been too preoccupied to notice the missed calls and unanswered texts on my phone.

"Coulter, I'm sorry," I said as I put the phone back into my pocket. "I was distracted. I didn't mean to make you worry."

There was nothing to be gained by telling him I'd been with Dina.

He slumped against the wall with a restless disorientation I couldn't place. Hanging my black leather jacket on the accordion rack next to the hallway table, I noticed the blue-and-white ashtray was askew. Coulter had stolen it years ago from a ritzy Paris hotel where we scraped together enough for cocktails in a plush velvet bar and vowed to return as guests one day. I lined up corners until the edges were straight.

"Sara, come with me," he said.

The light was on in our bedroom at the end of the hallway. *We could both use a good night's sleep*, I thought, but Coulter stopped short in the archway to our small living room. It took me a moment or two to understand what I was seeing.

There was a gaping hole in the ceiling by the window. The overstuffed green couch and the thick-legged wooden coffee table, cast-offs from Coulter's mother, were just as they had been when I left earlier this evening, but a giant slab of drywall had crushed Coulter's Swedish reading chair, a Craigslist prize bought off an elderly woman who gave it to him for a steal because he appreciated its worth. Now its wooden bones poked through torn sheepskin. The brass reading lamp jutted out from the dusty mass like a mangled leg.

"I was sitting there right before," he said, his voice faltering.

Nuggets of plaster littered the floor. White dust blanketed the couch, the coffee table, and the beige rug; I now understood why his gray T-shirt and jeans were dusted white. My eyes swept over the books on the shelves flanking the fireplace—stories I'd adored as a kid, each first edition a prize won at auction or hunted down through dealers with an ear to the ground. I didn't exhale until my eyes landed on the four books I treasured most: the three my mother gave to me when I turned eleven, twelve, and thirteen, and the last, a 1960 first edition of *To Kill a Mockingbird*, gifted when I was thirteen and a half. My mother's way of telling me she wouldn't make it to my fourteenth birthday.

Any relief I felt at finding my collection dusty but otherwise unscathed evaporated when I spied Coulter's incredulity: Did I really care more for my books than I did about him? I reached for him; he turned away. Feeling slighted, I busied myself with examining the hole. A thick, desiccated beam with rust-colored stains looked plucked from a seventeenth-century ship. In the dim light, it was hard to tell if the marks were old or new—not that it mattered. Fixing a hole this size would require money we didn't have. It seemed the question of whether I should take the commercial job had been decided for me.

Footsteps creaked above, followed by the scrape of a chair being pushed around. The elderly Scheitelmans in 6A, who didn't sleep. A thump landed overhead, powdering me with white dust.

Crouching down, I turned over a fragment of plaster. One side was damp. Did someone need to come and assess the evidence? What did people do when the ceiling came down?

"I texted five or six times," Coulter said, examining the rubble. Glancing up at the hole, I hoped the Scheitelmans weren't listening.

"I'm really sorry," I said, trying to wade past a pang of guilt that I'd been sipping champagne with Dina while our apartment was coming down around him. "I had no idea."

He yanked the brass lamp from the mess.

"Leave it," I said, then worried I sounded short. "So the condo board can see you could've been hurt."

He held down the lamp with his bare foot, wrestling its crooked stem, hell-bent on straightening it out. When it wouldn't yield to his will, he threw it down, smashing it apart.

I was no stranger to Coulter's temper, but he'd tamped it down over the years. Long runs and braising marathons helped. Only once in a while would I come home to find a vase smashed up against the fireplace, swept away quickly and added to the list of things we didn't talk about by morning.

I should take pictures, I thought. I flipped on one of the table lamps flanking the couch and backed up to the doorway, instinctively lining up the window casing with the broken arm of the Swedish chair. Coulter was blocking the shot. His hair flopped across his eyes with a tender vulnerability that took me back to our younger selves, when we were both at the bank and I was the associate charged with making sure he and the rest of the junior analysts didn't humiliate our bosses. Born three weeks apart, he a Leo to my Cancer, we graduated the same year, he from a small college in Minnesota. When his Uncle Chuck got sick the first time, Coulter put his budding career as a travel writer on hold and came home to New York to help run his family's restaurant for a year. Chuck beat the cancer, and Coulter showed up at the bank armed with tales of ancient mountain villages and remote herding festivals that made him seem so much worldlier and wiser than the rest of us. But I could tell he didn't really want to be there. I discovered much later Coulter had taken the banking job to prove his father wrong, an overreaction to some stupid, offhand comment his father made about Coulter not wanting to grow up and get serious about anything. Even so, Coulter was irresistible. Bright blue eyes and a lopsided grin, sweetly funny with a self-deprecating air you'd mistake for upper-class wit if you didn't know he'd grown up with a single mom in Brooklyn and had worked hard to get rid of his accent. It wasn't long before he'd won me over.

Once our relationship cover at the bank was blown, and HR warned me I was crossing a line as his manager, Coulter volunteered to move on; he insisted the insane hours were burning him out anyway. For a few years, he hopped between start-ups, hoping to strike it rich so that he could return to travel writing, his true love. I thought his decision to take over the restaurant when Uncle Chuck passed away six years ago was selfless and good-hearted, but to Coulter it wasn't a choice; he knew what the restaurant meant to his mother, even if the price was shelving his own dream for a few more years.

As I repositioned myself and framed him in the shot, I could see he was troubled by something bigger than the ceiling falling on his favorite chair. He was wincing, straining against a phantom pain.

"Are you hurt?" I asked, lowering my phone.

"No," he said flatly.

"We should stay clear," I said, nodding up at the hole. A rotten crossbeam could be serious; we might be in real danger. Like most

New Yorkers, I had the image of a building collapsing upon itself inked indelibly on my brain.

Coulter sank into a cross-legged seat in front of the fireplace and plucked a shard from the floor, turning it in his hands. He began to stack pieces of plaster the way people balance rocks at the beach.

"We should start with the condo board," I said, picking at the callus on my thumb, and when he didn't answer, I rambled on. "Make our case. Show them this wasn't our fault. I'll call the insurance company too. I don't know how long that process will take—they'll probably need to come out and do an inspection."

My voice trailed off. His expression had turned pensive, withdrawn. Maybe he, too, was thinking about the pact we made when we got married. A promise to squirrel away as much money as we could and seize the first chance that came our way to travel. I'd only been out of the country that one time with him, and I was dying to pack up my camera and see more, but now all of that seemed like a charming story we once told.

Coulter lowered a shard on top of the four already stacked, and I inched close enough to smell the briny musk of his cologne.

Jaw clenched, he contemplated his tower. I didn't know how to ease his anxiety or his pain, other than to put my arms around him. He nestled his chin in my hair, his body heaving with each breath. I buried myself in the warm scent of him: wood, citrus, the salty sea.

"Maybe this is a sign," I said quietly, feeling my way along. "The right time for a change. There's a full-time job. Shooting products for online and print ads. They're interested, if I can start next month. We'll have a little more coming in."

He pulled away to look at me.

"Sara, you walked away from a big-time banking job to pursue your photography. No way you're giving up now."

"But we're barely making it," I said without thinking, and immediately regretted it. He already felt hemmed in by the expectations of a previous generation raised on the back of a once-flourishing restaurant. And we had pooled the entirety of our savings to buy the apartment when I was still at the bank, thinking we could stretch because I had a steady income. Everything we had was tied up here, and what we earned went to paying down the mortgage.

I thought of the question Claudine kept coming back to as part of her either/or game: money or passion? I picked passion a few times until the day Bee marched into our shared bedroom and declared Claudine's choice a false one. Bee demanded to know why we couldn't have both, which was the most Bee answer imaginable. Now I felt sure Bee was wrong. You couldn't have both. And maybe some people couldn't have either, but I couldn't see a way to keep my passion alive without money.

"I have a plan," Coulter said.

"Aunt Judy is seventy-five. She won't take the restaurant back."

"I'm not talking about Aunt Judy," he said. "If I can come up with a little more investment capital, I can get some buzz going with a more creative menu. The *Times* has a new critic—she likes old classics with a seasonal spin."

He must've seen my concern because he held me in his arms.

"Sara, have faith," he said. "We'll figure this out."

"We will," I said with the enthusiasm he deserved, even while knowing we were going to need much more than faith.

4

It seemed impossible, and the most natural thing in the world, that the five of us were gathered again to usher in another round of the Circus. Any other year, I would've been swept up in the thrill of their company, Bee and Dina arguing over the direction of our country, Allie catching us up on people we didn't see anymore. We'd relive our favorite memories of the Circus: Dina and I miming the heart-stopping moment I reached for a carton of milk at the supermarket, only to have Dina grab my hand from inside the stockroom and shoot me, and Allie acting out the time she got locked out on the tiny balcony of Wesley's first apartment, forced to endure Wesley and her boyfriend's vigorous afternoon sex.

The mood was ebullient and the others had turned up as their sparkling, witty selves, but I couldn't shake the deepening dread that had taken hold of me since seeing Claudine ten days earlier. Sooner or later, Allie would read the rules, and I still hadn't figured out how to tell them I was ending our beloved game.

We took turns hosting these kickoff dinners, and this year it was Wesley's turn. When she revealed she'd gotten into a swanky new private members' club, we bashed her for being elitist, then insisted she bring us. The club was far from the sleek modern hideaway I expected, but rather a throwback to the tartan-and-leather final clubs we thought we'd left behind in Cambridge. Wesley was in her element, though, blond hair and wide-set blue eyes shimmering with cool-girl elegance as she walked Allie, Bee, and me through the downstairs rooms to greet friends who summered together in Southampton or Sconset.

As we trailed along, laughing at jokes and serving up compliments, the stark homogeneity of the club surprised me. The city and its private rooms had for the most part progressed to where I didn't often feel conspicuous for being half-Asian, but Bee, who was half-Black, and I exchanged a relieved look when we were shown to a crimson-hued jewel box bar on the second floor, complete with a stone fireplace and a table laid for five, that was all ours for the evening.

We settled in at the cozy bar, and I was reminded that Dina hadn't yet arrived. My texts went unanswered, but the radio silence wasn't unusual, so after giving her another half hour, we sorted ourselves around the table in the same old hierarchy. Bee held court by the fireplace with Allie and Wesley flanking her. That left a seat next to Allie and another next to Wesley, facing away from the French doors. Putting myself between Dina and Wesley would've prolonged the peace, but I was thinking of my mother's old warning that it was bad luck to put your back to the door. Figuring I needed all the luck I could get given the bomb I was about to drop, I slid in next to Allie.

We caught up on husbands, boyfriends, and kids; gossiped about classmates who had bested expectations or fallen on hard times; and raised a solemn toast to an acquaintance who had been tragically killed by a stray bullet a few months before. Bee, who had grown up on Staten Island, and Allie, who was raising her three girls in New Jersey, traded Staten Island–New Jersey barbs that had us gasping for air. Wesley scandalized us with tales of her everyday life—a dinner party where dessert was a few lines of coke in the shape of the host's first initial, and a well-known actor's proposal that she sleep with him in exchange for a standing reservation at a hot new West Village eatery, which she was seriously considering.

We'd been sitting for more than an hour when Allie asked, "What's keeping Dina?"

"She should've been here by now," I said, ashamed that I'd momentarily forgotten her. Here we were, drinking and eating with abandon when something terrible might've happened. Dina preferred to navigate the city by bike, even in the rain. What if she'd been hit by a car? I checked my phone as I pushed out of my seat—still no answer to my rapid-fire texts. Pacing at the bar, I kept getting her voicemail. It occurred to me then that Dina knew I was planning to tell our roommates at tonight's dinner that I wasn't playing. She was always a step ahead; if she really did want to play, was her absence a gambit to weaken my resolve? Let the wolves wear me down before she stepped in for the kill? She knew we couldn't decide anything until she arrived.

"I can't play," I said after I'd retaken my seat.

Everyone stared.

"I knew it," Allie said, slapping the table and looking pointedly at Bee and Wesley. "Didn't I tell you?"

"Hold on," Bee chimed in, extending an arm in Allie's direction. "Let's hear Sara out."

"It doesn't make sense anymore," I said, my voice a meek impersonation of the one I'd rehearsed.

"I get it," Bee said. "Coulter isn't exactly a fan."

Before I could clarify, Allie cut in.

"I'm with Sara," Allie said to my enormous relief. "Playing doesn't feel right."

"Maybe it is time," Bee said agreeably. "I have the best PR guy in town, but even he can't walk back a story that the DA plays a killing game, even if the guns are fake."

I wasn't expecting Bee to give up so easily. Had I been worried about this conversation for no reason? Was it possible we were all secretly relieved the Circus had run its course?

"What are we saying?" Wesley asked. "Are we done?"

All eyes landed on Bee, her brows furrowed under the apparent weight of this decision. She'd gone back to relaxing her hair and the polished, shoulder-length style suited her, though I wondered if this was a look her image consultants had insisted on so she could appeal to people her advisers euphemistically called "mainstream voters."

"Hell, there are good reasons to call it quits," Bee said. "And I certainly don't want this to be the thing that sinks my campaign."

She swirled her wine—a pause I suspected was intended for dramatic effect, but performed with such ease that I felt cruel doubting her—then set the glass down purposefully. "Let me ask you guys a question. What do you have that's for you and you alone?"

She held up a hand.

"Think about it for a sec," she said and made a point of studying the coffered wood ceiling before turning her gaze back on us. "I know for a fact you've worked harder than all the guys who came up with you to get to where you are, which is to say you're finally making decent money and hopefully getting the respect that comes along with that. Maybe you're even getting to the gym now and then. And fucking three nights a week."

I didn't see myself in Bee's words, but I couldn't help laughing along as we glared at Wesley with mock menace. She was the only one who lived such a charmed life.

"It's five nights a week, thank you," Wesley cracked with a naughty grin.

Bee smiled, waiting until we had settled down again before continuing.

"In any case, if you already have the life you want, then by all means, tell me to shut up."

None of us said a word.

"Do you remember why we kept playing after graduation?" Bee asked, cocking her head.

A chill fell over the table; we knew she was talking about Claudine, who cajoled us into playing the Winthrop House game sophomore year. I could still feel the rush of skittering in pairs to the library and back, the anxiety as we peered around corners and under bathroom stalls. The thrill of narrowing in on a target, pulling the trigger, and getting a kill. Growing up, Claudine hadn't been allowed to play sports, only take dance lessons—the consequence of her mother's antiquated view of what was appropriate for young ladies—so she'd been fanatical freshman year about trying every club team that would have her. Sophomore year, she played ferociously in the Winthrop House game and placed fourth, which the cutthroat among us would've swallowed with a dose of disappointment, but Claudine didn't see it that way. She was elated. The following year, no one was surprised when she came in second. We were sure she'd win the whole thing when we were seniors.

"I'll never forget what Claudine said to me once about the Circus," Bee said. "You probably remember that night. It was January of junior year and we were sitting around our common room. Claudine was cradling that silver cup, saying it was the first trophy she'd ever won. I assumed she loved the competition."

We nodded. How clearly I could picture the six of us strewn across our two futons and a fraying Persian rug, rehashing the golden glory of that afternoon, when the winners of the game were crowned. None of us could forget the sight of an ecstatic Claudine, a paper crown nestled in her golden hair, riding high on the shoulders of two seniors around the Winthrop House courtyard to the epic strains of *Carmina Burana* thundering from speakers turned out of third-floor windows.

"She said that was part of it," Bee continued. "But the thing she loved most about the game was that we all played together. She was sure in ten years it would be the thing we'd remember the most."

Bee paused, letting us feel the weight of her words.

"I've always felt she would've wanted us to keep it going," Bee said.

I traced a stain of red wine bleeding across the tablecloth, remembering how subversive and special our decision to keep the Circus going after graduation had felt. A tribute to Claudine, of course, but also a protest against the misfortune that had befallen us senior year, an attempt to cast off the pallor that had settled over us after her death. And a way to remind ourselves that we were tougher than even we believed ourselves to be.

"The thing is," Bee said, "if we were guys, we wouldn't be sitting here second-guessing ourselves. And we could've let this thing die a million times, but we haven't. We all know we're different when we play. Sharper. More alive. This"—she tapped the table urgently—"is for us."

It was a convincing speech—Bee was a seasoned prosecutor, after all—but I couldn't figure out why she was working so hard to convince us. Maybe I'd underestimated her loyalty to Claudine. I always saw the two of them as friendly, but not nearly as close as Wesley and I were to Claudine. Then again, Bee's superpower was her ability to forge instant connections with people. And yet we all knew the rules. If I was bowing out, then the Circus was over.

"I know Wesley isn't afraid of a little healthy competition," Bee said, and Allie snorted. We all knew Wesley wasn't afraid of anything.

Wesley gave a little shrug without looking up from her glass, and I wondered if Bee had gotten to her beforehand.

"Allie, you've got three kids, a mortgage, and an hour-long commute each way," Bee said, donning a sympathetic expression she probably used to curry favor with hostile witnesses and juries: a tilt of the head, eyebrows slightly raised, unassuming smile. "What do you have that's just for you?"

Allie looked flustered, repeatedly tucking strands of auburn hair behind her ears, but she had seemed out of sorts most of the evening. Of course she was the same loyal, generous friend she'd always been—a grown-up Ginny Weasley—but she wore a fatigue I hadn't seen before. This wasn't the exhaustion that set in after a long day spent wrangling colleagues and kids, but something more entrenched. When I had asked earlier if everything was okay, she'd put on a brave smile, insisting she'd never been better. She was Allie, after all—the rock who shouldered our problems and rarely burdened us with her own.

"A girls' weekend on the Jersey shore seems so banal, but we're not kids anymore," Allie said. "What does it matter, though? Sara's made up her mind."

Allie looked to me to weigh in; I nodded.

"Well, let's hold off on making any final decisions until Dina gets here," Bee said, shooting Wesley a look I couldn't decipher. Wesley didn't seem to understand either, for she held up her empty glass and waved at the barman to bring us another bottle of wine, though it was the last thing any of us needed.

If this last round of the Circus had gone like the others before it, it might've passed into our collective memory like all the others. Our madness condensed into one-liners trotted out to prove how young and crazy we once were. The details of that kickoff dinner and the days that followed rush back to me at the strangest times, piercing me with the sinking certainty that what happened afterward was my fault. Why hadn't I listened to the alarm bells ringing in my head? Why hadn't I put up more of a fight?

One thing I know for sure: I could've done more for Dina.

I was standing at the bar when Wesley climbed up on her chair, balancing determinedly with one arm outstretched. Not even our hollers and groans could deter her when she was in the mood for Latin.

"*Amici, Harvardiani, familiae, commodate mihi aliquantis per aures vestras*," she thundered in her gravelly voice—the opening to the Latin oration she famously delivered at our graduation in the way only Wesley could, lecturing thirty thousand people on the life lessons to be gleaned from *The Simpsons*. The undergrads were given a translation, and so we laughed in all the right places, which impressed our parents to no end. The hammy way she delivered it still cracked us up, and she was undeterred when halfway through she lost the thread. Searching for some other way to make us laugh, she seized on Dina's empty chair and cocked her head with a devilish smile. Allie and Bee were still convulsing with laughter, but I knew where this was headed. Glancing at the doors, I prayed for crosstown traffic or a sudden downpour—anything to keep Dina away a little longer.

Wesley slipped off imaginary glasses and twirled them around the way Dina did when she was nervous, an unconscious quirk.

"Wesley, don't," I said, waving at her to get down, but she brushed me off and began to mime the scene from Bee's wedding when Dina stood up to read a poem everyone assumed she penned, only to have a bridesmaid recite the same poem, attributed to a French poet, later in the service. Wesley wasn't mean, but she and Dina had gotten off on the wrong foot junior year when the housing office shoehorned Dina into our rooming group as a transfer. Back then, Dina was skinny, with thick glasses. She wore thrifted clothes that hung off her. She was brilliant—not even Wesley would dispute that—and Harvard had poached her from Chicago after she'd published a paper that dazzled the philosophy kings. But Dina hadn't yet learned that there was an art to human relationships and it was rarely about being right.

Sensing a presence behind me, I twisted back to the French doors. My breath caught. There, in the doorway, stood Dina. Taking us in.

I rushed over and threw an arm around her shoulders. She stiffened, but I didn't know how else to reassure her. The crimson cashmere scarf I gave her two years ago for Christmas hung around her neck in bright contrast to her lucky tweed blazer, which looked a little ratty in a place like this. I offered to take her jacket, but Dina shook her head with a pinched expression, so I steered her into the room. The laughter died too late.

Wesley climbed down from her chair, and Dina looked like she might run.

"Glad you made it," I said, aware of how quiet the room had become. "We were worried."

Allie, who was good to everyone, stood up and hugged Dina. Bee rose and leaned over with a hand up for a high five, but their timing was off, and Dina's fingers struck Bee's palm with a thin pat. Dina looked past Wesley, who feigned a sudden preoccupation with her drink. When Dina dropped in next to Allie, I eased in next to Wesley with my back to the door.

"What are you drinking? The usual?"

I leaned in closer to Dina, trying to crowd the others out of her view. When she didn't answer, I beckoned the barman to bring us two Fernets.

"Any problem finding us?" I asked.

Dina took off her glasses to rub at one eye, and I glimpsed an aching sadness that vanished when she realized she was being observed. I set a hand on her shoulder, bony and taut under her jacket.

"I walk by this place all the time," Dina said, shifting out of my reach. "Always wondered what goes on inside."

Allie asked after Dina's book, and Bee offered to help with a connection at Princeton University Press. I appreciated what they were trying to do. While I didn't blame her, Dina's rigid, mannered responses did nothing to dispel the chill that had settled over the room. I felt a vibration climbing up through my seat and glanced down to find Dina's foot nestled against the leg of my chair, shaking at a frenetic pace.

"Well, I know she hates being the center of attention," I said, plunging into the stilted silence, "but I have good news. We all know how dedicated Dina is. How determined. Years of hard work are finally paying off."

I waved off Dina's sharp glance.

"I know, I know. They still have to vote, sign the papers and all that, but they'd be idiots not to make it official." I raised my glass and beamed at her. "To Dina, on getting tenure."

A cheer erupted, and all eyes turned to Dina, who hunched over with a wan smile. They peppered her with questions. Was she moving back to Cambridge full-time? She hadn't worked it out yet. When would she know for sure? Sometime soon. How did she feel?

She didn't know. Dina's eyes darted around the room, searching for a place to land. My seat vibrated as her leg shook furiously.

"Congratulations, Dina," Wesley said.

Dina looked skeptical, as if she thought Wesley was still mocking her, but reciprocated with a thin-lipped smile. A truce, I thought, for the moment.

"Dina, you might have heard," Bee said breezily as our dinner plates were being cleared. "Sara doesn't want to play."

Time was doing that funny thing it did when we got together: feigning elasticity, then snapping back with a jolt of conscience. Dina had pulled the linen napkin out from under her glass, and her fingers ran over the club monogram like a blind woman reading braille.

"Just curious," Bee said, propping her elbows on the table and fixing her gaze on Dina. "You and I have five wins apiece. Wesley four, Allie three. Sara has two. Which brings us to now. Hypothetically, would you be up for another round? One last shot at glory forevermore?"

I was bewildered by Bee's doggedness, but I had to give her credit. Dangling the prospect of beating the others once and for all was a smart play—Dina relished winning, maybe even more than Bee.

Dina placed the napkin back under her glass, taking her time.

"If Sara says she doesn't want to play," Dina said, "then I guess we're not playing."

Breathing a little easier, I looked up to find the barman laying a leather folder at my elbow. Opening it, I tried to hide my alarm. Surely some error had been made—drinks double counted or a mix-up with the boisterous guys in the party room next door. Wesley was waving wildly at me from across the table, amused by my consternation. She came around to pluck the check from my hands, raising her own in surrender.

"I have a confession to make," she said. "Any of you remember entrusting me with the pot?"

WITH FRIENDS LIKE THESE

The year after graduation, we had chipped in to a shared account: a pot to be awarded to the winner of the last round of the Circus. It was a joke, a way to thumb our nose at patriarchy and privilege, specifically the myth swirling around the most secretive and selective of the Harvard final clubs, the Porcellian.

In those days, supposedly only 10 percent of Harvard men belonged to a final club. One or two women's clubs had gotten off the ground, and a few other social clubs, like the posh Hasty Pudding, the artsy Signet, and the satirical Lampoon, were coed, but the men's clubs were the most storied, founded in the late nineteenth century as refuges for privileged upperclassmen. They owned mansions around Harvard Square that boasted billiard rooms, smoking lounges, and professional bouncers who manned the doors during frequent, debauched bacchanals. The two-month punch during the fall of sophomore year was a gauntlet of parties where club members looked the hopefuls over at every turn—a thrill for well-connected extroverts and a terrifying trial for introverts. Wesley, Bee, and I were punched for the Pudding, but unlike them, I wasn't any good at small talk, and when cocktail parties turned into competitive sport, there was little hope for me.

No Harvard man would publicly hang his hopes on getting punched for the Porcellian, or the PC, as it was known, but most of our male counterparts secretly hoped they'd wake one November morning to discover a crisp envelope with a porcine seal slipped under his door in the dead of night. The PC picked eight men each year, ostensibly from the masses, but in reality only from a handful of Brahmin families with surnames like Ames, Coolidge, and Weld. According to rumor, if a member hadn't made his first million by the time he turned thirty, the club would simply bestow it on him. We didn't know if this was true—no one close to us made the cut, and the PC guys were so tight-lipped, so bought into the cult, that we decided to create our own fuck-you fund, doled out to the woman who won the last round of the Circus. Our pot was paltry by comparison, but it was always just for laughs. Besides, none of us dreamed we'd still be playing in our forties.

"Yeah, well," Wesley said, "you guys stuck me with managing the pot. Some misguided theory that one shitty year in investment banking made me a financial genius. Should've given it to Sara—you lasted what, six or seven years? Anyway, I didn't want to deal, so I asked a friend to babysit."

I was about to correct her—I was proud of myself for toughing it out in banking for nine whole years—when Dina jumped in.

"You could've checked with us first," she said, but Wesley held up a hand.

"When we started—how is it possible that was twenty fucking years ago?—we had a few grand. I doubled it and turned it over to a friend. Class of '97. Smart guy. Steve Camerino. Anyone know him?"

Steve had graduated before we arrived on campus, but I recognized his name. I had no idea why.

"Hedge fund guy," Bee said. "Big fucking deal."

Then it came to me. Coulter dropped in now and then on a monthly poker game hosted by Tad, his first roommate in New York. After the last one—September, no, it was October—he had come home slurring excitedly over the money he'd won, and by the way, he'd sat next to a guy named Steve, who'd turned out to be an old friend of Wesley's. In fact, this Steve Camerino had invested a little money for Wesley, as a favor really, and returned her a small fortune.

"Steve is a family friend," Wesley said. "He had left Goldman and was putting together his first fund."

"Are you saying he put our money in that fund?" Bee asked.

Wesley nodded.

"No clue why he took us," Wesley said. "We were itty-bitty potatoes."

Bee held up a hand.

"Don't say another word. He probably broke half a dozen securities laws. I don't want to know."

"Well then," Wesley said, taking her time. "Does that mean you also don't want to know that we're sitting on nine hundred and forty-seven grand?"

I was speechless. Bee clapped a hand over her mouth. Allie leapt up to high-five Wesley. Even Dina was smiling.

"Split five ways," Allie tapped on her phone, then held it up as proof. "That's a hundred and eighty-nine thousand each."

"Except for one thing," Wesley said.

Allie's glee evaporated.

"What?"

"The pot goes to the winner of the last round. We agreed."

"Wesley, don't be an asshole," Allie said. "I know this doesn't mean anything to you. You don't have three kids in private school and zero put away for college. To me this is real money, even split five ways. And who says this is up to you? We all contributed. We should all get something out."

Allie looked to Bee as the lawyer in the bunch, but Bee, who didn't take orders from anyone, wasn't about to switch sides.

"No, no way," Allie said with such bite that my back stiffened. "Playing has implications for all of us." She swung around to Dina. "Can't imagine the tenure committee would be okay with this."

When Dina shrugged, Allie threw her hands up, training her sights on Bee again.

"You really want to go through with this? You're the DA, for god's sake."

"We're not technically breaking any laws," Bee said.

"Technically? Is that your standard now? What about your campaign promises to stamp out crime and make sure no one is above the law? I guess none of that applies anymore because you're the one calling the shots?"

Bee folded her hands together and flashed a self-effacing smile.

"I agree the optics aren't ideal," Bee said.

"Aren't ideal?" Allie shouted. "Are you crazy? Do you really need me to spell this out for you? If the press gets wind of this, you'll be the poster child for everything that's wrong in this city, and you can kiss the mayor's office goodbye."

"I'm not gonna let that happen," Bee said.

"You think you can control this?" Allie said. "Even you can't spin your way out of the shitstorm we'll be dealing with if this leaks."

Bee drained what was left in her glass, then started in quietly.

"My life is scheduled in fifteen-minute increments, seven days a week, from eight in the morning until ten at night. I have a social media person, a PR guy, an assistant, a stylist, a campaign manager, a fundraiser, an accountant, a lawyer, and a full-time bodyguard, since some psycho is offended by the audacity of a Black Italian woman from Staten Island running for public office. Do you think what I say goes? No. Every minute of every day I have to be all things to all people. Just enough of myself, but not so much that people can't project their hopes onto me. Believe me when I say I understand the risk. But I need this. I need to prove I'm not some product. That somewhere beneath this cooked-up exterior, where my hair changes after every focus group, I'm still who I think I am."

None of us said anything for a while after that, but it was obvious Bee's mind was made up. Allie helped herself to Bee's margarita, polishing it off.

"I hope you know you're all batshit crazy," Allie said as she slammed the glass down and stormed off.

"You might've forgotten about the contract," Bee said when we were assembled around the table again, Wesley having cajoled Allie into at least hearing what Bee had to say.

I lowered my drink; Wesley's hung in midair. None of us had any idea what Bee was talking about.

"The contract we signed when we decided to keep this thing

going after graduation," Bee said. "When we all paid into the pot. Overkill at five pages, I admit it. I was a 1L at the time."

We looked at her like she was speaking a different language.

"Really? You don't remember?"

I had a faint memory of Bee asking us to sign something—a promise not to sue one another if anyone got hurt, a few pages of jargon she swore was boilerplate—but I couldn't dredge up more than that.

"Remind us what exactly is in this contract?" Dina asked huffily.

"Here's a copy," Bee said, pulling a stapled sheaf of papers from her suit jacket and laying it in the center of the table, where we could see plainly that all of us signed. "The point is we have a choice to make. According to the contract, if anyone refuses to play, we can either end the whole thing and donate the pot to our alma mater, or we play one more time—winner takes all."

"So if we don't play, Harvard gets the money?" Allie asked, incredulous.

Bee nodded, her expression impressively neutral.

"Who decides?" Dina asked. "I mean between those two options?"

"Well, that's the problem," Bee said. "We didn't stipulate. Like I said, I was a 1L when I drafted this."

"Screw that," Allie said, her voice hard-edged. "We're here now. We should split the money."

"They won't agree to that," Dina said to Allie with a nod to Bee and Wesley.

Allie's face was bright red; she looked like she was going to blow.

"So what do we do?" I asked. "Take a vote?"

We waited for Dina, who was taking a slow sip of Fernet. As a professor of philosophy, she was our compass when fairness was at stake.

"Assuming all of us signed this thing and the contract is valid," Dina said, gesturing at the agreement lying on the table and Bee nodding forcefully, "then yes, we should take a majority vote as long as everyone agrees to go along with the result."

Nine hundred and forty-seven thousand dollars. It was a lot of money. Money that could ease the pressure Coulter felt from the restaurant, fix the hole in the ceiling, and pay down the mortgage. But I couldn't get past the constant anxiety I'd been feeling since seeing Claudine.

"Sara, you've been pretty quiet," Allie said. "What do you think?"

I did a quick tally in my head. Allie and I would vote to scrap the game. Dina would back us up—if not out of sound judgment, then out of loyalty—which meant we were the majority. We would win. Maybe we'd also have the leverage to change the terms of the contract and everyone could walk away with a generous payday.

"A vote seems fair," I said, feeling a little disingenuous.

"All right, then," Dina said. "Everyone agree they'll accept the outcome if we vote?"

Nods around the table. Dina gestured at Allie to start us off.

"No way," Allie said, obviously annoyed. "We should absolutely divvy up the money. But if we're really locked into this stupid contract, then fine. Put the game out to pasture and give the money to dear old Harvard."

We moved on to Bee.

"We owe this to ourselves," Bee said. "One more time."

We turned to Wesley then, whose clenched expression gave her a coiled intensity. I followed her gaze to the portraits flanking the mantel, men who had built industrial empires or clawed their way to great political heights. She looked as if she might leap up and smash the paintings over a chair; I wouldn't blame her.

"I think we move on," Wesley said in a small, faraway voice. "We tell Harvard to put the money toward financial aid."

Bee frowned at this unexpected defection. Allie arched an eyebrow at me. We had this in the bag.

"That makes one for playing, two against," Dina said flatly, giving no indication of her own leanings. I folded my hands in my lap, feeling more at ease. Dina was nothing if not rational.

"Let's play," Dina said.

I couldn't hide my surprise. I had assumed that Dina and I shared an understanding; her abrupt reversal stung.

"I guess we have a tie," Bee said resignedly. "It's back to you, then, Sara."

Dina looked over at me. The hunch of her shoulders wasn't new, but there was an anguish in her eyes that seemed deeper than whatever Wesley's stupid stunt might've inflicted. And I saw something in Dina's face I initially couldn't parse: a pleading, tangled in humility and shame. Then I understood what she was asking.

Every fiber of my body told me we should walk away from the Circus. Heed our better judgment and quit before our fortunes reversed, contenting ourselves with the wild tales we'd accumulated over the years of near misses and close calls. So why was I hesitating?

In the span of our history together, I could count on one hand the number of times Dina had asked for my help. I had no sense of what the going salary was for an associate professor, but Dina never took vacations. She mostly cooked at home and wore her clothes until they were frayed beyond repair. When the two of us got together, we met up for drinks, rarely dinner. Being tenured would finally net her a decent paycheck, but Dina was still carrying student loans and supporting the aunt who'd raised her after her mom upended their quiet life in a Minneapolis suburb by running off with a Brazilian dentist when Dina was a teenager. Nine hundred and forty-seven grand might not be fuck-you money in New York, but in another city it could get Dina back to even. Besides, Dina was tied with Bee for the most wins, which meant she had a good chance of pulling it off.

The tumult I felt took me back to the morning of our graduation, when Dina and I sat with our backs pushed up against the stone balusters of Weeks Bridge. The Charles River was still, except for a sculler slicing through the water beneath us. The air was fresh with mud and flowers after a long, wet spring, the city still shaking off its winter sleep. When I suggested it was time to head back to Winthrop House to don our robes, Dina said only one word: *kenzoku*. It was a Japanese word for family, she explained, but it was deeper than that. Like two soldiers on the same path, committed to a similar destiny. A bond that doesn't lessen with time or distance, a connection Dina professed to only ever feeling with me. The admission had embarrassed me, and I hurried us back with a flimsy excuse about needing to find a misplaced tassel. Dina never brought it up again. I still regretted not showing her more decency.

I thought of the stunt Wesley had pulled earlier, the humiliation Dina must've felt, and how I hadn't stood up for her. If the tables were turned, she wouldn't hesitate to stand up for me.

"I need your word," I said, pushing away lingering doubt, "that you'll keep the game away from Coulter and actually follow the rules this time."

Bee nodded, Allie shot me a dangerous look, and Wesley tilted her head as if she was trying to figure me out, but they had heard me.

"What I guess I'm saying is that I'm up for playing one last time," I said.

Bee let out a triumphant whoop, and Allie would've stormed off again had Wesley not grabbed her arm, but my attention was on Dina, who was twirling a toothpick absently in one hand. She was always working some tchotchke—a lock, a squishy ball, a Rubik's Cube. She said it helped her focus.

When the others migrated to the bar, Dina said quietly, "All of you have done amazing things and made a difference."

"And you're about to get tenure," I answered a little too sharply.

It was crazy to think we had reached a point in our lives when we were landing jobs intended for adults, where people expected things like leadership and authority from us. Dina had always underestimated herself.

She shrugged as if to say tenure was no big deal, then thanked me, but her gratitude embarrassed me. I wasn't being generous; I was atoning for past failings.

I could feel Dina studying me as I gulped down the water that was left on the table.

"Are you still hung up on the ghost?" Dina asked, and I had to temper myself. She didn't understand—how could she? She hadn't known Claudine as well as I had. And no one blamed her for Claudine's death.

"Sara, everything's going to be fine," Dina said.

This time, I didn't believe her.

Wesley began to chant. Softly at first, then like a mallet striking a drum: rules, rules, rules. Her blue eyes moved deliberately around the table, entreating each of us to join the crescendoing chorus. Allie looked hesitant, so Bee got up and threw her arms around Allie, whispering in her ear. Soon Allie was clapping along too. Wesley conducted us, whipping us into a frenzy, our voices hammering on like a deafening train. I searched for the barman and found him kneeling at the French doors, unhooking the latches and swinging them shut. We were no different from the drunken frat boys in the room next door.

Allie, who had always been fiercely loyal, usually to her own detriment, stood then and pulled a piece of paper from her back pocket with a dramatic flourish. We howled like dogs. Unfolding the white sheet, she held it a little too far away—a concession to the passage of time. She tried to speak, but faltered and bowed her head for a moment. I suspected she was realizing, as I was, that an important chapter was coming to an end.

"Ladies, welcome to the twentieth round of the Circus," Allie said quietly.

Each of us could probably recite the rules from memory, but the way Allie read them was unparalleled. Her voice rose and fell in all the right places, whipping us up while faithfully leading us down a path we had traveled so many times together.

"This is a game of wits and smarts," she said, "where you are both killer and prey, but there is no great genius without a touch of madness. When you are shot on any part of your body, you die. Once dead, you surrender your medallion and the name of your target to the shooter, who shall assume your target. The first person to collect all five medallions shall be the winner."

She looked us over. Dina and Bee followed along with rapt appreciation. I must've been deep in my own thoughts; Wesley elbowed me to pay attention.

"One. The world is our battlefield, and as such, there are no safe zones. Two. It is up to you, and only you, to evade your killer and eliminate your prey. Three. Each kill must be in secret and without witness. Four. No collaborators. That includes spouses, boyfriends, kids, hired guns, and fellow players."

We turned to Dina with knowing smiles, recalling the year UPS delivered a duffel bag to the guy Wesley was dating. Wesley and her boyfriend didn't think much of it—she was sure we didn't know about him and she could ride out the Circus in his Midtown apartment—so they went back to whatever movie they were watching. When the boyfriend stepped out to the bathroom, Dina unzipped herself and shot Wesley. I was the only one Dina told about paying off the boyfriend with tickets to the Knicks.

"Five. No hostages. And since kids are off-limits, Wesley—"

"Allie's kids were fine," Wesley said. "They thought we were doing a hotel pajama party. An Eloise thing."

We groaned.

"Six, aka the Dina Aoki Rule. You may not impersonate an authority figure, including any firefighter or police officer."

"But other costumes are fine," Dina said with a raised finger, and we shook our heads warily, knowing Dina had a virtuosic talent for disguise.

"Rule seven, the Katherine Wesley Anderson Hale Amendment. No one may use, manufacture, or lie about a fire alarm, security alert, or medical emergency to gain an advantage in an attempt to kill another player or gain information about them."

We howled with laughter even before Allie could finish, remembering the time Wesley snuck into Bee's apartment in the middle of the night and hid all of Bee's and Doye's clothes. When the fire alarm sounded and a mortified Bee came down to the lobby in a towel, Wesley was waiting for her.

"Rule eight, the Bee Colasanti Catchall. Do no harm; respect yourself and your fellow players. Breaking the law and destroying other people's property will be frowned upon."

Allie looked down her nose at Bee, prompting laughter all around. No one could forget the year Bee slid off the roof of Wesley's parents' house in Rhode Island and spent six weeks in a leg cast. Bee's husband, Doye, reminded us every chance he got.

"And finally, nine. Play to your fullest, but bear in mind that this is only a game."

We leapt out of our chairs, raising our glasses in uncanny synchronicity, Teddy Roosevelt's words on the tips of our tongues.

"Far better it is to dare mighty things," we shouted fiercely, "to win glorious triumphs, even though checkered by failure, than to take rank with those poor spirits who neither enjoy much nor suffer much, because they live in the gray twilight that knows not victory nor defeat."

While the others cheered and pumped their fists, an unexpected hollowness took hold of me. The speech felt hackneyed and grandiose, the work of self-absorbed college kids yearning to be adults. I thought of the girl I was when I helped pen those rules and felt as if we were distant strangers.

"One more thing," Bee said when we had settled down. "According to the contract—"

"My god, enough with the fucking contract," Wesley said with an exasperation that made even Bee smile.

"—there are no rules for this last round. Well, that's not exactly true. There are two. Kills still have to take place in the order they're assigned. And no witnesses. Crowded places are fine as long as no one sees you take the shot. Other than that," Bee said with a shrug, "it's all fair game."

"You couldn't have told us that before?" I asked, and Bee laughed.

"And miss that spectacle?" Bee asked, gesturing at Allie. "Not in a million years would I have given up hearing Allie's speech one more time."

Allie grabbed her carefully preserved list of rules off the table, balled it up, and threw it at Bee, who caught it with aplomb. It should've made us laugh, but a sudden hesitation hung over us. Maybe we were feeling nostalgic, knowing that this was the end of a ritual that had figured so prominently in our lives. Others—Dina most likely—were probably thinking through the implications of a game with no guardrails. For years, Allie had laid down rule after rule to slow the arms race among women determined to get a leg up. We were ambitious, and yet no one wanted to repeat the catastrophe that had destroyed the Winthrop House game our senior year. But now it felt like we were headed straight back to where we'd started.

Allie returned from the bar holding a bowl partially draped with a napkin. She lowered it in front of Dina, who pulled out a crisp white card bearing the name of her first kill, then made the rounds to the rest of us. The name on my card filled me with relief: an easy first target.

"So we have our names," Wesley called out from where she was standing next to the windows, lighting a cigarette and turning away now and then to blow smoke out one of the cranked-open panes. "Everyone have their medallion?"

We held up the gold talismans hanging from thin chains around our necks: graduation gifts from Wesley. One side was stamped with a lion on a shield with three chevrons—the Winthrop family coat of arms and the crest of our beloved Winthrop House. The other side was engraved with our initials. For the past nineteen years, they'd been prizes in our game, relinquished along with the names of our targets to our killers.

"Same as before," Wesley said, tapping her cigarette against the window frame. "Seven days, starting New Year's Day. The first person to hand all five medallions to Hugo by Friday night at nine gets the money."

Hugo and Wesley had been friends since their first day of kindergarten. His pride and joy was the diner he ran near the West Side Highway, where you could find him most days flipping pancakes on the griddle. He was quirky, but he was grounded and real. He would keep our secret and our money safe, although we probably should have chosen a trustee who was slightly less eccentric if we'd known we'd be handing him a small fortune.

"What happens if no one claims it by the deadline?" I asked.

"We become the anonymous donors of a generous gift to Harvard," Dina said.

"Screw that," Wesley shouted as Allie retrieved a purple backpack from a hook under the bar, which she must've stashed on her way in. Allie rounded the table, placing a black pistol in front of each of us like it was our next course. Other than the orange tips, the guns were close enough to the real thing that we didn't take them out in public. We understood the risk of waving them around, even if they were toys. We were placing our reputations in one another's hands; a single misstep could bring us all down.

Allie skipped her usual lecture on how they stopped making this model years ago, how they weren't technically legal, how she couldn't fix them if they broke, or how she could get a fortune for them online.

"If this really is our last time," Allie said, "they're yours to keep."

Bee weighed her gun in her palm, bobbing it up and down like a scale. She gave it a shake, then pointed it sideways at Wesley like in the movies. Wesley straightened up, her eyes narrowed in warning, cigarette frozen in midair. Bee grinned as she pulled the trigger; water exploded everywhere. A dark circle expanded across Wesley's chest, white silk clinging to her skin.

"Shit," Wesley said, and everyone, even Dina, burst into laughter. Allie refilled us with the red wine left on the table, and we raised a toast as we always did at the end of the night. To Claudine, we chimed in. Glasses hurled toward one another; a crack rang out; wine splattered across the table. The barman rushed over. As far as I could tell, there was no blood.

5

IN the cold, predawn darkness of January first, I jolted awake with an urgent start. Reassured by the man-shaped heap of comforter next to me, I lay back down, my head throbbing with the recollection of the curious New Year's Eve party at Tad's Tribeca apartment the night before. Coulter showed up in a way he hadn't in ages. He was the life of the party, impressing, delighting, and coaxing the shy and sober out onto the makeshift living room dance floor. At one point, I spied him guzzling champagne tête-à-tête with Wesley on the terrace, and it delighted me to see Coulter giving her a chance. He was sweet, too, squeezing my shoulder, whispering how much he adored me every time our paths crossed. But my memory of what happened later was hazy. Had Coulter really admitted to Wesley that he didn't want to come between my college roommates and me anymore? Wesley swore she hadn't brought up the Circus, but he had revealed to her that he envied the closeness my roommates and I shared. He had family, but he didn't have old friends like I did.

I wondered what had prompted Coulter's confession to Wesley; she and Coulter weren't particularly close. Of my roommates, Allie was the only one who didn't offend him because she was so down-to-earth, the most relatable among us. He respected Bee—she was formidable—but he thought her fake; she would say anything to score a political win. He disapproved of Wesley, or as he liked to say with a snooty lockjaw, Katherine Wesley Anderson Hale, because she had more fun than everyone else, but Dina, whose intelligence and single-minded determination he found unnerving, rattled him the most.

Still, New Year's Eve had been a good night for us and exactly what we needed. The project I'd spent a year on—stark images highlighting the invisibility of women at work in laundries, factories, kitchens—had landed with a silent thud in the laps of gallery owners, and old demons had returned to convince me I wasn't good enough. We'd been going out less because I couldn't face the questions strangers lobbed at me. *Would I have seen your work in any museums? Could I take pictures of their baby or their dog?* And their inevitable advice: *Have you thought about looking for work that is more practical?* Coulter and I had been fighting about money, where to cut back. We used to make fun of couples who had grown rigid with age, so afraid of discomfort and uncertainty, utterly convinced we would never become them.

I was burrowing into my warm cocoon when I remembered it was the first of January. New Year's Day.

The twentieth round of the Circus had begun.

I checked the time on my phone. Already late. My usual tactic was to set out on the first day earlier than anyone else, when the others would be sleeping off a hangover or (in Wesley's case) crawling home, bleary and disoriented. Now any advantage to be had was shrinking by the minute. I should've been driving out to New Jersey to catch Allie before Brad and the kids woke—but first I had to slip out without waking Coulter.

I shimmied toward the edge of the bed and the comforter came with me too easily. Turning back, I slid a leg in his direction, careful not to rouse him. Expecting to feel the warmth of his body, I was surprised to find his side cold. When I reached for him, the blanket hollowed out. He hadn't been sleeping well lately.

There was a note on the floor outside our bedroom; he needed to catch up at the restaurant. He was taking the beater car we kept in a garage two blocks away. I was frustrated he'd gotten a jump on me—the train to New Jersey would take twice as long—but I figured he'd be gone for at least a few hours. Enough time for me to pay Allie a visit and be back on the couch before he returned. I wouldn't have to explain myself, even though we both knew the significance of today's date. And we wouldn't have to engage in the same old argument about my college roommates and their reckless privilege.

If I'd learned anything from the Circus, however, it was that very little went according to plan.

As the westbound local rattled away from Penn Station, thin-sliced row houses expanded into grassy, split-level colonials in the slow-breaking light. I yanked my coat tighter at the neck to fight a chill coming off the windows. I could've slept in, listened to my intuition that this last round of the Circus was an ill-advised undertaking, and made the prudent choice of letting it pass me by. But my imagination was galloping ahead. I was already picturing Coulter's reaction when I delivered the news that I'd won and what that meant for us. I could see his fatigue giving way to the joyous incredulity he used to wear so often. Coulter had been the kind of guy who stopped in the middle of a crowded sidewalk to marvel at a rainbow breaking over Manhattan, and got up early so he could enjoy a perfectly still morning in Central Park. The thought of seeing that Coulter again was enough to make my body hum with electric possibility.

A sharp laugh turned my head to the kids across the aisle. Two raccoon-eyed girls were settled in across from a rumpled boy with inky-black hair. I could tell they were high school kids from the *likes* that peppered their speech and their vehement dismissal of classes and teachers who were the worst ever. I could have easily been one of them at their age, but I didn't go out all that much in high school. I was too intimidated by the social scene to do much more than lurk on the fringe. Most nights I worked at the town pizza joint, and when it was slow, Carlos, the cook, and I watched reruns of *Fantasy Island*, one-upping each other on what we'd ask for if we got a turn on that seaplane.

By tenth grade, my mother had been dead a year, and my father worked plumbing jobs when he wasn't drinking. The only person who noticed I was spiraling was a teacher named Mr. Byrd, who conscripted me into math league and cross-country. Junior year, I agreed to be his teaching assistant for AP Calc, and when no one ran for student body president, Mr. Byrd told the principal I would do it. Only years later did I understand what Mr. Byrd was doing. I couldn't cruise around town after school in Jenny O'Dowd's convertible or kill time at Lara Miller's house, which was empty after her parents split and where everyone went to party. It was Mr. Byrd who planted the seed of an Ivy League school, Mr. Byrd who wrote the recommendation that undoubtedly got me in, and Mr. Byrd, in his quiet, unassuming way, who saved me.

We wrote to each other the fall of my freshman year, matter-of-fact stuff about classes and news of people we knew, but when Wesley read one of Mr. Byrd's letters out loud to Allie and Bee, I was furious. I swore I'd never lay myself bare like that again, but the thing I regretted more was not writing him back.

"Maplewood," the conductor cried with a twangy call. The train braked, throwing me against the brown padded seat. I hurried to the front of the car and peered through the window, careful to stay out of sight. A shadowy figure was sprinting across the parking lot toward the train. I checked behind me—still only the three kids. The aisle was clear in case I needed a quick escape. The figure—brown parka, knitted hat pulled down low—had reached the platform, closing in. Braced to run, my body seized with panicked excitement, then unclenched. It was only a guy running to catch his train.

As the train sputtered and rolled forward, I swayed back to my seat, thinking of sophomore year, when we added Claudine to our little troupe and became five. Winthrop House hadn't been our top choice, but its quirkiness grew on us, and we soon felt like we knew too much about one another to live anywhere else. The awkward layout of the U-shaped buildings demanded you key through multiple doors and cross at least one courtyard in the cold and dark to get to our entryway, then trudge up four or five flights of stairs to our rooms, all while shouldering a loaded backpack—how fit we were in those days! The sunken, wood-paneled dining hall resembled the steamy hull of an old schooner, and the spring formal on the courtyard patio made us feel like royals. Although the personalities of each upper-class house started to fade when the college randomized housing assignments a few years before us, the stereotypes still rang true. Eliot House, our next-door neighbor, poured champagne at elegant soirees to St. Paul's scions and Park Avenue princesses. Rambling, tucked-away Adams was artsy and alternative, and once had a swimming pool that hosted the occasional orgy, where everyone slept with everyone regardless of gender or orientation. Kirkland, which sat diagonally across from us, was for jocks. Winthrop, where we landed, was the high school house. I had no idea what that meant, but given that we were turning forty-three this year and still playing a game we started in college, there seemed to be something to it.

A shriek brought me back to the train. One of the girls across the aisle had put her back to me, blocking my view; the other was kneeling in the well between the bench seats. The boy moaned softly.

I envied their freedom, or at least the illusion of being free. I'd felt that way only once in my life: the year I met Coulter. We were twenty-five, and everything about him thrilled me—his confident optimism, his deadpan wit, his sweet determination. How quickly he became my whole world. We talked incessantly on weekend trips to a friend's summer share house on the Jersey shore, through movies at the Angelika, over dinners in an East Village restaurant we thought of as our own, dreaming of sleepy beach towns we'd explore, cultures we would soak up, fellow travelers we would befriend. Now we slid past each other like roommates. I had buried my desire, telling myself I would find it again when we had room to breathe.

"Short Hills," the conductor bellowed, and a jolt of anticipation shot through me.

The kids raced off the train, bundling into an old woody station wagon, but I hung back. When I was sure the platform was clear, I crossed over and climbed into an idling taxi. The driver wished me a happy new year in the rearview mirror, and I gave him the address I knew by heart.

"You have new year decisions?" he asked as we nosed past renovated ranch houses and cedar-clad colonials I imagined were filled with needlepoint monograms and ceramic soup tureens. He meant resolutions, I knew. Would anyone believe that I could rake in almost a million dollars for hunting down and tagging my college roommates with an illegal toy gun? How absurd it sounded. I told him I hadn't gotten around to making any, and he told me he was saving up to get his five-year-old a cat.

The suburbs made sense for Allie, the only one of my roommates who wasn't terrified by the prospect of settling down in a small town resembling the one where she grew up. Her parents were therapists, so she showed up freshman year with a conviction that no one else had: a belief that she was enough. Allie had genuine passions—debate, the school paper, softball—and she was one of the few kids who didn't try to reinvent herself as soon as she crossed the iron gates of Harvard Yard. Still, from the day we met, Allie dreamed of teaching, preferably in some remote town in Southeast Asia or West Africa, where she might learn more than she taught. She might have done it, too—she signed up for a two-year stint teaching English with the Peace Corps in Cape Verde after graduation, but a week before shipping out, she discovered she was pregnant. She miscarried two months later and dumped the boyfriend, but by then she had lost her taste for adventure. She interviewed for grown-up jobs, telling herself she would teach once she had a little saved up, and landed a junior marketing gig at Amex in the city only so she wouldn't have to move back in with her parents. No one thought she'd stay at Amex for the next twenty years, but Allie has done well for herself. A big title, a decent budget, a windowed office. Even so, I worried that she had stumbled into a career without ever asking herself if it was what she wanted.

When the cab rolled by a low-slung redbrick school and Allie's street lay around the corner, I asked the driver to pull over.

"Icy," he said without slowing down.

"It's all right," I said. "I'll walk."

I didn't want to tip anyone off.

When the cab stopped, I opened my wallet; my throat clenched. I swore I'd had twenty bucks left when I paid for my train ticket. I rifled through old receipts and maxed-out credit cards I kept for show. A panic washed over me. Coulter had taken over our finances a few years ago, after we had drained my savings and his salary became steadier than mine. I tried to carry half of the mortgage payment each month by working for Fabby and moonlighting as a backup wedding photographer, but most of the time I had to ask Coulter for money. He rarely questioned my spending, but I couldn't ask him for money right now. Not with the ceiling coming down. And definitely not with the Circus on.

I searched the seat, the floor, my pockets. I apologized a few times to the driver, who lectured me in a language I didn't recognize. I pointed to my gloves—coffee-stained brown leather—but the driver shook his head, holding up his own pair of wool gloves. He pointed at my plaid scarf—a gift from Wesley. It made no sense to pay a ten-dollar cab fare with a scarf worth ten times that, but I unlooped it from my neck and handed it over. The driver felt the material and studied the tag, then nodded. I thanked him and scrambled out.

The morning was devastatingly bright; a quick glance at the snow sent up floaters at the edge of my vision. I treaded carefully on the icy road toward number twenty, a sweet white colonial at the end of a short, shoveled walk. Allie and Brad moved in right before Chloe was born, and the house held so many memories: a rollicking engagement party for Wesley (the marriage lasted four months), a baby shower for Bee and Doye's oldest, and a thirtieth birthday party for Allie the week before her dad died. It was the kind of home where neighborhood kids ran in and out and Allie wasn't shy about asking people to wash dishes.

I tried to remember the last time I was here. Two years, maybe three? It must've been the Easter egg hunt when I'd brought my goddaughter, Chloe, a stuffed bunny, not expecting a lanky teenager who thanked me politely before slinking off to rejoin a gaggle of girls in sweatpants and cropped tees that showed off their abs.

I patted my coat pocket for my pistol and regretted wearing loafers. I was usually better prepared, better equipped for the running, jumping, and dodging the Circus demanded. Plunging into the ankle-deep snow on the neighbor's corner property, I trudged toward a thicket bordering Allie's lot, struggling to keep my shoes on.

As I clambered onto the snow-covered patio at the back of the house, I imagined Brad at the griddle, flipping his famously fluffy chocolate chip pancakes, regaling the three girls perched at the counter with stories of the stages he danced on in Vienna, Moscow, and Paris. Allie would be leaning against the fridge in her old white robe and gray wool slippers, her weary expression not hiding how proud she was of her girls, how grateful she was to Brad for staying home with them. At times I envied her—how rich her life seemed in comparison to mine.

The picture window afforded a wide view of Allie's kitchen, oddly dark and empty at this hour. The table was strewn with the detritus of teenagers—pastel highlighters, crumpled foil wrappers, stapled homework packets—but the electric coffee maker wasn't even plugged in. I checked the time on my phone again; it was nearly seven, which didn't seem right given that Allie was always up by five thirty, reading the paper or squeezing in a few extra emails.

I glanced up at the primary bedroom, which sat over the kitchen. There was a faint light on in one of the kids' rooms, but Allie's room was dark. Maybe she and Brad had stayed out late the night before, ringing in the new year.

Flattening myself against the gray stone siding that ran between the kitchen and family room, I fished in my pocket for the key Allie had given me ages ago, when I babysat Chloe for a weekend. Once inside, I'd make my way to the living room at the front of the house;

from there I'd have a good view of the stairs and a clean shot at Allie when she came down. Maybe it was a good thing nobody was up early.

A grackle whistled loudly overhead, repeating its piercing call like an overzealous watchdog intent on waking up everyone on the street. I searched the trees and found the bird perched on a branch jutting out above me, black feathers glinting emerald green. I hissed and waved a hand, thinking I could scare it off, but it turned a rounded head and whistled determinedly at me. Pulling my gun out, I took a shot to scare it off. My aim had always been spotty, so I was stunned when the stream hit the bird in the full of its breast. To my horror, the little guy fell and landed with a thump on the pristine snow, twiggy legs sticking straight up. I whispered to him, urging him to get up. I wanted to pick him up, cradle him, but I couldn't seem to unstick myself from the stone siding. I'd never killed anything real before.

A light flicked on in Allie's bedroom, urging me to keep moving. I murmured a solemn apology to the dead bird before trying the key in the kitchen door. *Damn*—it didn't fit. I scrambled for another way in. Wasn't Allie complaining a few months ago about Chloe always forgetting her key? I felt around underneath the three planters at the edge of the patio, pawing the frozen dirt. Nothing.

I was wondering if I could jimmy the bathroom window around the side of the house when on a lark, I tried the family room patio door. I couldn't believe my dumb luck when the door swung open. Of course, this was Allie, who still believed people could be trusted to do the right thing.

She had redecorated since my last visit. The hulking brown suede sectional had been replaced by a round wooden coffee table and a pair of beige linen sofas. The same built-in bookshelves lined the far wall, but even with a squint I couldn't make out the photos across the room.

At the sound of a man's voice, I slid headfirst into the crevice between the sofa and the wall. I couldn't see him with my head buried in the dusty gap, but I felt him enter the room. A whiff of sandalwood and black leather took me back to the Drakkar the boys wore in high school, and I bit down hard on my lip to stifle a cough. The sofa shifted as he sat. The television sprang to life with the brassy sound of a high school marching band and the chatter of New Year's Day parade announcers.

Lean and muscular with a deep voice and a wicked sense of humor, Allie's husband, Brad, had trained at a ballet school in Europe as a teenager and danced with the New York City Ballet for a year before landing in Boston for college after he tore his ACL. Allie met him two years after graduating, and she fell hard. A few years ago, I asked her how they managed to seem so much in love after decades of marriage. After laughing so hard Diet Coke bubbled from her nose, she realized I was serious. She told me they had a pact. They didn't badmouth each other to anyone. Not to the kids, not to their friends, and definitely not to their parents. And it was true. To this day, I'd never heard her utter a critical word about him.

Footsteps pattered in the hall, followed by the high-pitched squeal of a young girl. The couch exhaled as Brad rose.

"They'll be here in half an hour," he barked. "If you're not done picking up in the kitchen, there'll be hell to pay."

The irritation in his voice was jarring; this wasn't the Brad I knew. A vacuum whirred; I prairie dogged over the back of the sofa. Brad was gone and in his place, a towheaded girl was pushing the vacuum back and forth half-heartedly in front of the television, her attention captivated by the twirling Minneola cheerleaders. She was a kid—too young to be Chloe. Had to be Allie's middle daughter, whose name I'd forgotten.

I swung my head up, biding my time. The wall above the sofa was blank, painted over, with no trace of the pictures of kids, grandparents, and cousins or the teaching certificate Allie had earned in college that had hung there before. Allie had doubled up on classes for a few tough semesters, never missed the fourth-grade class she co-taught that was an hour-long bus ride away, and took one of the kids out for breakfast three times a week after discovering he was bringing in a chocolate bar for lunch because there was nothing else to eat at home. Every time I saw that certificate on the wall, I felt proud of what she had done, but also a little more regretful with each passing year that she hadn't found a way to follow her dream. I couldn't think why she would've taken everything down.

The girl made a few more distracted passes near the back door, and when she dragged the vacuum away, I seized my chance. Backing out of my hiding place, I sprinted from the family room. I was careening through the dining room to the front hall when I heard a man's voice on the landing at the top of the stairs. I froze—I was completely exposed beside the stairs, and in a second, my path to the living room would be cut off.

I'd never been a gambler, but I prayed that I'd have enough time to slide by without being seen. Scurrying through the entryway, I skittered around the corner into the living room. Just past the Christmas tree, I dropped into a crouch at the far end of the sofa. I held my breath, and the house seemed to do the same. The living room was open to the front hall, and from here I had a long but straight shot at anyone coming down the stairs. I was weighing whether to venture upstairs or wait for Allie to come down when I heard a rustling at the foot of the tree. I jumped at the sight of a little girl in pink-footed pajamas crawling out from under the furry red tree skirt. Standing upright, she was a tiny thing. Brown pigtails sprouting out of her head like fountains. Too small to be Allie's youngest. A niece, maybe? Was Allie's brother visiting from South Jersey?

The girl watched me with interest. She jumped up and down, thumping loudly. I held a finger to my lips. When that didn't work, I whispered, "What's your name?" with a smile as wide as it would go. Distraction seemed like a sound strategy.

She stopped jumping and furrowed her eyebrows at me like I had ruined her game. I figured she couldn't be more than two or three. At what age did kids understand full sentences?

"Is Chloe here?" I asked in my most playful voice.

The girl shook her head. Pigtails flapped from side to side, swatting her nose.

"What about Auntie Allie? Mrs. Kohlstedt?"

She stared, unblinking. Allie's brother had two kids—were they boys?—who were probably in high school by now. Who was this kid? And where was Allie?

My gaze shifted to the Christmas tree in the bay window, a perfect triangle hung with plain silver balls. Wesley called Allie and Brad "Christmas Crazy" because they started decorating the day after Thanksgiving and for the month of December, the house was covered in electric trains, mini Santas, and stuffed elves collected on their travels over the years, not to mention the life-size herd of reindeer frozen mid-liftoff in the front yard. The hand-painted menorah that Allie inherited from her Bubby took pride of place on the sideboard in the dining room. But this tree looked like it had been drop-shipped from a catalog; it was perfect and all wrong. Where were the paper chains and clay angels the girls had made over the years? The topper fashioned from the star that Chloe wore in her third-grade pageant? The photo ornament of Brad in tights with a mullet?

The vacuum revved up again, louder now, around the corner.

I surveyed the room. The photograph of Allie, Brad, and the kids that hung over the sofa had been swapped out for a glossy aerial view of a crowded, sun-drenched beach. White wooden candlesticks sat on the mantel where the silver clock marking Allie's fifteenth anniversary at Amex should've been. The scrolled iron banister, usually ribboned with cards, was tragically bare, and the only other nod to the holidays besides the tree was a pair of yellow poinsettias. Allie hated yellow.

My understanding of Allie and Brad was intertwined with this house. They talked about this place as their forever home. The patio and grassy backyard were made for their summer cookouts, the girls' elementary school sat a block away, and the neighbors were family.

Still, Chloe was headed off to college in the fall, and I knew Allie, the sole breadwinner, had been beating herself up about how she was going to pay for it all. Winning would certainly solve that. Hiding out in a place where none of us would know to look was a smart play on Allie's part.

A disturbing thought struck me: Had I broken into the house of a stranger?

I needed to get out now, but the girl was standing between me and the front door. I was about to make a break for it when a beefy guy with a wrestler's build tromped down the stairs and swung toward the kitchen. He didn't strike me as the kind of guy who would forgive a woman skulking around his living room with a gun in her hand, even if it was a fake. The head of the vacuum peeked in and out from the hallway; the man was shouting something I couldn't make out over the din. I needed to move, but my right foot was asleep. I shifted my weight to my left, lifting up the tiniest bit, and the girl unleashed a piercing scream. My hands flew out—an instinct to muffle the sound—but I didn't dare touch her.

The man came around the corner. Definitely not Brad. This guy was a foot taller and fifty pounds heavier. He seemed befuddled, then lunged for his daughter—the opening I needed. I beelined for the front door, fingers fumbling the storm door's latch. It gave way just in time, and I barely registered the yelling as I jumped the steps and skidded down the icy walk, forgetting that the front yard had a slight downward pitch. My legs slipped out from under me, and I landed hard on my back, eyes watering. The man lunged, but I twisted, scrambling out from under him, plunging into the snow and cutting the corner off the yard. When I hit the road, I slipped and slid in a frozen, treaded path, not stopping until I rounded the redbrick school. When police lights flashed in the distance, I dove behind a bush, only exhaling after the cop car flew around the corner and turned up Allie's street, disappearing out of sight.

I forged a shortcut through backyards, losing a shoe along the way. When the throbbing in my frozen foot became more than I could bear, I called a cab and bartered my gloves for a ride to the PATH station in Hoboken. In the back seat with the window down, the wind whipped my hair across my face as I tried to make sense of what I'd done.

I replayed what I'd seen, and the details—the blank wall behind the sofa, the half-hearted Christmas decorations, the beach photo above the living room fireplace that Allie would hate—told a convincing story: Allie had moved the family out without a word. Was this her way of getting a leg up in the Circus? It was a clever strategy, but moving a family of five was no small task, especially for a woman who worked eighty hours a week. More likely, she'd been planning this move for some time. Had Wesley tipped her off about the pot? Had they brought Bee in on it too?

On the subway back to the city, I wondered if there was another explanation for why Allie hadn't told me about the move. Allie and I weren't inseparable anymore in the way that we'd been when we were younger, working ungodly hours while still finding time to meet up for happy hours and picnics in Central Park. Yet I still thought of us as close. Was it possible that she was drifting away? What else had she kept from me?

I knew I should've made more of an effort with her and Chloe. Maybe Allie was disappointed that I wasn't the most attentive godparent, but it wasn't because I didn't care. I often thought about taking Chloe to a concert at Lincoln Center or to dinner, but the idea always fell away, buried under the five or ten other things that felt more urgent. Now Chloe had to be seventeen or eighteen, a senior in high school. She'd be off to college in the fall.

As I leaned against the wall of the subway car, I figured Allie's move was an act of either desperation or genius—which, I wasn't sure. What I did know was that we were pushing to extremes and I had sorely underestimated the lengths to which my roommates would go to win this last round of the Circus.

6

By eleven forty-five that morning, I was lying opposite Coulter on the green couch in our living room, the previous Sunday's *Times* and a stack of unopened Christmas cards fanned out between us. Beating Coulter home was a welcome bit of luck. A hastily plucked bag of groceries was my intended pretext, but it wouldn't have explained why I was wearing one shoe and missing my favorite scarf and gloves when I hurried in just before eleven. Coulter stormed in a few minutes after me, mumbling about one of his chefs, and I didn't press.

He handed me the arts section and began to leaf through the sports pages. I pretended to be engrossed in the paper, but my thoughts were still twisting around my narrow escape at Allie's house. What would've happened if I had been caught? Even if Allie still owned the place, I knew too well from past rounds of the Circus that forcing your way into another person's home was a felony—even if the owner of the house stood next to you at your wedding as you exchanged your vows.

Allie's move would've required planning and forethought. The more I thought about it, the more convinced I was that Allie had been tipped off about the money. Was this confirmation that Allie and Wesley were working together? We had scrapped the old rule against collaborators; the others were clearly taking advantage of this new, unfettered version of the Circus. By dinnertime, they'd be fanned across the city, into Jersey, and up to Cambridge after Dina. I was itching to get back out there; every second on the couch was an opportunity for the others to get ahead, but I also couldn't afford to upset the delicate peace that I had struck with Coulter. He was headed to work in a few hours for the Saturday dinner service. Maybe I could find a reason for him to leave earlier.

Coulter had spread the paper across his lap and he was reading an article about athletes upping their game after forty while picking absently at the skin tag behind his ear, the one that bled now and then.

"Everything okay?" I asked.

He sighed, his hands dropping into his lap.

"I had to fire Evan."

"Your prep guy? Didn't he have a baby a few weeks ago?"

Coulter's frown hardened.

"Twins. A month ago."

It was a harsh move for a guy so devoted to his staff, especially his beloved chefs.

"What did he do?"

"Interviewed at Bottega."

Coulter viewed the neighborhood Michelin one-star as his archnemesis; I doubted they held Sempre in the same regard.

"Why not let him leave?" I asked.

He turned the page, sinking back into the paper.

"He didn't get the job."

"I'm confused. You let him go anyway? I thought he was good."

"He's a rock star, but I had no choice. Keeping him would've set the wrong example."

Coulter had no tolerance for disloyalty, especially from a guy like Evan, who'd been with the restaurant for five or six years now and was like a little brother to Coulter. I made a mental note to pull Marcella aside at the next family lunch. Coulter wouldn't change his mind, but maybe his mother could change it for him.

My gaze floated up to the hole in the ceiling.

"I think he's avoiding me," I said. "The guy who runs the condo board. What's his name—plaid bow tie?"

"Gary," he said.

"Yes. I ran into Gary on the stairs yesterday. Asked if he'd read my email and he got all flustered. The condo docs aren't clear about leaks, but he won't even have a conversation about whether the association's insurance will cover this. Do you think they're trying to get out of it?"

"Absolutely," he said without hesitation.

It was hard for Coulter to believe in people. I blamed his father for that. Coulter was fifteen when his dad left him and his mom for a neighbor's German au pair; he hadn't spoken more than a few words to his father since. I'd come to accept that Coulter might never forgive his dad for living happily ever after with Rinske and their four kids in Chappaqua, and I didn't bring it up. I could see it was still painful, even if Coulter insisted it was ancient history, and it colored the way he saw the world. He worked hard to make people think he was an open, easygoing guy, but in private he would double-check every contract and line up fallback options in case someone double-crossed him. It took years of showing up precisely when I promised I would to convince him I wasn't going to desert him in the middle of the night. I did what I could to reassure him he didn't need to prove his worth to an absent father, but his insecurity threatened to become a wedge between us. He wasn't the only one who'd been abandoned by a parent.

My phone vibrated. I leaned over to grab it from the coffee table and found a new text from Bee with a link to an article in yesterday's *Boston Globe*. The Middlesex County DA's office had solved the oldest case in its history, a decades-old murder of a Tufts student, through the use of advanced DNA testing. The victim's sister expressed her relief in finally getting answers, and the DA was pleased that he could provide closure to the victim's family, who had been haunted for years by their tragic loss.

The article hit me with a jolt. I told myself the facts of my case were completely different. There was no murder, for god's sake, but this was political gold for the DA, an impetus to dredge up more of the past. I felt like I might be sick.

"Bones, what is it?"

Bones was what Coulter called me when we were good together, a callback to a time when we were more adventurous, striking out across the city in search of little-known dishes revered in other cultures. Swimming, blackened, fermented, we ate it all, but he was scandalized when we found ourselves in a Cantonese hole-in-the-wall one night and I christened chicken feet simmered in salt and spice the perfect late-night snack. Far too bony, way too little meat, he countered with a dubious yet charming smile. Afterward, he started calling me Bones, and the pet name stuck.

"Am I in trouble again?" he asked with a teasing smile.

"The Middlesex County DA might be opening an investigation into Claudine's death."

"Middlesex County?" he asked, his playfulness draining away.

"Cambridge."

His mouth rounded into an O.

"Where did you hear this?" he asked.

"Bee told me a few weeks ago."

"It's been twenty years. What do they think they'll find?"

"I don't know," I said. "The whole thing with Claudine is never going to end, is it?"

Up until two weeks ago, I was convinced I had turned a corner. In the aftermath of her death all those years ago, I thought of Claudine obsessively. My guilt was a corset, strangling my happiness, constricting every desire. A few years after she passed, a therapist helped me loosen the strings. The constant tightness gripping my chest and throat eased into an intermittent pain. I would be skating along contentedly until I suddenly crashed into a reminder of Claudine—a sweetened tea, baked oysters, the lilt of a Southern accent—and all the anguish I'd locked away would come rushing back. The only reliable reprieve was the Circus, which I attributed to its unyielding demand that for a week in January I give it my undivided attention. In recent years, my grief had settled into a sense of incompleteness, a phantom discomfort humming at a low frequency, but this, too, unraveled after seeing Claudine again.

"Isn't there a time limit on these things?" he asked.

"Not on murder," I said, and he sat up a little taller.

"That's serious."

"Bee's going to find out more, but I'll probably have to get a lawyer. It'll be expensive, and I—"

"That's why you want to take the commercial job," he said, and I nodded.

"Her parents have this vendetta against us, against me. They're never going to stop until they—"

"Okay, okay," he said, coming over to hold me in his arms. The stress I'd bottled up was clawing its way to the surface.

"I can't go through it again, Coulter. I can't."

"I know. We'll come up with the money and fight. We'll figure this out."

We sat like this, his arms around me, neither of us moving. The weight of him kept me from spinning out. When I felt like some semblance of myself again, I pulled away gently, and he searched my face until he was convinced my anxiety had subsided. I hated keeping things from him. I wanted to tell him about seeing Claudine and the pot, but conversations about the Circus always ended badly.

"Do you believe me when I say that I won't in a million years let anything happen to you?" he asked.

"Yes," I said, but there was a hollowness in my voice that I hoped he hadn't heard.

He looked at me skeptically for a moment, but instead of calling me out, he muttered that he was off to do battle. They were seating a few large parties tonight, which was a good thing, even if it didn't sound that way from his disgruntled tone. As he thumped around the bedroom, gathering his things, I tried to take comfort in his reassurances. I believed him. Trusted him. But I'd be a fool to rely on the restaurant to save us when the solution to our problems lay in my hands. As soon as the front door closed behind him, I picked myself up, closed my eyes, and stretched my arms as high as they would go, prepping for a battle of my own.

7

"How do you spell that?" the security guard asked when I presented myself at the reception desk in the Amex lobby later that afternoon. Clad in my black moto jacket and black jeans with Coulter's old messenger bag slung across my body, I was hoping to be forgettable.

Glancing down at the thick envelope I'd bought at the drugstore around the corner, I spelled out Allie's last name like I was seeing it for the first time. Allie had been grousing at the kickoff dinner about how her whole holiday was screwed up, which told me she'd be holed up in the office this week on an important deal.

"Needs a John Hancock," I added.

"Yeah, we can't let people up anymore unless they're on the pre-approved list," the guard said.

"My boss isn't gonna be happy if I don't put this in the hands of the right person. How do I get on the list?"

"It's gotta come through the right channels," he said and gestured to the package. I held it up and he looked it over, then typed a few words on a keyboard I couldn't see behind the shoulder-high desk. "You know what department?"

"Marketing," I said, realizing too late that a real courier wouldn't know this. "VP of marketing, maybe? Do they have a special process for bigwigs?"

"Nah, everyone's gotta follow the same rules," he said. "Someone in the department comes down and signs, or you can leave it with me."

"You mind calling up?"

The guy peered at his screen, then punched in the extension. Even with the handset to his ear, I could hear it ringing.

"Nada," he said, shrugging at me.

Allie was playing smart. I leaned on the counter, surveying a cluster of sleek black sofas.

"Mind if I wait?"

The guard seemed uneasy.

"Sorry, miss. Against the rules. Security's tightened up in a big way."

"Yeah, I get it. Thanks anyway."

I made my way back out to the street, emptied of its usual bustle due to the New Year's holiday, and stuffed the fake package into a can. How could I hope to win if I didn't have the faintest idea where Allie was? The wind howled through the empty plaza in front of Allie's building and I zipped up my leather jacket. I needed to get off these deserted streets. I was easy prey out in the open.

"Come, come, you try," a man beckoned from his peanut cart, and I glanced around, unsure if he was talking to me. He nodded encouragingly and I approached a pair of food carts with familiar blue-and-yellow umbrellas. The hot dogs in the first cart lolled in murky, ancient water, but my stomach, which wasn't terribly discerning, answered with a loud grumble. The man scooped candied nuts from a heaping pile and poured them into my cupped hands. I popped two into my mouth, not expecting the warm, sweet, crunchy hit. I'd lived in this city for almost twenty years; how had I missed out on this simple pleasure for so long? A few bucks and a promise to come back got me a full paper sack. I cupped the nuts in my hand, their warmth comforting, and their salty sweetness lifted me out of my funk.

Just then I spied a woman watching us from ten or fifteen feet down the sidewalk. Blond hair, army-green puffer, jeans. My stomach clenched. I had forgotten to check for a tail.

Wesley came at me like a sprinter off the blocks and I ran. I was a tourist in this part of town, wary of the broad plazas that left me exposed. I swerved east in search of tight streets and dark corners, zigzagging madly between cars with a giddy laugh, and careening around an oblivious foursome fanned across the sidewalk. I skirted barricades shutting down the street for a festival and raced past trucks hawking foot-long hot dogs, my body electric. I liked to think I was in decent shape thanks to my obsessive walking and fifth-floor apartment, but I was huffing. Wesley hadn't been to a gym since we were twenty—her idea of exercise was dancing at all-night raves; how was she hard on my heels? There was no way she was catching me; this wasn't how I was going down.

Veering off West Broadway onto smaller, more familiar streets where tiny shops bore Chinese names, I spotted a dinner crowd gathering in front of a glittering gold facade. Wesley was closing the gap quickly. A bustling restaurant seemed like a good place to hide.

Tugging at the glass door, I pushed my way to the front of the messy queue, where the hostess shouted out names. The smell of sizzling beef and fried noodles gnawed at me as I took in the packed dining room, the huge round tables, the families and friends indulging in honor of the New Year. I hustled down the aisle, nearly colliding with a waiter expertly balancing platters of steaming noodles, and ducked through a swinging door.

In the smoky kitchen, a string of men in white undershirts stood shoulder to shoulder against griddles, fryers, and burners. They manned stockpots and woks the size of huge drums and shouted orders down the line over the sizzle of hot oil. I kept moving, giving wide berth to cooks decimating chickens with enormous cleavers, and jumped when a prep cook waved a knife at me like a gruesome appendage. He shouted in a language I didn't speak, but I knew what he was saying. I had no business being here.

Hurling past a bank of refrigerators, I aimed for a door propped open to what I hoped was a back alley when I noticed a child-sized opening on my left—easy to miss in a hurry. I loathed confined spaces, but I wasn't sure I could beat Wesley in a footrace down the alley, so I ducked inside the narrow, airless storeroom. The light slanted in enough to make out huge sacks of rice stacked five and six high, thick as a bunker wall. I had just touched down beside the sacks, pumping with adrenaline, when jeans and white sneakers raced by. Unmistakably Wesley.

Intent on doubling back to give Wesley the slip, I crawled awkwardly out the opening and was barely back on my feet when a woman crashed into me so hard I fell backward, slamming into the wall.

"Sorry, Sara," Dina said, her gun in one hand, the other hand held out in apology.

Before I could say anything, she slid by me and bolted after Wesley.

I shook off the dizziness and raced after them, but by the time I hit the alley, Dina was turning the corner onto the main thoroughfare, and I lost both of them in a weaving sea of dark coats. Thinking Wesley or Dina might come back for me, I kept watch from the shadows on the corner, praying Dina had chased Wesley halfway to the Bronx. My whole body pulsed with the same delicious rush I got from the roller coasters I still loved: the clenched anticipation, the stomach flutters, that moment of exhilarating lightness just before you fall.

When the dinner crowds began to dissipate with still no sign of any roommate, I headed home, relieved that I had survived the first day of the Circus. Knowing Coulter would stay late at the restaurant to accommodate the Saturday-night stragglers, I found myself alone in the kitchen, exhausted and unsure what would quell my restlessness. At the back of the fridge, I found a can of hard cider, Claudine's favorite drink, and thought of those early days. How in the spring of our freshman year, the four of us—Wesley, Bee, Allie, and me—convinced ourselves we needed a fifth roommate to boost our chances of getting into the upper-class house we so badly wanted. Wesley proposed some girl in her Latin class, who was smart and funny, but because she was a free spirit and a bit of a loner, she might be open to joining us.

WITH FRIENDS LIKE THESE

When the five of us met over lunch in the freshman dining hall, Claudine was nothing like what I'd expected. With tousled blond hair and a light dusting of freckles across her nose, she looked like an earthy goddess, but anyone who spent five minutes with her could tell her mind didn't run in straight lines. Her thoughts hopscotched across eras and disciplines, making unexpected connections that we didn't always follow, but Wesley had been right. She was warm and funny. We were sold.

Once we landed in Winthrop House, Claudine and I drew the short straws, which stuck us together in a walk-through double—a rest stop on the way to the more comfortable room where Bee and Wesley slept in twin beds flanking a window, and a world away from Allie's single, which felt absolutely palatial in comparison. Claudine slept on the bottom bunk and I on the top, our two dressers lining the opposite wall, so close I could set my book on top of my dresser when I settled in for the night.

After the first few weeks, I wouldn't have traded that crappy little room for anything. Claudine and I would stay up for hours whispering from one bunk to the other. In the beginning, we skated along on the surface, dishing about professors we loved and loathed and imagining our bright futures. I hadn't decided on my direction yet, but she dreamed of setting up in some high desert town like Santa Fe, where she'd capture the sky, the stars, and the wind with her paintbrush like her idol Georgia O'Keeffe. Claudine wanted to live simply with people who honored history and tradition but didn't feel imprisoned by it.

Over time, we tunneled under the surface into territory that felt more real. Claudine had a way of asking questions that I'd never answer for anyone else. She never judged, always made me feel like she desperately wanted to inhabit my perspective, as if being a half-Asian woman from a Maryland suburb with a dead mother and a drunk father was a skin she could actually slip into. She knew how devastated I felt after my mother's death. How when I was fourteen my grilled cheese set the kitchen on fire and my father developed a habit of locking me in a closet when he got called out at night to fix a broken toilet. She told me how she was scared of her own mother, who had a vengeful streak. Her mother had once tried to drown her father in a hotel pool during a family vacation to Disney World.

Had you asked, I would've denied it at the time, but Claudine was the first real friend I'd ever had. The first person who saw me, who knew me in a way I barely even knew myself, and made me feel comfortable revealing parts of me I'd hidden away. For the first time at school—maybe for the first time since my mother died—I was happy. I had no idea how soon it would come to an end.

8

COULTER'S restaurant sat on an unassuming street in a neighborhood that had gentrified with surprising speed over the last few years. Sempre was sandwiched between a cash-only bakery that had sold cannoli for seven decades and a hip bring-your-own-vinyl bar hawking succulents over the counter of a Dutch barn door. Though Coulter had been dragging Sempre into this decade bit by bit, swapping out the eighties faux-stone facade for steel mullioned windows and red vinyl banquettes for beige leather chairs, it seemed fitting that the restaurant should sit between these neighbors, between tradition and trend, chasing relevance in both directions.

When I walked up late the next morning, Coulter's extended family was already gathered inside, just as they'd been one Sunday a month for a decade, and it was apparent this place hadn't lost its soul. I looked forward to these gatherings, to the noise and chaos, to good-natured teasing and heated debates, and to the way Coulter's relatives inserted themselves into one another's lives when it would've been so much easier to skim the surface and leave other people's problems alone. I tossed my coat and scarf over a bar stool and dove into the fray, double-kissing aunts and uncles, hugging cousins. Aunt Bettina eyed my stomach, asked when I was going to give them another cousin. I told her when the time was right, which was the answer Coulter and I had settled on—not committing, but not needlessly squashing hopes either. The truth was that some days I worried we'd regret not having kids. Other days, I felt relieved; the responsibility terrified me. What if I was no better at parenting than my own parents? What if motherhood pinned me down and swallowed me whole? For the better part of a year, when we were a little younger, I tried to get pregnant. When nothing took, I suggested we take a break, try again later. "Later" stretched into a year, then two, then three. I let go. Since motherhood had always seemed amorphous and distant, I didn't suffer it as a loss.

Uncle Tony put his hands on my shoulders, told me I got more beautiful every month. I'd never been good with compliments, so I was grateful when his daughter, Venezia, threw an arm around her dad and chided: "Dad, we talked about this. You can't say that kind of stuff anymore. Remember #MeToo?" Tony shrugged, regarding us with a sheepish grin. Venezia gave me a peck on both cheeks.

Coulter had wanted to skip the family lunch this week, desperate for a break from the restaurant, but I wasn't about to miss the shot of big, boisterous energy I got from Coulter's family. I pointed out he might gain an extra hour on the couch, but would hear about it from his mom for *weeks*. He should save his fire for the battle he and his mother were waging over the menu, I reasoned. Marcella insisted the old favorites would bring people back, but he knew a bigger menu meant higher fixed costs. It didn't matter that she had no official role at the restaurant; she was a strong personality and didn't hesitate to share her opinions. The cloth napkins weren't white enough, the entrée portions were too generous, the servers should be pushing cocktails. Coulter was right, but Marcella meant well. And maybe I was able to overlook her minor transgressions because she treated me like a daughter and made the rest of the family fall in line behind her.

As we arranged ourselves around the table, Marcella appeared suddenly behind me, squeezing my arm and whispering that Coulter looked thin. I glanced over to find him engrossed in conversation with his eleven-year-old niece. He looked sharp in a blue checkered button-down that brought out his eyes, his mop of brown hair tousled to one side—but I, too, could see that his shirt was hanging a little more loosely than usual. She patted the top of my arm, her way of saying that this was a situation that I, his wife, should fix.

Once we were seated, we bowed our heads in honor of Grandpa Vito and Uncle Chuck, who took the restaurant over after Vito passed. As soon as the moment lifted, the school-age cousins barreled through the swinging door, bearing platters laden with bresaola, polpettone, and manicotti. The table was so full that we rearranged glasses and bottles of wine, pulling our place settings close so that everything fit. For the next two hours, I didn't think about Claudine, the DA's intentions, or who was coming for me. I soaked up an aunt's tutorial on the proper way to make eggplant Parmesan, took the right side in a debate over whether air-conditioning was bad for your health, and helped to convince the elder generation that double kissing on the cheek was too presumptuous for a standard greeting. Coulter sat diagonally across from me, and it was good to see him laughing too.

Though I considered my college roommates a kind of family, I didn't have much in the way of my own family. My mom, an only child, was an elementary school librarian who immigrated from China and landed at a small college in Northern Virginia on a full scholarship. Cancer took her a few months before I turned fourteen, which struck me as preordained because the number four in Chinese sounds like the word for death. She had a thing about it too; she'd order one more steamed bun or egg tart if they arrived in a box of four, ask to change hotel rooms if we were assigned a room with an unlucky number. I still felt her absence like a dull throbbing. I often wondered how different my life would be—how different I would be—had she survived. Mostly, I regretted pushing her chopsticks away when she gave me the last dumpling or emptied a platter of noodles onto my plate. Now I knew better; this had been her way of showing her love.

My father, also an only child, had no idea how to express his emotions, and something inside him broke when she left us. He'd grown up on a farm and had always been reserved, content to stand in her warm shadow as she struck up conversations with strangers in line at the supermarket or the library. She had a talent for asking questions that put people at ease, a habit she attributed to her self-consciousness about her accent. When she died, my father didn't know what to do with the handwritten notes, the poppyseed cakes, the barbecue invitations. His drinking seeped into every corner of our life, and as he became more volatile, we became an island. At night, I dreamed of a life I conjured from the glossy brochures in our high school guidance counselor's office: a picturesque New England university with pristine, rolling lawns and shiny friends who would teach me how to drink and smoke and discuss highbrow things like philosophy and geopolitics. I counted down the days until my new life would start on a wall calendar I hid in my desk drawer.

"Let's ask Sara what she thinks," Coulter's cousin Rocco was saying to his sister, Annelise, before turning to me expectantly. "Don't you think dating the new waitress is totally fine?"

Annelise, who was roughly my age, gave me a conspiratorial look: "Coulter hired a new waitress. Mid-twenties, blond. And yes, I will concede she's hot." Then, turning back to Rocco: "But you coming on to her is the definition of a hostile workplace."

Coulter had forgotten to mention that his newest employee was attractive.

"I don't even work here that often," Rocco insisted. "I'm a part-time bartender, barely getting minimum wage. The management obviously doesn't appreciate my talents."

"Sounds like you need to take it up with the guy in charge," I said. "I think you're worth at least minimum wage." Rocco shot me an exaggerated side-eye, and Annelise laughed. I was relieved neither of them noticed my concern. Coulter had a weakness for bubbly blondes. A few years ago, I caught him texting with a marketing manager at his first start-up. He'd left the bank the previous year and was drifting in a sea of uncertainty and self-doubt; when he landed a sales job at a buzzy tech company, I should've known he was vulnerable. The text chain I stumbled on was a month long, salacious at times, but what bothered me more was that he was confiding in her in a way he wasn't in me. We worked through it. Couples therapy had helped repair trust, but we both had scars.

"Rocco, how about we move on to a subject more interesting than your love life?" Annelise asked. "Sara, I hear Barbara Colasanti is a friend of yours."

"My college roommate, actually," I said in between bites of manicotti.

"A Black mayor from Staten Island," Rocco said approvingly. "Could be good for the city. You know, shake things up."

"She's biracial, and yes, I think she'd do a fantastic job," I said. I didn't think of Bee as a candidate who would bring radical change, although I knew that for some, having a woman of color in the mayor's office would in itself be a dramatic departure from the status quo.

"Have you been to Gracie Mansion?" Rocco asked. "What's it like?"

"Not yet, but if you vote for her, I'll take you when she's elected."

"I don't know—she's a little progressive for me," Rocco said, and Annelise punched him in the arm. "But hook us up, okay? Marcella says you have friends in high places."

I scanned the long table and found Marcella chatting with Aunt Bettina at the far end. So she thought I had friends in high places?

The younger cousins came around to clear the table, but we'd barely dented the generous servings on our plates, so we dug in with gusto. Only when I felt sated did I realize Coulter's chair was empty. I surveyed the dining room and found him huddled with his mother near the kitchen door. His head was bent, his arms crossed over his chest, and Marcella was talking in his ear. He suddenly squared up against her, his hand slashing the air. I couldn't make out what he was saying, but I could tell from the way she recoiled that it wasn't what Marcella wanted to hear.

Coulter's mother was what you'd expect from a woman of her generation who grew up in a hardworking immigrant family. The

Russos landed on Ellis Island with pennies in their pockets, and the early years were filled with setbacks. Marcella told stories of how men shouted slurs at her on the street and how she was once fired from a good waitressing job after dumping a pitcher of water on a man who insulted her Southern Italian heritage. The family was turned out of their apartment more than once, and while her mother found steady work as a babysitter, her father took what he could find, which usually meant building roads and digging ditches.

It was no surprise that Marcella became strong and scrappy, and I respected her resilience. She climbed her way up from hostess to waitress, typist to secretary, lounge singer to nightclub manager. After her divorce from Coulter's dad, she sold real estate on Long Island. Despite her capacity for reinvention, she held on to traditions—dishes drawn from the old recipes, Catholic baptisms and weddings, Italian aphorisms peppering her speech—that felt stuck in the past. Marcella wouldn't let us move in together until we were married; she'd be livid if she knew we were sleeping over every night for a year before the wedding. Even though she'd worked her whole life, she believed in the primacy of wives building up and supporting their husbands, and every gift she gave me—a frilly apron, a silky nightgown, a pasta machine—doubled down on her worldview. At times, her embrace felt conditioned on my ability to fulfill the role of a good wife.

Marcella retook her seat, but Coulter still hadn't returned when the table was cleared. I excused myself and peeked into the kitchen to find three middle-school nieces washing dishes with varying degrees of enthusiasm. The teenage nephews were putting the finishing touches on tiramisu, all terse efficiency and intense focus. No sign of Coulter, but Aunt Bettina perched on a tall wooden stool was a welcome sight. Her dark thinning hair was coiffed in an elegant blowout, her navy-blue knit suit a little tighter than it used to be, but she was vibrant and aware at eighty-two, barking orders at her grandnieces and grandnephews.

I felt a presence behind me.

"Sara," Marcella said, her accent still thick after all these years. "You know the saying we have in this family—*Chi si volta, e chi si gira, sempre a casa va finire.*"

I recognized it, though I couldn't remember its exact translation. I kicked myself for not having kept up with the online Italian classes I dabbled in a few years ago.

"He always had big dreams, but this is not part of it," she said, gesturing to the dining room.

"Coulter loves this place," I said. "He knows what it means to you."

I hoped to reassure her, but she was right. This life had been thrust upon Coulter, accepted out of a sense of duty that had seeded a growing resentment. I wondered if this explained his dislike of my roommates; they were forging their own paths and living on their own terms, both of which he craved for himself.

She put her hand on my arm.

"The restaurant is in trouble," Marcella said.

I glanced past her to the dining room that Coulter had fixed up on a shoestring budget, fighting for the long oak bar, the beige leather chairs, and the brown shaded wall lamps that added a little refinement. He could barely afford the updates on the heels of the kitchen fire three years ago that nearly took the whole building down, but I thought he had dragged the restaurant's finances back onto stable ground.

"He took out a loan, and we have a big payment coming due," she said, crossing her arms over her chest. "Too big."

Neither Coulter nor I had any illusion we'd retire early or rich, but the goal had always been to keep the staff in their jobs and cover our basic expenses. I didn't dare ask how big of a payment she was talking about, perhaps to hide my embarrassment that Coulter hadn't mentioned it. I rifled back through recent conversations. He'd shared worries about his front-of-house guy leaving, the rising cost of ground beef, the shiny newcomers opening up and down the street. Nothing about a loan.

"You may not have a good job now, but you are the dependable one," she said, and I tried not to take offense at being described like a pair of old shoes. "My son is . . ." She paused, waving a hand around as she searched for the right word. "Well, he wants life to be fun. Always la dolce vita. He was that way in school, and I'm afraid he has not changed."

I had heard stories about Coulter's college antics.

"This is not a good combination with *una testa calda*," she said, wagging a finger at me.

My Italian was poor, but I understood. He could be hotheaded.

"Talk to him," she said. "Make him see this is the time to focus. We cannot lose this."

I nodded vigorously.

"I will," I said, and she gave me an approving nod before starting back to the table.

"Marcella?"

She swung around, eyebrows raised.

"The family saying. Can you remind me what it means?"

She looked surprised, even a touch amused, by my question.

"*Chi si volta, e chi si gira, sempre a casa va finire*," she said. "No matter where you go or where you turn, you'll always come home."

A satisfied expression moved across her face, but I was caught up in something I'd missed before.

"That's where the name of the restaurant comes from? Sempre?"

She seemed pleased that I had made this connection.

"Under my grandfather, it was called Sempre a Casa. Chuck thought Americans would have a hard time with that, so he shortened it to Sempre."

She patted me on the arm and headed back to the table.

When we had devoured our tiramisu, we pushed away from the table and made the rounds to say our goodbyes. Out of the corner of my eye, I spied Coulter emerging from his office at the far end of the bar. Had he been hiding from his mother this whole time?

Bettina and the middle-school nieces swarmed the dining room with brown paper boxes stacked high. One of the nieces placed a heavy box in my hands. Maybe I was thinking about the past more than usual, but it reminded me of the brown bag lunches my mother used to pack for me. Lo mein, fried rice with bits of sausage, or a steamed bun filled with barbecued pork. The language of love was always the same.

The girls ran back to the kitchen. Through the swinging door, I caught a glimpse of Coulter, head bowed, chopping furiously in preparation for the Sunday-night dinner service. I had just started toward him when Marcella emerged from the kitchen with a furious look on her face. She smoothed her hair and donned a pleasant smile, the transformation instantaneous, and I wondered what else had transpired between them. She was right about Coulter—he did have big dreams, which didn't include the restaurant—and I wondered how much longer he and his mother could exist like this, locked in a struggle that neither of them could win.

9

FABBY gave me Monday off unexpectedly—she was holed up with a new boyfriend in her place upstate—so I spent a good chunk of the day skulking around in the cold outside Allie's office, accosting anyone who looked like they worked in corporate marketing to ask if they'd seen Allie recently. By the time I got home, deflated and chilled to the bone, all I wanted to do was warm myself in front of the fire. Coulter always stayed late at work on Mondays to catch up on orders and payroll. To be honest, I was grateful for the time alone, since I was dreading the conversation I'd promised Marcella I'd have with him.

I figured I'd forage for something to eat and watch a few shows to get the Circus out of my head, but before flopping on the couch, I did a sweep of the kitchen, bedroom, and bathroom, where the doorknob was still loose despite Coulter's repeated promises he would fix it. Terrified I'd get locked inside, I made a mental note to bring it up with him when he got home.

I checked that the front door was chained and double bolted, both of which I'd reinforced a few years ago because of Dina. She could pick most locks, although given what I knew about her rough upbringing downtown, I suspected this was a skill she acquired long before the Circus. Even so, I could tell the paranoia was setting in. It was day three, and I was checking over my shoulder obsessively. I would've barricaded the bedroom door if Coulter wasn't coming home. The anxiety would only increase as we marched toward the final day—if I was lucky enough to last that long.

When I was satisfied I was alone, I retreated to the living room to build a fire. I was rolling newspaper to prime the flue when a strange feeling tripped down my spine—a springing awareness that I had company. I turned and jumped back at the sight of a figure standing in the corner.

"Jesus Christ," I said. "How did you get in here?"

Dina was leaning against the wall at the far end of the sofa, clad entirely in black. Her eyes were fixed on the hole in the ceiling.

"What the hell happened here?" she asked.

"It collapsed. Coulter was sitting there just before it happened."

Dina skirted the coffee table to peer up at the hole. The mess had been mostly cleaned up, but Dina knew Coulter liked to read by the window in his sheepskin chair. Her presence had me on high alert; it could only mean she'd taken out Wesley and I was her new target.

Flipping on the lights, I surveyed the bar Coulter kept on the cabinet near the window, figuring a drink would buy me time. Coulter thought of himself as a mixologist, and he wasn't half bad—every season he came up with the restaurant's featured drink, and the Dumbo Dumbwaiter had been a recent hit. He was particular about his setup—a tray of spirits and mixers, a silvery cup for the vintage bar tools he collected, a creased notebook of his own recipes—so I left the cocktails to him and stuck to the straight stuff when he wasn't around. I poured two glasses of Fernet, the bitter digestif we drank because it was known to settle stomachs and nerves.

"He'll be home soon," I said, handing Dina her drink as I leaned against the shelves near the door.

She laughed.

"No, he won't," she said without an ounce of doubt.

"How do you know?"

"Because you just did that thing with your eyes—blinking up and to the right."

It was hard to outsmart someone who knew me so well.

"And he always works late on Mondays," she said. "But don't worry. I'll be gone before he gets back."

I'd grown accustomed to the way Dina pared things down to bare fact, discarding the skin of emotion that colored other people's worlds, but I hated the dynamic between my husband and my closest friend. The two of them simply approached life from opposite poles. Coulter went out and took what he wanted. Dina worked harder than anyone I knew, and never wanted to impose. It didn't help that years ago during Coulter's stint at a Silicon Alley start-up, Dina brought the Circus to a dinner he was hosting at a fancy Midtown restaurant for an important investor. It was a mess: Dina thought Coulter and I were eating with mutual friends. She ambushed me on the way to the bathroom, causing a melee that ended in getting all of us thrown out. Coulter was mortified. The investor stopped returning his calls and Coulter was nearly fired. He never forgave Dina for that fiasco.

Dina was too good to criticize him, but I sensed she didn't trust him. He'd probably given her good reason to be skeptical, but it sometimes felt like she was hoping he would slip up and expose his affable exterior as a cheap facade. And Dina could be possessive. She and I were friends before I met Coulter. These days, it was easier to keep the two of them apart.

"Come on," I said. "You know you're always welcome here. Well, not this week, but you know what I'm saying."

"How is he, anyway?" Dina asked, which surprised me because our conversations usually steered clear of Coulter. "What's going on with him?"

"He's fine, I guess. Working all the time. Trying to keep Sempre's doors open."

"Is it that bad out there for good Italian restaurants?"

"In this economy, yes."

"Well then, maybe it's time you convinced Coulter that we'd all be better off under a matriarchy," she said slyly, knowing I'd been tossing around the idea of a new photography series on women in power, and I laughed at how impossible her suggestion sounded. I'd always thought of Coulter as one of the good guys, an ally to women and people of color, but he was blind to how easily he moved through the world. He gave little thought to running in Central Park or walking home at any time of night, when I wouldn't jog around the block after dark or take the subway alone after a certain hour. What frustrated me was when he climbed up on his lefty stump, insisting that health care and college should be free for all, and people thought him unrealistic or out of touch, but still clever and charming. When I tried to point out the ways that women had to work harder to get paid the same as men, people lowered their eyes and thought me shrill.

"God, that would be so much better," I agreed. "But no, we can't even figure out a vacation, much less flying to the other side of the world for a photography project no one is asking for, so I'm applying to travel fellowships instead. There's one at the Tibet Society that sounds interesting."

It was a secret I hadn't even told Coulter. I had applied to a bunch of programs over the past year, and last summer I'd been shortlisted for an emerging artist grant, only to lose out to a guy Fabby deemed a middling photographer. I was crushed when I found out he went to high school with one of the jurors, but Fabby talked me down. She planted the seed for the matriarchal societies project. She thought it was the kind of thing the Tibet Society would back if I pitched it the right way. The director had ties to the Mosuo in Western China, and he'd been looking for ways to highlight minority ethnic groups. More important, Fabby said, glaring at me in that stern but loving way of hers, success was the best revenge.

"I know you'll get it," Dina said, and I knew she wanted this for me as much as I wanted it for myself. That was the thing about our friendship—we weren't friends because one of us was useful to the other, nor were we coasting on the long tail of history. From the start, we understood each other. Daughters of absent mothers, introverts in a world that preferred extroverts, Dina and I did the best we could. Under the wings of selfless teachers, we beat the odds, but we still weren't sure how either of us landed at a place like Harvard. I'd never touch the word *love*—it was too loaded, left you too exposed—but I felt there was something true about our friendship. Something authentic and unassailable, solidified over the last twenty years. I'd never felt this way with anyone else. Except, for a time, Claudine.

"She'd be happy, you know," Dina said. "Claudine thought you had this way of observing things that gave you a certain clarity. She wanted you to do something creative with it."

How had Dina read my thoughts so easily? I never wanted Dina to feel that our friendship was lessened by the closeness I had felt with Claudine. But the kindness that Dina relayed—Claudine's generous spirit—reminded me of what I had lost and left me with a dull aching.

The truth was that Claudine and I had begun to drift apart by the late spring of our junior year. People who didn't know us might've thought this was because Claudine and Wesley had started dating guys in the same final club, their foursome quickly becoming a popular fixture at campus parties. But the real cause had been seeded in the fall, when Dina joined our roommate group unexpectedly as a transfer. She had no problem fitting in academically, but it was clear from the start that she was otherwise lost. Allie and I took it upon ourselves to show her around and to include her whenever we could, but Dina kept to herself in those first few months, and there were times when I thought we might simply coexist as roommates before going our separate ways. As winter turned to spring, I was surprised to discover that behind her quiet brilliance was a fantastic dry wit, a constant generosity, and a passion for house music that she would crank up and dance to when no one else was around. Maybe Dina needed to know that she could trust me, and I suppose I had passed her test.

That spring, Claudine made a huge effort to bring me along to dinners and parties, but I begged off with increasing frequency, aware that the invitations rarely extended to Dina. I'll admit that I was envious when I heard reports of all the fun Claudine and Wesley seemed to be having—Wesley described their foursome as young, irresponsible, and having a hell of a good time—but their partying grew more determined. They drank until one of them blacked out. And Claudine picked up smoking; she developed a habit of sitting on our window ledge to light up when she couldn't sleep.

By senior year, the mood had grown tense in our suite, mostly because of the widening rift between Claudine and me. She and Wesley were still carousing loudly around Cambridge, though with much less conviction than the previous spring. They were no longer college girls looking for good trouble, but women who drank to feel more like themselves.

"Did you hear about the stunt Bee pulled?" Dina was asking. "Called pretending to be the university police. Claimed some kid broke into my office and I needed to get down there right away to see if anything was taken. I fell for it too."

"Isn't that against the rules? Pretending to be a cop?"

She gave me an arch look, and I realized my mistake. The rules didn't apply anymore.

"She's good," Dina said. "Never said she was a cop. Just put on a good accent. And the call came up on my phone as the university police."

"Impressive," I said. "How did you get away?"

"The building was too quiet. And she didn't know there's a back staircase up to my office."

I nodded. This was what I was up against: four smart, capable women pouring everything they had into winning.

I had been inching closer to the doorway while we spoke, subtly enough that Dina didn't seem to notice. I couldn't fathom why she hadn't attacked already when I was in such close range. With Dina, there had to be a reason why she was stringing me along. I wasn't going to wait around and find out.

A police siren blared, followed by the rapid-fire rumbling that you could feel in your bones. Dina turned to the window for a look; it was my opening. I tore out of the room and somehow flung open the front door without getting shot. Flying down the stairs, I kept running when I hit the sidewalk.

I felt the impact first on my neck and shoulders, the weight of her on my back. We tumbled, went down hard on the concrete, which was unforgiving and bitterly cold. I rolled over, pain shooting up through my shoulder. Dina, sprawled on the sidewalk next to me, pushed up first and offered me a hand. I waved it away.

Dina paced a tight circle, then bent over with her hands on her knees, panting like a high school sprinter.

"Allie's right," I said, sitting up with my legs splayed out in front of me. "We're too old for this shit."

The shooting would be a formality. The Circus was over for me. I expected a wave of disappointment. Instead, I was surprised to find I could breathe again.

"You okay?" Dina asked, pointing at her cheek.

I put a hand to my throbbing cheek, scraped but not bleeding too badly. I nodded.

"You?"

"I'll live," Dina said, grimacing.

"Well, congrats," I said.

"For what?"

Dina could be so dense sometimes.

"Getting Wesley. And now me."

"Oh," Dina said. "You're not my target. And I haven't gotten Wesley. Not yet."

I got to my feet, confused.

"Then what was all this?"

"I just wanted to talk to you."

"Talk to me? What were we doing upstairs?"

"You ran before I could ask you the thing I wanted to ask."

"Well, now seems like a good time."

She held up a finger to tell me she needed a second, and when she caught her breath, she said: "Help me win."

The request caught me flat-footed. Except for her veiled plea at the kickoff dinner, Dina wasn't in the habit of asking for help. She preferred to go it alone.

"We can tag-team Bee after you take care of Allie," she said.

"How do you know Allie's my target?"

"Your reaction at dinner: relief," Dina said as if this were the most obvious thing in the world. "You wouldn't have felt that way if you had gotten anyone other than Allie. And she's only won three times."

There was a hint of judgment in her voice. She'd clearly forgotten I'd won only twice—once by disguising myself as the kind of older woman who garners little notice in public and a second time with Coulter's help.

"I'll admit Bee's the hardest get," she said. "I'm systematic. Wesley's crazy. But Bee is a dangerous combination of daring and smarts."

For someone who had a hard time reading people, Dina could be incredibly perceptive, or just thoroughly logical. And she was right about us. The Circus allowed us to indulge our baser instincts, show our true colors. Some of us crossed lines and took risks we wouldn't usually dream of; others couldn't fathom doing anything in the Circus they wouldn't do in real life. Allie was definitely in the latter camp. She'd steal your trash, reconstruct your shredded bills, and glean that you saw your trainer every Tuesday morning at eight, but she didn't have a wily bone in her body, which made her an easier kill than the others. Still, only a fool assumed the Circus would play out the same way each year.

"Dina, I don't know."

She fiddled with the zipper on her black windbreaker. She usually came at me with logic and reason—never a quiet admission that she needed help.

"Did you hear back from the tenure committee?"

"No," she said curtly. "But I could use this win."

The wind kicked up, reminding me I had run out without a jacket.

"Dina, everything's gonna be fine. Do you remember when you finished your PhD? You were so stressed your hair fell out, and then you landed teaching jobs at your top three. And when you thought they wouldn't move you up from assistant to associate professor?"

"Took them a hell of a long time."

I arched my back; a small pain radiated up and down my side.

"It was your fifth year. Isn't that when everyone moves up?"

"Yes, but—" she said, stopping short. I knew what she was thinking. She wasn't like everybody else. She was supposed to be better.

Dina's relentless perfectionism was rearing its head. After being told all her life that she was smarter than everyone else, she believed she should get things right on the first try. It was a combustible formula. Disaster could only be prevented by achieving the impossible.

"So what do you say?" she asked, changing the subject abruptly.

"I wouldn't be any help," I said. "I can't find Allie. I've looked everywhere."

It wasn't a lie. On top of standing outside Allie's office building for the past two days, I'd scoured social media, political donation logs, and real estate sale sites, even wasted $39.95 on a website claiming they could find anyone through public records. I called Allie's gym, her dry cleaner, a mom she knew from her kids' school, and the leader of her toastmasters group. Aside from the kickoff dinner, no one had seen Allie in weeks.

"You might want to check Chloe's music school," Dina said so casually it took me a minute to recognize the magnitude of what she was saying. "Morningside Heights. Allie's picking her up Thursday."

"Wait—how do you know that?"

She shrugged sheepishly. She'd never reveal her methods, but this was a sweetener. A carrot to lure me over to her side.

"Dina," I said, unsure what to say. I wanted to help, but I couldn't. I knew she was still paying off student loans, that she didn't make nearly enough as an associate professor as she should. She needed this, but Coulter and I did too. Dina seemed puzzled by my hesitation, at least until her confusion turned to sympathy.

"You're leaving him," she said.

"What? No."

"Oh. I just . . ." She didn't finish the thought, but she didn't need to; I knew how she felt about Coulter, even if she didn't often voice her animosity. Flustered and embarrassed, she mumbled that she needed to go and stalked off, eager to put distance between us.

"Dina, wait," I shouted, feeling awful. When she didn't stop, I called after her. "Fine. I'll do it. I'll help."

She stopped. I knew she'd heard me, but she didn't turn back. She simply waved over her shoulder and resumed her brisk pace.

10

I ARRIVED at Sempre the following morning to find Bee at the center of a dark-suited huddle, staffers gathered around her, listening with rapt attention. She was a commanding presence in a red jacket and the three-inch heels she favored so she could tower over men. The gaggle of twentysomethings thought so, too, watching her with such bright admiration. They nodded as she walked through how she wanted the fundraising lunch to unfold, explained the backgrounds of the big hitters who would be in the room, and highlighted campaign talking points. I thought of the recent headline in the metro section of the *Times* that had caught my eye: "Cash Pouring into Heated NYC Mayoral Race, Colasanti at Risk." I tore through the article, which noted the top two candidates had already raised record amounts of money while Bee trailed at a distant third place. If Bee didn't close the gap by the end of this month, the article claimed, her campaign would face tough choices. She'd be forced to lay off the bulk of her staff. A death knell, according to this columnist.

This was why Bee wanted to play so desperately. This was why she had to win the Circus.

The dining room was transformed—long tables of eight and ten draped in crisp white cloths, with stunning flower arrangements, and a buzz the restaurant didn't usually have—but a cursory glance told me we'd be cutting it close, with barely an hour until the first guests arrived. Some of the tables weren't fully set, there were no clean glasses behind the bar, and water hadn't been poured. Through the kitchen window, I could see the waitstaff nodding, their expressions serious. Coulter must be briefing them. Stashing my coat and purse behind the bar, I got to work.

I was hauling a stack of plates from the kitchen when I spotted Bee chomping on carrot sticks from a plastic baggie, an aide walking her through the name tags at the welcome table.

When Coulter had told me about this booking two weeks ago, neither of us acknowledged what we were both thinking: Why would Bee schedule a fundraiser right in the middle of the Circus? I figured this lunch must've been planned by a staffer in the dark about her boss's pastime, and Coulter wasn't about to object. This was a fantastic booking for him. These days, lunch was rarely more than a quarter full, and Coulter might even garner a mention in the press.

I'll admit that I was grateful for the temporary respite from the Circus. A crowded dining room wasn't out of the question for a kill, but getting a shot off without any witnesses would be nearly impossible, especially if I stayed close to the tables. I took this to mean that none of my roommates would touch me for a few hours, even while I was holding out hope that since Bee was Allie's target, Allie might be tempted to show her face today. When she did, I'd have my opportunity.

I had laid the last of the bread plates and was dropping off a tray of clean glasses behind the bar when I heard a familiar voice.

"Bones."

I spun around to find Coulter behind the bar with me. He had changed into a fresh white button-down and dark pants. For a guy sweating through his undershirt, he looked convincingly at ease.

"Thank god you're here," Coulter said with a murderous expression. "My new server called in sick two hours ago and didn't get anyone to cover."

I wondered if he was talking about the blonde Rocco was chasing, but I knew it wasn't the time to bring it up. We were expecting eighty for lunch, including a raft of city officials and major donors from the neighborhood. Today needed to go perfectly.

"What can I do?"

He ran his fingers through his hair, then nodded at three pink boxes tied with red-and-white string sitting on the bar—the hallmark of a well-known Italian bakery nearby.

"Maybe it's for the best," he said. "Bee's team brought in pignoli cookies for one of the donors, and the new girl is deathly allergic to every single kind of nut known to man."

"Seriously?"

He nodded.

"Where do you need me?"

He checked the yellow pad in his hand. Coulter was forever scribbling lists—provisions to buy, vendors to call, equipment needing to be fixed—and leaving a trail of sticky notes behind.

"Finish the tables?"

"Already done," I said, and he scanned the dining room, surprised to find I was right.

"Fill water glasses?"

"On it," I said, motioning toward the service station, where the pitchers were kept. Suddenly aware he was blocking my path, he kissed the top of my head and raced back to the kitchen. I was pouring the last few glasses when I felt an arm snake around my waist. Thinking it was Coulter, I batted it away, afraid I'd spill. Bee laughed at my prickly reaction.

"Don't you have more important things to do than grope the waitstaff?" I asked.

"Top of my list is murdering the person who thought it was a good idea to plan this lunch today of all days," she said.

"Buck stops at the top," I said. "Pretty sure that's on you."

"The team plots these things months in advance. I couldn't exactly tell them I needed the week off."

Bee scooted out of the way as I came around the table to reach the last glass.

"How do you escape them?"

"Not easily," she said, shooting me a rueful look. "They literally schedule in fifteen-minute intervals, so I told them Doye and I are going through a rough patch. That I need some space this week."

"Smart," I said, but this left me wondering if the two of them were actually having a tough time. When she ran for DA, Doye had been everywhere—shaking hands at neighborhood block parties, handing out paper signs at street festivals, making the rounds at community meetings. I hadn't seen him in any of the gossipy papers that followed her around. Were Bee and Doye keeping a low profile because of friction at home? They'd secretly bought a house in New Jersey in her mother's name a few years ago when Bee had a stalker and they needed more security. Was Doye hiding out there with the kids?

"I feel like I have a giant target on my back. Like Allie's gonna jump out any second."

"Too many witnesses," I said. "You're safe here."

"Maybe, but I'm not peeing without three interns blockading the stall," she said, and I laughed.

"While I have you," Bee said, glancing around to double-check we were out of earshot. "I heard from my friend in the Middlesex County DA's office. She thinks the reason why Shanahan has taken an interest in Claudine's case is that he's dug up new evidence."

Bee had described Shanahan, the Middlesex County DA, as a self-aggrandizing operator who cared only about quick political scores, but now it sounded like he had actual proof of our guilt.

"What kind of new evidence?" I asked, trying to fathom what they could have unearthed after all these years.

"Don't know. Could be emails. Or a new witness. Shanahan's facing a tough reelection this November. Word is he's chasing all kinds of cases. Seeing what sticks." She shook her head. Her stump speeches weren't empty rhetoric; she loathed people who used the office as a political stepping stone instead of a tool for protecting the most vulnerable among us. "It's bad timing. He's trying to prove he's tough on crime, but you'd think he'd pick a case from this decade."

"So it's actually happening? They're going to press charges?"
She frowned.

"It's possible. But something's not adding up."

I put a hand to my forehead; I was desperate for a reason, however remote, to believe this wasn't happening.

"I'll do more digging," she said. "I'm getting the sense that someone's pushing for this off camera. It feels personal."

"Claudine's mom?"

"I don't know," Bee said, crossing her arms over her chest, "but I'll find out."

A dark suit appeared at Bee's side to suggest they run through her comments one last time. Bee motioned for him to give her a minute. She turned to me, her expression solemn. "If this goes forward, we have to tell the others. It'll get press, and we'll all be dragged into it. I'll try to quash any mention of the Circus, but we have to be prepared for the exposure."

The nightmare was just getting started.

"I think it's time to interview lawyers," Bee said. "I'll send some names over."

"Okay," I said, not knowing what else to say. "Thank you."

"Sara," Bee said, with a hand on my shoulder. "Don't worry."

As Bee strode across the room, I felt awash in an old terror. The looming threat took me right back to senior year, when the six of us lived in a Winthrop House suite that stretched over the entire fifth floor. We had singles off a long hallway with a shared common room at one end. I could still see the view from Claudine's bedroom window: tall black gates fronting the Charles River, dark water snaking past frozen banks. And if I looked down, I'd see her body lying on the grass five stories below.

It was January, and we were four days into the Winthrop House game. A few sophomores had been tossing around a Frisbee in the courtyard when Claudine fell. The university police interrogated the boys, but they each told a different story. One described an argument that ended with me pushing Claudine. Another recounted a commotion that had to be more than two girls—more like a whole pack taunting her. The third boy insisted the others had it all wrong. I was trying to help Claudine and it was some other girl entirely who pushed her out the window. A full-blown investigation followed.

The entire campus was set ablaze with vicious chatter and countless theories on who among our roommate group was more jealous, more vengeful, and more desperate to win. Dining hall conversations cited our cliquey behavior, the pettiness and infighting that must have infected our rooming group. Debates raged over whether our selfish cruelty was endemic to the college or limited to a few bad apples. One of the boys, realizing the power of his newfound fame, launched a campaign to raise awareness around mental health, citing the trauma he was experiencing from seeing a woman pushed to her death.

Bee spotted Claudine's parents outside the university president's office in Harvard Yard a few days after Claudine's fall. We assumed they wanted to see us—if not to hear our story, then to find solace in the company of those who knew her and loved her as they did. When the knock came that night, it was the Winthrop head tutor, an innocuous guy getting his PhD in anthropology or sociology or something good-natured like that. He asked us in soft-spoken, roundabout ways what our friendship with Claudine had been like, if we'd had any disagreements with her, if there was any reason we'd want to harm her—questions we'd already been asked by the university police. It was clear once he'd left that he'd been sent by Claudine's parents, who didn't think her death was an accident at all.

Claudine's mother had never liked me—I had the sense she thought me unworthy of her daughter, who was admittedly prettier, smarter, and better liked by our classmates than I was. I'd only met Mrs. Abernathy a few times, and I knew the tempestuous relationship she had with Claudine, but still I'd worked hard to show her respect, even when she prefaced every question with *your people*—and it was apparent she wasn't talking about my family. My suspicions were borne out years later, when Bee was running for the Manhattan DA's office, and we found out Claudine's mother had backed a political action committee that ran attack ads against Bee. Bee wrote it off as the dirty lint of the political process—nothing she couldn't handle—but I always felt like Claudine's mother was waiting in the wings, biding her time until she could ruin us.

In the days after Claudine's death, Bee sprang into action, heeding what were already keen political instincts. She took it upon herself to defend me, arranging meetings with the house master and the college deans, pleading my innocence. She was well-known around campus by then—a soccer star and president of the Harvard Political Union—so her advocacy carried some weight. Two weeks later, sagging yellow tape still draped across our courtyard, she warned me that charges might be filed, but then the boys inexplicably changed their tune. They swore they'd been in shock, had let their imaginations get the better of them. They hadn't seen a push at all—only me leaning out of a fifth-floor window, trying to hold on to Claudine—and could the press keep their names out of it in the future? Without their star witnesses, the university had no choice but to close the investigation, deeming Claudine's death a terrible, tragic accident and making it known that anyone found playing the game would be summarily expelled. I knew the boys were trying to save their own necks, steering clear of any taint on med school or PhD program applications. And could I blame them? Since their cowardice ran in our favor, my roommates and I agreed to leave them alone.

Now I caught Coulter waving to get my attention from the kitchen door. I snapped to work, running cranberry, walnut, and chèvre salads to the tables. As we cleared plates and moved on to mains, I was impressed by Coulter's operation. The waitstaff was hitting all the right notes: present but not intrusive, plates laid and cleared without a single clanging fork or dropped knife. Coulter would be thrilled to know that despite an absent server, his team had performed beautifully.

I was filling water glasses when Bee placed herself at the front of the room and delivered a rousing call for a return to civility, underlining the importance of simple, carefree pleasures like running in the park, taking your kids to the neighborhood playground, and strolling neighborhood streets after dark. She expounded on her commitment to put jobs in the hands of locals, clean up the city, stamp out crime. Her expression was charged but optimistic, her command of the issues and the room never in question. In short, Bee was dazzling.

When she was done, I wanted to jump up and down, screaming her name. A few of the younger women leapt to their feet and hollered, and the entire room rushed in with thunderous applause. A woman in the back started a cheer—"Barbara, Barbara"—and Bee struck the perfect note of humble and confident as she shook hands at every table.

I was still riding an exuberant wave when Bee found me pulling espresso shots behind the bar. I was about to tell her how amazing she'd been, how proud I was, but all of that fell away when I saw her face. She was furious.

"Bee, what is it?"

"This."

She thrust a half-folded slip of paper at me. I took it gingerly, afraid of what I'd find inside. Written in blocky black letters: **WHAT WOULD VOTERS THINK ABOUT THE GAME YOU'RE PLAYING?** As a public official, Bee had suffered her fair share of harassment—threatening letters, stalking, a dead squirrel once mailed to her apartment. This seemed innocuous by comparison, but her stern expression kept me in check. She was right to be concerned about a threat that could topple her career. When I handed the note back, she held up her hands like she didn't want to catch anything.

"Where was it?" I asked.

"Folded into my napkin," she said, and this got my attention.

"Did you see anyone?" I asked.

It was a stupid question; Bee had been mobbed the whole time.

I'd been working, but not so busy that I didn't have one eye scanning the room continuously for Allie. The older woman working Bee's table had been with the restaurant for years. She was warm, nonintrusive, and reliably good. I couldn't imagine her being mixed up in this.

Bee stared at me, agape.

"This is your place," she said brusquely, and although the restaurant was Coulter's, I understood what she was implying. "Where the hell did this come from?"

I studied the slip of paper. This was clearly an attempt to intimidate her. Was this a political adversary? Someone mentally unwell?

"Is Allie still in?" Bee asked.

"She is."

"How do you know?"

"She's my target."

"Well, I'm hers," Bee said. "Could she have gotten in here without you seeing?"

The suggestion seemed ludicrous. Not just because we would never wage this kind of psychological warfare, but because the window of opportunity would've been extremely small. Bee's table wasn't completely set when I arrived, so the culprit had to have slipped the note into Bee's napkin after I finished setting the table and before Bee sat for lunch. The dining room had been buzzing with activity the whole time.

"Not likely," I said. "And this doesn't feel like Allie. Or any of us. Who else here knows about the Circus? Have you told anyone on your staff?"

"Of course not," she said, offended.

She tugged at the base of her jacket, straightening herself out.

"I'm betting Allie got in and out right under your nose. And if it wasn't Allie, the next person down the chain is you," Bee said, and the accusation stung.

"Bee, this wasn't me," I said hurriedly. "I swear. And there's no way Allie could've gotten in here without me seeing her. But I'll find out who did this. I promise."

She scowled, then spun on a spiky heel and strode back to the crowd. Did she really believe that one of us would've done something this underhanded? I headed to the kitchen, remembering that I had talked Coulter out of installing cameras last year in favor of paying his chefs a little more. Cameras would've been useful right now.

Thinking of what Dina had said at the gallery about the others being all in on the Circus, I pulled up a picture of Allie on my phone and waved it around the kitchen, accosting the chefs, the waitstaff, and the two busboys. No one had seen her. I double-checked that the door to the alleyway was locked, then as a last-ditch effort asked the women at the welcome table. One of them nodded, saying yes, she saw Allie a few minutes ago on her way out. Allie was wearing a trench coat over a white shirt and black pants, and for that reason the woman assumed Allie was a server ducking out early.

Flustered, I asked which way Allie went. When the woman pointed, I hurried out onto the street, searching frantically for a flash of Allie's ginger hair. Stumped, I stood on the sidewalk, completely unaware of the bus pulling away, and the woman in a beige trench coat twisting around in her seat to watch me from its window. I stamped a foot in frustration, feeling duped, for Allie was so much better at this game than I had thought.

11

THE silver railcar diner marooned near the West Side Highway had the feel of a ship, set adrift and forgotten—acrid smoke, vinyl stools bolted to the floor, a sprinkling of customers at the counter and at the tables along the windows in no apparent hurry. Setting my umbrella down near the door, I spotted Wesley nursing a mug of coffee in the far corner. She was wearing her favorite white silk blouse, the one she'd worn to the kickoff dinner, but now it looked wrinkled and even a little disheveled—almost as if she'd slept in it. A harried waitress pushed by with a meaty sandwich in hand, and I could see why Wesley had dragged me out to Hugo's diner. It was the perfect place for an execution.

After Bee's luncheon the day before, I was even more determined to find Allie after she had slipped by me at the restaurant. I'd been hanging around in the freezing rain outside Allie's gym all morning, praying I'd catch her sneaking in a midmorning workout, when I got a text from Wesley saying we needed to talk. Urgently. I ignored the ploy, but when she insisted this had nothing to do with the Circus and would I please come, I allowed that she might actually have something pressing on her mind. In return, maybe she'd clue me in on where Allie was hiding or even shed some light on why I'd seen Claudine.

"The way I like it?" Wesley asked the waitress as an enormous sandwich—ham, egg, and melted cheese on a puffed-up kaiser roll—nestled in a pile of greasy potato chips landed in front of her.

"Honey, how long you been coming here? If I wanted you dead, I would've done it already. Gluten-free, nut-free, taste-free." She enlisted me in her cause with a wink. "Doesn't trust nobody, does she?"

Wesley had been one of those kids who was allergic to everything. She'd grown out of most allergies, but she still had a list that made impatient waiters roll their eyes. Since her relationship to food had always been complicated, she leaned on drink and drugs to make her feel sated. I'd seen her at enough parties to know she wasn't careful about what she bummed off other people, but she always waved me away, insisting at least she'd go down happy.

The waitress shook her head in mock exasperation before circling back to the counter. Wesley gestured for me to sit. Her eyes, usually such a vivid blue, were red-rimmed and dull, her skin ashen. The Circus was taking its toll. None of us was sleeping or eating well, and the paranoia made us aggressive, skittish, and short.

"No kill for at least an hour after I walk out of here."

The look on Wesley's face made me feel like I was being uptight, but she waved to show her grudging acceptance of my terms.

"What are you having?" Wesley gestured up at the menu over the counter. I turned, but even with a squint, the fuzzy white letters refused to sharpen—another unwelcome reminder we were turning forty-three this year. Allie would be first—the end of February. My birthday was in July, an obvious Cancer. Wesley was August and Dina September. Bee, who always seemed older, was December.

"I'm good," I said, even though my stomach sounded like the trucks that rumbled down the street at dawn every morning. I wasn't planning on staying long.

Wesley's jaw moved from side to side with a deliberate rhythm, one eye fluttering as she gulped down the sandwich. It was good to see her enjoying a meal for once.

"Are you, though?"

"Yes," I said, a little too defensively.

"You taking the Xanax?" Wesley asked, and I considered the orange bottle at the back of my bathroom drawer—pills she had slipped me three years ago, when the panic attacks first started.

"Don't need it," I said, stealing a napkin from the table and folding its corners into neat triangles. I didn't want a lecture on the importance of vulnerability, on how transformative a healing retreat upstate for people who feel stuck could be, or how much better my relationships would be if I'd just do the work.

"Yeah, well," Wesley said, and I knew she didn't agree.

The cook shouted at the waitress, and I startled. Wesley guffawed through a stuffed mouth, mustard clinging to her lower lip. I balled up the napkin and chucked it at her, narrowly missing her mouth. She pretended to be hurt, and I laughed despite myself.

"Hey, I never thanked you for talking to Aaron a few weeks ago. He's pretty fired up about photography."

Wesley had taken a bunch of high school kids outside Santa Fe under her wing. She had met them through a retreat center she visited a few years ago, and came home so moved that she'd committed to cover college tuition for four kids if they graduated with decent grades. I always wondered if Wesley had gone to Santa Fe because of Claudine, who had talked about moving there after graduation. Claudine's senior thesis had been a combination of a paper on Georgia O'Keeffe and a painting of her own that incorporated O'Keeffe's influence while pushing into new territory, which to me, an English major, sounded like an impossible task. I thought of the night I found Claudine belly-down on the common room floor, poring over an oversized book on O'Keeffe in short pink pajamas, her thick, slouchy socks kicking the air. She rolled onto her back, arms butterflied behind her head, and asked without looking over: "Summer at a lake house with friends or all alone in the desert under a vast cloudless sky?" Certainly I could picture myself in a cabin at the edge of a glittering lake, picnicking by the water, splashing around on inflatable rafts, and winding down the day at a long table crowded with friends. It seemed the very picture of bliss, and embodied the cozy belonging I'd been craving my whole life. I picked the lake house. She raised her head up off the rug to look quizzically at me, as if this was the first time we'd wound up on opposing teams.

"Yeah, no problem," I said. "He seems like a good kid."

"He has big fucking dreams. Pisses me off that he and his mom have to drive into town to get decent Wi-Fi. Kind of makes it hard if you're trying to take AP classes online."

Wesley shook her head. This was a good direction for her.

"I hope this place never changes," Wesley said. "Reminds me of the Tasty."

I hadn't thought about that dump in years. Back in school, one drink with Wesley always snowballed into three or four, and in the small hours we would end up at the Tasty's linoleum counter, where the gruff owner bowed mockingly to the princes and princesses of Cambridge before slapping half-cooked burgers down on paper plates. While the rest of the world slept, we argued ferociously over things that didn't matter and stumbled back to our beds with our arms around each other, the sisters we never had.

"What did you want to talk about?" I asked.

She tilted her head and looked up at the tin ceiling, which told me she wasn't ready to come out with it yet. The waitress handed Wesley a mug of coffee and set down a glass of water in front of me. I figured I might as well make good use of our time together.

"I thought I saw Claudine on the street two weeks ago."

"She shows up in my dreams now and then," Wesley concurred.

"No, like I really saw her."

Wesley looked puzzled for a second.

"Well, I wouldn't put anything past our roommates, especially with the ban on costumes out the window. This round's a free-for-all with a million bucks in play."

"This was before Allie scrapped the rules," I said. "But you actually think someone would dress up like Claudine?"

She shrugged, not as bothered by this as I was. She was gripping her mug with both hands, tapping a foot underneath the table—desperate for a smoke. Her nails, painted a bluish gray, were bitten down to the quick.

"Dina broke into my place while I was in the shower," Wesley said. "Creeping around like Norman fucking Bates. Ballsy, but not smart when we're this jumpy. Thank god Nick was over and scared her off before I got to her. Otherwise one of us would've ended up bleeding out in the bathtub."

She was trying to be funny, but it landed a little too close given the dynamic between Wesley and Dina.

"Now I see Dina everywhere," she said. "Saw her face in my coffee yesterday—you know, like latte art?"

She stared down into her mug, then looked up at me with real fear in her eyes.

"Wes, what did you want to talk about?"

She looked around to confirm the tables closest to us weren't eavesdropping, then handed me her phone. It was open to an email from the night before titled *does your father know*. The message continued below: *about the games you play?* And that was it. The sender's handle was a mix of letters and numbers—a ghost account, untraceable. It was then that I noticed an attachment at the bottom of the screen. I scrolled down to find a photo and my stomach knotted. It had been taken at Wesley's thirtieth birthday bash a decade ago at her family's house in Rhode Island, and she looked radiant in a strapless black dress. She was kneeling behind a glass coffee table, a credit card in one hand. The problem was that she was looking down eagerly, smiling at the line of white powder on the table.

I was at that party—we all were. It was a memorable night, but we were adults, or at least pretending to be, in the mansion Wesley's parents had lent us for the weekend. The picture was taken by an (ex-)friend of Wesley's who thought he was being funny by sending it to the hundred people who'd partied with us that weekend. When Wesley saw it, she went ballistic. She couldn't afford for the image to get back to her father, who used her trust fund to keep her on a short leash. She ordered everyone at the party to delete the photo right away. Most probably blew it off, or never got around to it, and the picture was still lurking somewhere deep in their inboxes. I was at the bank then and slammed with work. Not a good excuse, but it wasn't at the top of my priority list. I could probably find a copy in my email if I searched hard enough.

"Did you do this?" she asked.

"Of course not," I said, handing the phone back.

"If my dad gets this, he won't care the picture is ten years old, or that I'm clean," Wesley said, her voice high and tight. "He'll cut me off for sure. I can cover my day-to-day if I stay in orthopedics, but I have nothing saved up."

I didn't know the particulars of Wesley's trust fund. She moved into the West Village apartment a few years ago and received an allowance, but I had no idea if the bulk of the money was coming to her in a lump sum or if her dad was doling out smaller payments to keep her perpetually under his thumb. Either way, I worried for her. Her dad was a narcissist, her relationship with him a roller coaster. When we were sophomores, the elder Dr. Hale invented some kind of surgical implement that made him a wealthy man in his own right. It should've been a triumphant victory for a guy who'd married into one of New York City's most prominent families, but I suspected he could've made ten times the fortune his wife inherited and it still wouldn't have been enough. Wesley's dad was generous when we were in school, insisting I come along whenever he swooped into town to take Wesley out to dinner, but he was always scanning the room, looking for something better, even with his only child sitting right next to him.

"I know how this sounds," she said. "Whining over a trust fund. The problem is . . ."

"You've already spent it," I said.

She was surprised that I had divined the truth; we weren't as good at hiding our ugly secrets as we thought we were.

"Not everything. He was supposed to release the rest of it last summer," she said. "But he's obsessed with control, so he rolled it over for one more year."

"So you'll get it this August? On your birthday?"

Wesley shrugged as if to say, *We'll see.*

"The medical clinic outside Santa Fe where I volunteered has had a hell of a time recruiting doctors. Well, *clinic* is an overstatement. It's a shack with secondhand supplies that's supposed to serve a hundred and fifty people. If anyone gets more than a scrape, they have to drive two hours to a real hospital and wait most of the day. Missing out on a day's pay is bad enough, but people also lose their jobs when that happens. I'm helping them build a real facility."

"Wesley, that's amazing."

She brushed past the compliment.

"The problem is that I fronted the money six months ago, thinking I'd have the whole thing in August," she said. "Construction is supposed to start in two weeks, and I can't back out now. This photo is going to blow the whole thing up."

"What if you stopped playing?"

She clutched her chest like she was having a bout of heartburn.

"And give in to the asshole who sent this?"

I'd never known Wesley to choose the sensible path, especially if she was standing up for what she thought was right.

"What about the apartment? Can you sell it?"

"Not mine to sell. My father will take it back if he's feeling vindictive. Which is always."

She took an aggressive bite of her sandwich.

"Everything's lawyered up in a revocable trust," she said with a full mouth. "Basically, he has veto rights every time I want to take a piss. So I'll have no money and no place to live, and I'll have screwed over the community I was trying to help."

I didn't know what to say, other than to agree that we shouldn't let her dad see that picture.

"Does your father know about the games you play?" she mimicked. "Who the fuck would've sent this?"

It was clear that Wesley didn't know about Bee's note, which must have been sent by the same person. Someone who knew the Circus, attended Wesley's thirtieth (or was close enough to get a copy of that photo), and had the opportunity to slip the note into Bee's napkin. It was a pretty small circle. Unless Bee's outrage at the luncheon had been a well-acted ruse, the signs pointed to Allie.

"Have you told anyone else about the Circus? Is Nick the guy you met at Burning Man last year? Does he know?"

"It's not him," she said. "I made him take a blood oath. And he's constantly broke, so he's even more excited about the trust money than I am."

"An actual blood oath?"

She nodded as if this was normal.

"So who do you think sent that email?" I asked.

"Isn't it obvious?" she asked, throwing her hands up at my apparent cluelessness.

"Allie," I said emphatically.

"What? No, I was talking about Dina."

"Wesley, you can't bring up the same old beef you have with Dina."

"Fine. Here's the proof. She knows about the money, obviously. She was at my party. I'm sure she's been saving that photo for the perfect opportunity."

She took a breath, gauging my reaction with hopeful interest, then doubled down.

"For the record, she's always had it out for me. Now I'm her fucking target. Of course she's going to do whatever it takes to bury me."

I felt like an idiot for not remembering this. I was so used to defending Dina.

"We don't even know if she's still in the game," I said feebly. "Bee's probably taken her out already."

Wesley sighed, and I couldn't tell if she was frustrated by my misplaced loyalty to Dina or because I wasn't taking her seriously.

"Sara, we've been through some pretty screwy stuff together," she said. "You've always been the one person I can talk to about my messed-up family. You were there for me when I was having a hard time with the drinking, and everything with my dad."

No one in their right mind would pity Wesley for growing up on Park Avenue, but I knew it wasn't as easy as it sounded. I'd overheard a few troubling things over the years, and even Wesley once said that after the staff went home for the night, her parents weren't afraid to throw dishes or punches behind closed doors. The tumultuous fall of our senior year, Wesley was hell-bent on drinking herself into oblivion. We staged an intervention of sorts, mostly stealing her cash and hiding the handle of vodka we found at the bottom of her laundry bag. Wesley admitted her parents were separating. Her mother had caught her father sleeping with his assistant. I couldn't tell what bothered Wesley more: the infidelity or her father's lack of imagination.

I thought of my own father then, how mortified I was by his short-sleeved shirts with his name embroidered on the breast pocket. How he'd ask for whiskey when a friend's mom offered him wine. How I had to pick him up—I didn't even have my license then—whenever the owner of the local pub called. For years, I would drop a check in the mail and push off thinking about him for a few more months, until one day three Septembers ago when I got a call from a woman named Carol, claiming in a Texan drawl to be my father's girlfriend of ten years. She told me in a quiet voice that my father had lost his fight with lung cancer. I thanked her for calling, but she kept on. "God must have a sense of humor," she said, "to take him like that when he'd been dry for nine years and a nonsmoker for fifteen." I tried to hang up, but she didn't stop. "Oh, he bragged about his daughter going to Harvard," she said. "That's not to say there weren't hard times with us working four jobs between us, but when your checks came it was like manna from heaven. Your father treated himself to a key lime pie. Bet you don't even know it, but you got us through some pretty dark days." I asked if my father had been good to her. Had they been happy together? She thought about this, and said, "Yes, very happy. But he always said he could've been better to you."

"I know you're still dealing with stuff that happened with your parents and it hasn't been easy for you to open up, but I hope you feel I've been there for you too," Wesley was saying.

"Yeah. Of course."

Wesley had stuck her neck out for me more times than I could count. Right out of college, she helped me land my old job at the bank. I stayed on her couch when I found out Coulter was texting some pretty intimate things with a woman at work. I didn't tell anyone when my dad died, but somehow Wesley knew, and she turned up at my door with two backpacks. We spent three days climbing the Gunks and roasting marshmallows around a fire. Exactly the break I didn't know I needed. I told Wesley everything about my dad: his alcoholism, the way he disappeared into himself after my mother died, leaving me to fend for myself. How despite everything he'd put me through, I regretted not patching things up with him when I had the chance. Apart from Claudine, Wesley was the only person I'd ever confided in about how bad things were after my mom passed away. I read somewhere that you stopped being a kid when your father died. But even with two dead parents, I still felt a generation away from adulthood.

She dabbed her mouth with a paper napkin, then balled her hands under her chin.

"I feel like you've been drifting since you left the bank," she said. "I know the Claudine thing hasn't been easy on you, but recently you've been more and more distant. I don't know what's really going on with you."

She was studying me, doing that thing Allie called her superpower. Dina claimed it was more like a reality distortion field, and evidently Bill Clinton did a pretty good version of it too. Others called it charisma, but it went way beyond charm. It was a combination of the way Wesley looked at you—unflinching and honest, like she wasn't afraid of your darkest truth—and closed in. Not crowding you, but enough to create a sense of intimacy. Like she was giving all of herself to you, which made you want to do the same.

And then it hit me like a kick in the ribs. Wesley was going to ask me to team up with her. She'd appeal to my altruism, convince me that the money would pay for the new clinic. But how could I agree when I had not only promised Dina my help, but if I was being honest, I still wanted the money for myself?

"I should go," I said, craning around to find that the two tables around us had cleared out, which likely meant lunch was over.

"We still need to talk about the urgent thing," Wesley said.

"Didn't we cover it? The email?"

She shook her head.

"I'll come right out with it. We need you to drop out."

My mouth hung open.

"Drop out of the Circus? Why?"

"Bee told me about the investigation. They'll start digging, and we can't get caught playing a game that killed Claudine."

"Killed Claudine?"

"That's the way they'll spin it."

"That's not what happened."

"It's what people will think."

"Let them think it. It's not true."

"Sara, whatever happened with Claudine, we're all on the hook for it now. But you need to distance yourself."

"Wouldn't it be cleaner if we all stopped playing? And what do you mean by 'whatever happened with Claudine'?"

"I'm just saying that we were there for you. No questions asked. But this time around, we're asking you to step aside."

The insinuation that I might've been responsible for Claudine's death had me reeling. Memories of that time came flooding back: Bee sitting down with every dean who would listen, Dina and Wesley meeting with the housemaster, Allie barking at kids in the dining hall who looked at me askance. I turned to the window; I didn't know if I was going to lash out or crumble.

When I turned back, Wesley had her gun out. Pointed at me.

I realized then that the diner had emptied out. The customers at the counter were gone. Hugo and the waitress were nowhere to be seen. Wesley had orchestrated this execution perfectly; I could either agree to withdraw from the Circus or she would take me out. Either way, she would get what she wanted.

I wasn't going without a fight. The problem was that my back was to the door and she had a clear line on me all the way down the aisle. I needed a distraction.

Wesley wouldn't forgive me, not when she was wearing her favorite white silk blouse, but I had no choice. I upended the table, dousing her in a soggy mix of half-eaten sandwich, ketchup, and fries, and I was out of my chair before the plate hit the floor. I thought for sure she'd kill me as I sprinted for the exit, so no one was more surprised than I was when I tumbled out the door. Plunging into the downpour, I tore away from the diner at breakneck speed. When I reached my building, I barely registered the squelch of my shoes or the wet-dog stench from my wool sweater. Even though I had left my umbrella and jacket behind, I was dizzy with relief that I had somehow escaped my own execution.

12

LATER that afternoon, Fabby's assistants and I were snapping at each other, frustrated by the complexities of moving neon signs around an enormous sandy desert. We had thought we were one step ahead of Fabby, having worked through most of the logistics for her spring shoot in White Sands. When she realized we hadn't yet convinced the park service to issue us a permit, which threatened to shut down the entire photo shoot, she berated us for being scattered and kicked us all out of the studio. Her dismissal stung, for we craved Fabby's approval like the late-spring sun after a long, cold winter, and I was already feeling like I was failing everyone I loved. The truth, of course, was that my college roommates and I had been pushing too hard, unconstrained by the rules we had created to keep us in line. No matter how tough or how impervious we thought we were, the Circus toyed with our bodies and minds. By now, we'd been revving in a constant state of alertness for five days straight. Like doctors operating back-to-back shifts, we couldn't focus, our reaction times were slower, and we had trouble reading people. We were working on instinct, baser versions of ourselves. The real problem, though, was that we thought we were fine.

I was surprised to find the rain had stopped and it was a beautiful afternoon, the golden hour washing everything in a soft light. I kicked myself for not having my camera; I could've woven through Chinatown, where I was trying to build relationships with the elderly women who have raised generations there. Coulter worried that I'd stuck my nose where it wasn't welcome, but I never felt uncomfortable in places where older women held sway.

Feeling untethered and out of sorts, I headed for the restaurant. The twenty-five-minute walk was risky, but I needed to feel the wind on my face. I turned onto Brooklyn's Fifth Avenue, a quieter, more neighborly version of Manhattan's, keeping a close eye over my shoulder. The light was fading quickly; the lunch places and coffee shops were done for the day, and the nicer restaurants were ushering in their first seating.

The burst of momentum we felt after each kill was the push that usually propelled us over the day-five hump, but this year I had none of that wind at my back. Even though Dina had tipped me off on Allie's Thursday-afternoon pickup, I still had no idea where Allie was hiding out, and Thursday was a full day away—a lifetime in the Circus. I was still miffed that I had allowed her to slip past me at the restaurant, and my altercation with Wesley in the diner played over and over in my head. She had repeatedly couched her demand that I drop out of the Circus as what "we" wanted. Did this mean the others shared her feeling that I was somehow responsible for Claudine's death? Were they, too, trying to distance themselves from me?

I shortcutted through a residential neighborhood that quickly turned too dark and quiet for my liking. Picking up my pace, I was rethinking the wisdom of walking alone as I hurried down a narrow spit of street hemmed in by brick row houses. Pockets of light dotted second-story windows, but the street level showed surprisingly few signs of life. My mind flitted back to that infamous case from the sixties, when a Queens woman was stabbed right in front of her apartment building—within sight and sound of thirty or so neighbors without a single one coming to her aid. I told myself as I speed-walked toward the corner, intending to cut right in search of more life a few blocks over, that this New York, my New York, wasn't that city.

At the crossing, I took the turn at a sharp angle and found myself face-to-face with a heavyset man in a dark coat, holding a paper bag in his hand. The sight of him there, standing so close to me, gave me such a fright that I screamed. He reached for me, causing me to stumble backward and fall. When he started waving both arms up and down, I realized he was trying to calm me down. He spoke softly in a language I didn't understand, and when my panic subsided, I could see he was an older man and didn't mean any harm. He pulled a bottle of vodka from the paper bag and offered it to me, but I shook my head. Picking myself up, I apologized, and we continued on our ways in opposite directions.

I hurried on to the restaurant after that, unsure of my footing. Shadows jumped out at me, and every rustle and hum seemed to be whispering my name. I was crossing the street in the middle of the block when I noticed a figure at the corner, obviously following me.

Toward the end of the block, I dared a glimpse over my shoulder. I couldn't make out much at this distance except for a black coat—maybe a black beanie—so I stopped in front of a restaurant on the next block and pretended to study the menu in the window. The figure also stopped. They were leaned up against the railing of a stoop, not pretending to be doing anything other than waiting for me to resume my walk. It was hard to gauge from a distance, but the woman—or perhaps a young man—looked too petite to be Wesley or Bee. Closer to Dina's size, but the gait was too casual, too easygoing, to be Dina's purposeful stride.

Claudine is dead, I reminded myself. And I mostly didn't believe in ghosts.

Wesley insisted at the diner that she wouldn't put anything past our roommates, but dressing up as Claudine was a step too far, even if this round of the Circus was unlike any that we had experienced before.

I grasped my medallion, running it back and forth along its chain. I thought of the time Bee fought bravely to convict a deputy who had shot an unarmed kid in the back, though she had to change her phone number twice because of the death threats.

A kind of insanity took hold of me then. I turned and charged.

The woman bolted away, and I raced after her. She was light on her feet, and fast, too, as I chased her toward the water. As we neared the highway, the glare of restaurants gave way to the blank stare of empty offices. The streetlights cast a dim haze; she faded in and out. The highway rose up overhead and she disappeared into an underpass. I slowed as I entered the darkness, bracing for what might be lurking in the shadows. When I emerged on the other side, the woman was gone.

"Mustang Sally" wafted out of a neighborhood bar on the next block. A jogger loped toward me, and I yelled—had he seen anyone? A woman in a dark coat?—but he shook his head and sped off. The screech of brakes on the highway overhead made me shudder.

I knew the Circus made us paranoid—it made us see things that weren't there. What if Dina was right? What if I was seeing ghosts?

A roaring kicked up in my head, and I was taken back to the night before exams that fall of our freshman year, when Wesley and I smoked Gitanes out our common room window. I watched in awe as she floated perfect little rings up into the dark night. Allie yelled that it was nearly nine, and we hurriedly ground out our butts. Bee and Allie crowded in with us at the window and we threw the sash up as high as it would go. When the clock struck nine, we leaned out together, howling as fiercely as we could, adding our voices to the hundreds around Harvard Yard in a harrowing, collective, primal scream.

13

LATER that night, I was perched on the fat rolled arm of the living room couch, craning up at the hole in the ceiling. A reddish stain bloomed across the wooden beam, making the opening resemble a fresh-cut wound.

"Do you think this was caused by something?" I asked when Coulter appeared in the arched doorway to the living room, having shed his coat and backpack in the hall.

"Everything's caused by something," he said unhelpfully as he slid by me so he could help himself to a drink.

"No, I mean could someone have done this on purpose?" I asked as he rifled through the julep cup that held his bar tools, plucking out a pair of silver tongs.

"So the Scheitelmans cut a hole in the ceiling and dropped it on me?"

Picturing one of those *Tom and Jerry* cartoons where Tom saws a hole in the floor that falls through in a perfect circle, I glared at Coulter, but he was focused on muddling sugar and bitters in the right proportions.

"Want one?" he asked as he plucked another sugar cube from a glass jar.

"No, thanks."

I thought of the voicemail I'd gotten earlier from a cop assigned to the Middlesex County DA's office. He had questions, and was there a good time for us to talk this week? I hadn't called him back.

"Actually, yeah," I said.

He padded to the kitchen for another glass, where the rush of water and the clink of ice followed. I was wondering if I could be arrested for not returning a phone call when he returned.

"I'm sure they'll find a leak," he said, tippling bourbon into two glasses and giving them each a vigorous stir. "Happened at the restaurant, too, right before Uncle Chuck got diagnosed. No one knew water was pooling in the crawl space over the kitchen. Whoever built the place used half the nails they were supposed to. Eventually, the whole ceiling came down."

After straining the mixture, he handed me a glass and settled onto the couch, crossing one leg over the other as he took a long, wearied sip. He usually relaxed after work with tequila, but turned to an old-fashioned when he was celebrating or decompressing after a particularly grueling day. Today was clearly the latter.

"Rough day?" I asked as I joined him on the couch, crossed-legged, feet tucked under my knees.

"Rough month," he said, staring down into his glass.

"The staff did a great job yesterday for Bee's lunch," I said, trying to keep the mood light. "Didn't even feel like you were down a server."

He murmured something that sounded like agreement while he took a long draw, the liquid draining out around a ridiculously large ice cube—his war on dilution. He got up to make himself another, and I couldn't help myself.

"Rocco has a crush on her," I said.

"Who?"

"The new server. The one who called in sick."

"Nellie," he said without turning around.

Before she had been a story; now a name made her real. I wondered if Coulter was thinking about her too.

"Rocco thinks she's hot," I said, and Coulter laughed. When he didn't say anything else, I asked, "Is she?"

"Is she what?" he asked, rejoining me on the couch.

"Hot."

He pressed his lips together, apparently giving this serious thought.

"The Southern accent doesn't hurt."

I grabbed a pillow off the couch and hurled it at him, but he saw it coming and batted it away with a sly grin.

"Come on, Sara. You have nothing to worry about. She talks too much, and she's allergic to every goddamned thing."

He knew Wesley had grown up with severe allergies; he had promised to be more sympathetic.

"Sorry, I know," he said. "The allergies aren't her fault, but it's a real fucking pain in the ass. Separate prep stations, extra handwashing, additional training, ingredient lists—all of it costs money I don't have. And everyone is already doing more than their share. All for a server who calls in sick two hours before the biggest event we've had in a year?"

I nodded to show him I understood, but also to hide my relief that there was nothing between him and Nellie. His mention of money reminded me of the promise I'd made to Marcella. I knew it wasn't the right time—this probably wouldn't end well—but I, too, was curious about the loan she'd mentioned.

"So how's the restaurant doing?"

"Meaning?"

"Financially."

"Fine," he said with a hint of wariness.

Marcella could be manipulative at times, which I attributed to her hardscrabble upbringing, but her love for the restaurant was constant. If the restaurant was in trouble, she'd have no reason to lie about it. And if she was telling the truth, then Coulter was lying.

"Is it?" I asked.

He gave me a sideways look.

"What?" I asked.

"Surprised is all. You've never shown an interest in the books before."

"Well, when the sky is falling," I said, gesturing at our torn-up ceiling, "I guess it's a good time to get interested."

I'd gone too far. Coulter had never been good with criticism, and now I was attacking his management of the restaurant.

"Sorry, that came out wrong," I said hurriedly. "Your mother asked me to talk to you."

He didn't answer right away, but took his time contemplating the contents of his glass. I could see he was chastened by his mother's doubt.

"Let me guess: She thinks I'm not focused. That I'll screw it all up."

He said this in a matter-of-fact way, without the bluster I would've expected. Maybe I'd erred in agreeing to do this favor.

"Coulter, she didn't mean it that way," I said. "She wanted to know what the plan is for paying back the loan."

He glared at me. I was making things worse.

"Well, the restaurant has always been her favorite child," he said, and the sudden vitriol took me by surprise. I was well aware of how he felt about his father, but I'd never heard bitterness toward his mother.

He downed his drink, then pulled himself to his feet.

"Coulter, I'm sorry, I shouldn't have—"

I was sitting up now, my legs unfolded.

"Are you worried too?" he asked, leaning up against the bookcase next to the doorway.

I hated seeing him this way—humbled, deflated—and I never wanted him to think I would side with his mother against him.

"A little," I said.

"But you're with me, right?"

This sudden need for affirmation wasn't like him; usually he was the one reassuring me. He set his glass down on the cabinet with a hard *thunk*.

"You know what?" he asked. "Enough of bending over backward for everyone else. I don't care what it costs; it's time we started putting ourselves first."

He kissed me good night and padded off to bed. I was glad to hear he was ready to stand up to his mother, maybe even turn the restaurant over to his cousin Rocco. And he was right. We had to fight for what we wanted. Hadn't Wesley once lectured me that the key to winning is being willing to push harder than everyone else? There were two days left in the Circus, and my roommates were undoubtedly crossing lines they wouldn't have touched before, so I had to shake off the old rules and become as daring as Bee, as calculated as Dina, and maybe even as crazy as Wesley. With more determination and a heavy dose of luck, maybe—just maybe—I could save us.

14

LATE on Thursday afternoon, I was lingering across the street from a graceful limestone building in Morningside Heights, the home of a well-known music school. I had no idea what it took to mold a kid into a musician, but I knew I was in the right place from the earnest teenagers who trickled out through arched doors with black cases of all shapes and sizes slung over their shoulders.

Hiding in the encroaching darkness, I pressed up against a buttressed stone wall that looked plucked from a medieval English abbey. The forecast was snow; thick, low-hanging clouds painted everything in a dull, gray shadow. I had layered up with wool socks inside my ankle boots and my black puffer jacket, but now and then when the wind died down, a sour mustiness pinched my nose, a reminder I hadn't showered since the Circus began. Too many kills took place in the shower.

There were good reasons why I shouldn't be here. The old rule making kids off-limits didn't apply, but I still felt like I was crossing a line. I wasn't one of those creeps who lurk outside park bathrooms, but anyone paying attention could tell that I—like any adult lying in wait for a high school girl, even if she was my goddaughter, Chloe— was up to no good.

I wiggled my jaw, stiff from clenching, and checked the time. Fourteen more minutes of violin lessons, music theory, or whatever it was that Chloe did here. I didn't intend to bother her; I simply needed to find her. She wouldn't even know I was here until Allie picked her up—then I'd have my kill.

The problem was that I hadn't seen Chloe in a few years, not since the Easter egg hunt at Allie's house when Chloe had slouched around with hair falling across her eyes. She must have changed since then; I wasn't sure I'd recognize her. I had to get in closer.

When a trio of kids toting black cases—a violin, a flute, maybe a French horn—spilled out of the glass doors at the front of the building, I knew my window was closing. I crossed over at the light and held the door for a kid valiantly heaving a double bass. As I stepped into the empty lobby, the sight of a security guard planted at a rounded desk sapped my nerve. I tried to channel Bee, who would march through like she owned the place, or Dina, who would come up with a clever way to avoid being seen.

A sudden thrum of music kicked up from across the foyer—the jolt I needed to scurry across the lobby and slip inside the auditorium. The hall was awash in a sea of blue velvet seats, and a full orchestra was crammed onstage. The cellos were sawing away, the music thick and lugubrious. The violins and violas sat upright, bows springing to attention as the conductor waved frantically to bring them into the fold. I lost myself in the rich tapestry, transfixed by their muscular sound.

The conductor tapped his baton on the edge of his music stand, barking at the woodwinds for missing their cue. Slowly, I edged my way down the left aisle for a better view of the first violins. They were young but serious—stick-straight backs, eyes on the conductor, no goofing around. I searched the line of violins and my gaze snagged on a girl in the second row, diagonally behind the concertmaster. When a door slammed behind me and she looked out across the empty seats, I could see her more clearly. She had Allie's fair complexion and the same reddish-brown hair pulled up in a ponytail, but it was her ears that gave her away. When we were younger, Allie had lamented that her ears stuck out a mile.

"This is a closed rehearsal," the conductor hollered, and I realized too late he was addressing me. I fumbled an apology, and a hundred pairs of eyes watched me skulk out of the auditorium. My cheeks were still ablaze when I reached the street.

Cars had doubled up in the loading zone at the front of the conservatory. I kept watch for Allie's gray minivan as I fingered the pistol in my pocket. I was about to check the time on my phone when the sidewalk flooded with kids chatting, laughing, thrilled to be done for the day. It was then that I noticed a guy in a pulled-up hoodie loitering a little farther down. I couldn't see his face in the darkness, but he was empty-handed—no instrument, no backpack, nothing. Suspicious, but the same could've been said about me. I trusted he was a parent until he sensed me watching and picked his head up, then hustled off in the opposite direction, holding a hand up in brief apology as he shouldered a student in his haste.

I was checking the carpool line again for Allie when I felt a tap on the shoulder.

"You here for pickup?"

The cop was about my size, sporting a turtleneck embroidered with NYPD in bright white letters under a navy jacket. Her badge was pinned to her chest, above a long name I couldn't make out.

"Um, yes."

"You got a kid at this school?"

"Well, my goddaughter."

"So you're picking her up?"

"Uh, I came by to, uh—"

"You got another purpose for being here, then?"

"I wanted to see my—"

The cop hoisted a flashlight, the beam forcing me to look away.

"My goddaughter. Chloe. She plays the violin."

It wasn't a lie. The cop asked to see some identification. It was stupid, really—I wasn't thinking. I patted my pockets, and in my nervous haste to find my wallet, I pulled out a tin of breath mints and the water pistol.

I was flat on my stomach then, and someone was yelling at the kids to get inside. One of the cops was barking at me not to move. Amid the panicked shouting, no one wanted to hear anything about a game.

A police car screamed up and the cops took charge of clearing the sidewalk, moving the carpoolers away from the curb. I lay face down on the frigid cement with cuffs pinching my wrists, shoulders wrenched back at a painful angle, watching red lights bounce off the limestone facade. *This stunt might end with me in a cell*, I thought, but what gnawed at me more was that I had put my roommates at risk. The cops would ask questions, and reporters would circle too. Once they got word of what I'd done, none of my roommates would ever speak to me again.

I listened as the cop called in my particulars. I expected they'd be calling Coulter next. After what felt like a frozen eternity, the commotion dissipated. When the sidewalk had been cleared of everyone except for half the precinct and me, I was yanked to my feet, uncuffed; my wrists ached.

"Against my better judgment, I'm giving this back to you," she said gruffly as she handed me the pistol. I squirreled it away, grateful but unsure why she was letting me go. "If I see you around here again, I'm gonna book you for trespassing. And don't take that out in public," she said, pointing to the pistol in my pocket. "You got that?"

"Yes, and thank you," I said. The flashing lights receded, and students trickled back onto the sidewalk. Most sped away in the opposite direction, but the brave averted their eyes and ran a wide circle past me. As the students thinned out, I noticed a girl loitering six or seven feet away. I sensed she had something to say, but was hesitating not out of fear but more of a grudging reluctance. When she realized I'd spotted her, she marched over.

"I know you," she said, her tone sharp but not hostile. "You're Aunt Sara."

"Chloe," I said, "I don't know what you said to them, but thank you."

Her navy down jacket was full of zippers, and her hair was knotted in a bun—an adult now, a stranger, yet still familiar. Her violin case was slung over one shoulder.

"I told them the truth."

"Which version?"

"That you're a friend of the family and you came to pick me up."

I hated myself for putting her in this position.

"Thank you."

"Everyone's stressed out after that shooting at Stuy," she said.

"That makes sense," I said.

"Does my mom know you're here?"

"No, she doesn't."

We stood together in an uneasy silence. I didn't think Chloe knew about the Circus, but if she did, I didn't want to contradict whatever Allie had told her about what we did in January. I certainly wouldn't ask Chloe to lie to her mother. Nor would I blame Chloe for telling her mother about seeing me here. What I wanted to say was that I was happy to see her, to acknowledge how she'd grown, how she was on a good path, but I didn't feel like I had the right to say any of these things.

"I know I haven't been around enough. You know—as your godmother."

"It's fine."

She clamped her mouth shut like she'd said too much.

"What?"

"My mom didn't tell you?"

I shrugged.

"She swapped you out two years ago."

"Who for?"

She looked at me sideways, unsure if she should tell me.

"Ms. Colasanti."

Of course. I didn't blame Allie for upgrading to Bee, our Golden Girl. Who wouldn't want the future mayor of New York as your kid's godmother? Birthday parties at Gracie Mansion, reservations at top restaurants, tickets to sold-out shows. I would've done the same— but I couldn't get past the sinking knowledge that I had not only let Chloe down, but I'd failed a good friend too.

"How is your mom?"

It was Chloe's turn to shrug.

"Did you guys move?"

Her eyes narrowed at my attempt to milk her for information. She was a smart kid. A good kid, too, which didn't surprise me.

"Sorry, I'm not trying to pry. She seemed tired when I saw her at dinner last week, that's all. Is she okay?"

"You're not gonna find her," Chloe said, and it dawned on me that a kid as bright as Chloe would have pieced together the particulars of the Circus years ago.

"Why's that?" I asked.

"She's acting deranged, even for January. My dad went to her office the other day. She's not even going to work. He thinks it's like a reverse midlife crisis or whatever because she's all obsessed with money. Cutting back and how we're gonna pay for stuff. She made my sisters drop their lessons, and Dad only let me keep coming here because we already paid for this semester. The game is making her so insane. I can't wait until it's over so we can go back to being normal."

Allie's preoccupation with finances didn't strike me as that strange. She was the primary breadwinner, after all, and she'd been worried about the hit they'd take for college tuition, but making her girls give up their lessons seemed out of character for a woman who'd been pushing them from the time they could walk to be competitive swimmers, softball players, and violinists. Was her situation more dire than she had let on? And was this somehow related to the fact that she wasn't going in to the office?

A gray minivan pulled up to the curb. When a cellist hobbled over with her instrument and lifted the rear door, I turned my attention back to Chloe.

"For the record," Chloe said, "I'm against your stupid game. It's violent. It makes you all crazy."

I wished everyone in my life were this honest.

"Do you like Halloween?" I asked.

"Yeah, sure."

"The game's not that different. We get to try on new things, see how they feel. Learn stuff that might be useful in real life."

"Still weird," she said, throwing her shoulders back and standing a little taller. "But winning means a lot to my mom too."

Her tone was suddenly fierce, but it wasn't a threat—more of a protectiveness that bowled me over.

A rusted gray Jetta lumbered up to the sidewalk. The driver, a young woman I assumed was Allie's nanny, hollered at Chloe through the passenger-side window.

There was more I wanted to say to make up for not being there for Chloe, for the adventures we should've had, for the closeness I had hoped to build between us. Instead, I told Chloe it was good to see her. She waved before tumbling inside the Jetta.

The car minnowed into traffic and sped away, carrying with it any hope of finding Allie. But the Circus was far from my mind, my thoughts sifting through memories of Allie and Chloe together. The delight that Chloe had brought Allie as an adorable piano-obsessed elementary school kid, the worry that Allie shouldered when Chloe was bullied in ninth grade, and the joy I saw in Allie's face when she told me about the good friends Chloe had made at camp the summer afterward. I was thinking about how much grit it took to be a parent and how good Allie was at being a mom, which made the phone call I got a few seconds later all the more strange.

Instinct urged me to let it roll over to voicemail, but curiosity won out.

"Hey," I said, not trusting my voice.

"Sara," Allie said briskly. I scanned the street. Had Allie been watching us the whole time? "You should get over here."

"Here?" I asked.

"The hospital."

I could hear Allie asking for the address.

"The hospital? Why? What's happened?"

"It's Bee. They just brought her in."

"What? Is she okay?"

"I don't know. Wesley and Dina are on their way. You should come too. Soon as you can."

Allie recited the address of an Upper East Side hospital.

"Where are you now?" Allie asked.

An enormous wave of guilt washed over me. I had always thought I was decent at friendship, but now I could see the ways in which I was falling short. With a pit in my stomach, I told Allie I was uptown and leaving now. Before hanging up, she told me to hurry.

I filled with the same awful dread I felt in the moments after Claudine's fall, when I pulled myself back from the window to stand alone in the middle of her room, vaguely aware of the shouting in the courtyard below and the wail of what must've been an army of ambulances and fire trucks racing toward Winthrop House. Paralyzed by shock and disbelief, all I could think was that Claudine didn't know what she meant to me, and never would. But what I remember most from the moments right after Claudine's fall—and what chills me now—is the damning irreversibility of it all. Then, as now, I was overcome with the harrowing sense that the world had changed. That my life, going forward, would never be the same.

15

WHEN I burst through the hospital's double glass doors, the sight of Dina hovering at the peach-colored reception desk filled me with relief that I wouldn't have to face whatever this was alone. I listened as Dina spelled out Bee's last name in staccato syllables—*Co-la-san-ti*—and spun her glasses around in one hand to the obvious consternation of the receptionist.

Dina didn't react when I sidled up next to her, except to spell out my name too. Like me, she was dressed in monochrome black—skater slip-ons, dark jeans, dutiful peacoat. Her mood was equally somber.

"All right, ladies, you're cleared for Barbara Colasanti in 246," the receptionist said as she handed us visitor stickers and pointed down a hallway past the elevators. Dina hurried off while I was still fumbling with my sticker. I, too, was dying to know what happened to Bee, but I couldn't seem to launch myself from the safety of the lobby. Hospitals were too bound up with a hopelessness I didn't want to feel again. The last time I stepped inside a hospital was the morning my mother died, her thin arm slipping out from under a sheet to hold my hand before she drained away. I still couldn't stomach the smell of bleach, bodies framed by darkened doorways, people slipping away the second you turned your back. I thought of the boorish woman in the room next to my mom's, who complained incessantly about her ungrateful kids, who never came to see her. One morning she was gone, the room cleaned and readied for its next guest. When I suggested hopefully that one of her kids had probably come to get her, the nurse regarded me ruefully. I was old enough to understand.

I knew my loathing of hospitals was as pointless as blaming the mailman for an upsetting letter. Closing my eyes, I puffed out a few fiery breaths, winning a show of concern from the receptionist, but for now it was enough to dig out from under the panicky feeling.

"So what happened?" Dina asked when I caught up with her near the elevators. I couldn't hide my surprise; I thought I was the only one in the dark.

"Well then," she said, "I guess we're paddling in the same unwitting boat."

Bee had tamped down her wild side by the time she graduated from law school, but to us she would always be the fun-starter who rallied us for Thursday-night dance parties at our favorite bar and led the charge at the Winthrop House formal into the fountain of a Boston office building when we were juniors, causing security to drag fifty sopping-wet undergrads in black tie from the water, after which Harvard was blacklisted from renting downtown for a while. She was also the one who kept us in the Circus year after year, reassuring us that Dina's arrest and her own broken leg were a fair price for our fun. Now she was the city's face of law and order. The press would whip itself into a frenzy—she was supposed to be preventing accidents, not having them.

We turned a hard left into the newer wing of the hospital, where the walls were painted a garish shade of orange. The faint smell of bleach made me queasy.

"Who didn't get the memo the guns are fake?" Dina asked, but I didn't find this as funny as she did. I had tried to convince myself on the way over that Allie's curt summons had to be an overreaction; Bee was probably taking charge of this place already, doing the rounds, shaking hands. Then I caught on to what Dina was implying.

"You think one of us did this?" I asked, and she wore a look that said she was sure of it. Bee had told me she was Allie's target; had Allie been too zealous in her pursuit? Was this what my gut had been warning me against for weeks?

The orange corridor opened into a lilac-hued waiting room, spidery potted plants and blocky tables punctuating lines of brown hopsack chairs. Quiet for a Thursday night. Dina nodded at the far side of the room, where Allie was leaning up against a vending machine in her old beige trench coat, one knee hiked up, a New Balance pressed against the glass. She saw us coming and ducked down a hallway, out of sight. The news couldn't be good.

Dina jerked a thumb toward the brown chairs in the middle of the room, but before we could sit, Wesley sauntered up and we flanked her, starved for information. It was rare to see Wesley so dressed down in an old NYAC sweatshirt and ratty jeans, her light hair unkempt, disheveled. She was frowning.

"How is she?" we asked.

"Skull fracture, broken hand, a few broken ribs," Wesley said, her voice taking on a heightened assurance as she flipped into doctor mode. "The real worry is head trauma and internal bleeding. She lost consciousness for a while."

I felt as if I was outside myself, observing but not part of what was happening around me. I couldn't parse what Wesley was saying—did this mean Bee was going to pull through, or should we be bracing for the worst? Wesley's tone was so even, so detached. I guessed that was the point of all those years of rotations and residency—you became inured to the gory realities of the human condition.

"What happened?" I asked.

"Bee fell onto the subway tracks in Times Square," Wesley said, and I gasped. I couldn't imagine the horror of being on the tracks with a train bearing down, but the image of a woman lying on the ground, unmoving, was uncomfortably familiar.

"The tracks are only a few feet below the platform in that station," Dina said, earning a side-eye from Wesley.

"She fell backward," Wesley said. "Landed on her head. You don't need a huge fall to sustain a serious head injury. The way you hit the ground can be more important than the distance you fall."

"Tell me she wasn't hit by a train," I said.

"No, thank god—some woman managed to get her up in time," Wesley said as she gnawed at a hangnail.

"She'll be okay, though, won't she?" I asked.

"They'll keep her here until they know more," Wesley said, the ambiguity frustrating.

Dina was mired in her own thoughts, and I wondered if she was thinking about the Circus, which was ending tomorrow. It had only just occurred to me that Bee was out of the running.

"Can we see her?" I asked.

"She's in pre-op, so no. Not for a while."

"How did you find out?" Dina asked. "About Bee, I mean."

It was a strange thing to ask, but Dina rarely posed a question without good reason. Did she think Wesley was behind this?

"Doye called," Wesley said testily, her impatience showing. "He was out of town, and I happened to be nearby."

I could tell Dina and I were wondering the same thing: Why would Bee's husband, Doye, call Wesley first? Everyone knew Allie was the person you called in an emergency. Still, the prospect of having to explain ourselves to Doye set off alarm bells in my head. A psychiatrist and a bright star in his own right, Doye had a preternatural calmness and a self-effacing wit that always made him seem like the adult in the room. But his deep gaze made me uncomfortable. I often felt like he was studying me, boring into the dark corners of my mind and seeing things I'd worked hard to bury. This time, he'd know what we'd been up to. He'd want to know who was responsible.

Over Wesley's shoulder, I could see two cops headed down the corridor toward us. I thought of the unanswered voicemail on my phone. Were they here for me? I held my breath as they nodded at Wesley and didn't exhale until they passed us by.

"What are they doing here?" Dina whispered.

We'd worked to stay on the right side of the law and out of the press. Even if the past stayed buried, we all knew that a single reporter getting wind of the Circus could sink Bee's career. My stunt at Chloe's music school wouldn't help; I was praying no one would link what I'd done to Bee.

"I've put them off for now," Wesley said with a new urgency. "But we need to get our story straight."

What did Wesley mean? Was this confirmation that Bee's accident was tied to the Circus? I thought of how Bee, Wesley, Allie, and Dina rallied around me after Claudine's death. We would do the same for Bee.

"How did she end up on the tracks?" I asked.

Wesley crossed her arms over her chest, her stare defiant. Allie had reappeared, and she was leaning against the vending machine once more, listening.

"Did they get it on camera?" Dina cut in. "They must have in a station that busy."

"The cops are working on it," Wesley said.

"So you don't think this was an accident," Dina said to Wesley, but Allie pulled herself off the vending machine and broke into our circle.

"We have no reason to think this wasn't an accident," Allie said in the slow, deliberate voice mothers use when they're trying to keep a child in check. Wesley scoffed.

"Allie, come on," Wesley said. "People don't just fall on the tracks."

"Sure they do," Allie said. "All the time."

Allie pulled out her phone, intent on proving Wesley wrong.

"Not really," Dina said. "Something like four million people ride the subway every day. Last year, just over two hundred were reported as accidentally falling onto the tracks. It's a pretty small percentage."

Allie didn't hide her annoyance, but none of us were surprised by Dina's command of what seemed like random statistics. We no longer fact-checked her; she was always right.

"Thank you, Dina," Wesley said. "For once we agree."

"On what exactly?" Dina asked.

It was Wesley's turn to display her irritation.

"That this wasn't an accident, especially on the heels of someone trying to run Bee and me out of the Circus. Bee was pushed."

Dina looked confused, and Wesley seemed surprised that I hadn't told Dina.

"I got an email threatening to send an incriminating photo to my father—get him to cut me off—if I don't stop playing," Wesley said.

I caught Allie watching me and gave her a quizzical look. She looked away. I'd talk to her later about her appearance at the restaurant. Give her a chance to come clean in private before telling the others.

"What kind of photo?" Dina asked.

"From my thirtieth—the one I asked everyone to delete," Wesley said indignantly. "They pulled the same stunt with Bee. Slipping her a note saying they were going to leak the Circus to voters if she didn't drop out."

How did Wesley know? Bee must've told her, but the luncheon was only two days ago. When would they have talked?

"Is that all it said?" Dina asked. "I mean, did they ask for anything else?"

"No," I cut in. "The whole thing happened at Bee's fundraiser Tuesday at Sempre. I was there helping out."

I didn't know what to say next.

"Wesley, you think this was an intimidation tactic by one of us," Dina said.

Wesley raised an eyebrow.

"A million dollars on the table?" Wesley asked. "Bee was Allie's target, so that's pretty hard to ignore."

Allie looked like she'd been slapped. Wesley was just winding up.

"Let me guess," Wesley said to Allie. "Bee's a hard woman to pin down. Getting her alone is practically impossible, but you did your homework. You knew she'd take the subway to the Guggenheim, and we all know she tries to ditch her security in public so no one thinks she's afraid of the streets. So you followed her down into the station.

Maybe Bee tripped and took a tumble on her own. Or maybe all that money was too tempting. A little push at the right moment would take care of all those college tuition bills."

Wesley pantomimed a two-handed shove. Allie was irate; she looked like she might make a run at Wesley.

"You're way out of line," Allie said through gritted teeth, and I angled myself between the two of them, arms spread to keep them at bay.

"Wesley, before you start putting Allie on trial, how about we figure out what we actually know?" Dina asked.

"I think we know what we need to," Wesley countered.

"If Allie's right about this being an accident, then we're arguing for no reason," Dina said. "But if it wasn't—if she was intentionally pushed onto the tracks—then we need to know why. Maybe it was one of us. But what if it wasn't? A kook who disagrees with Bee's politics is one thing, but if someone's after the pot, then we have a serious problem."

Wesley didn't protest. Allie was seething, but no longer looked ready to charge. I lowered my arms.

"Where should we start?" I asked.

"Let's find out if there were any witnesses," Dina said, slipping off her glasses and flipping them around in one hand. "Allie, can you ask the cops?"

Allie nodded. Dina started to pace.

"Has anyone heard if Bee's stalker is back?"

We shook our heads.

"Anyone else making threats? Or getting them?"

We shrugged.

"Who else knows about the money besides us?"

"Spouses, close friends," Allie said. "Hugo."

"It's definitely not Hugo," Wesley said adamantly.

"What about Steve Camerino?" Dina asked. "Isn't his firm under a pretty big cloud right now?"

"It's a smear campaign," Wesley said. "And he doesn't need our money."

We looked up then to see a nurse in pink scrubs waving at us from the double doors to the ER. She was holding a white plastic bag. Allie hustled over; they exchanged words we couldn't hear before Allie rejoined us.

"She wants us to hold on to Bee's things until Doye gets here."

"So, Allie," Wesley asked with her hands on her hips as Allie set the bag down on one of the brown chairs, "where were you earlier tonight?"

Allie spun around.

"Back off, Wes."

"No, really, there's an easy way out of this," Wesley said. "The cops are putting Bee's fall between five thirty and six, so all we have to do is figure out where everyone was at that time. Where were you?"

Anyone paying attention would've seen the color drain from my face, but Wesley and Allie were in too deep.

"You're so quick to accuse the rest of us, Wesley," Allie said. "How do we know it wasn't you?"

"You think I'd send a threatening email to *myself*?" Wesley asked.

"Yes, I do," Allie said.

"Stop it, both of you," I said, but Wesley wasn't finished.

"Sara," Wesley said, turning to me. "Leaving a note for Bee seems a little obvious, but maybe you were counting on that so we wouldn't suspect you. That's what you do, isn't it? Hide behind your camera, put up walls so no one can see what's going on inside? I hear the restaurant's struggling. Is it fair to say the money would ease the tensions at home?"

It was my turn to bristle.

"My mother used to say there's a limit to friendship when there's money to be made. I always pitied her for being cynical," Wesley said. "Now I see she was trying to warn me."

"Enough, Wesley," I said.

We shared too much history to splinter like this. I hoped Dina would step in, but she had wasted no time laying out Bee's things across the chairs like a weekend sidewalk sale. She was studying the array as if an answer lay in the folds of Bee's clothing.

"What do you notice?" Dina asked in a hopeful voice I imagined she used on her students.

We took in the phone, heels, black coat, silk blouse, and flowy pants. Seeing Bee's possessions laid out like this—the trappings of a woman whose resilience we'd taken for granted—drove home the seriousness of our situation. Bee was fighting for her life, and we were tearing one another apart.

"Her medallion is missing," Dina said finally, and we couldn't believe we had missed something so obvious.

"Isn't this proof Bee was targeted?" Wesley asked. "Someone snatched it before pushing her."

"We don't know that," Allie said adamantly.

I could see we were going in circles, making no progress when time wasn't on our side. Claudine's reappearance had been nagging at me and even though I didn't have an explanation of how it all fit together, she felt like the missing puzzle piece. Too important to keep to myself.

"Listen, I know what I'm about to say sounds crazy, but hear me out," I said, swallowing hard. "It's just that, well, someone's been following me. I think it's connected to all of this."

My mind was suddenly foggy under the heat of their scrutiny.

"It was Claudine," I said hurriedly, and Wesley threw up her hands. Allie pushed the clothes over and slumped into one of the chairs against the wall. "I swear. She was real, and it feels like she's trying to—"

"Exact her revenge?" Wesley asked.

"Yes," I said, nursing a faint hope that Wesley understood. The feeling didn't last long.

"That's the dumbest thing I've ever heard," Wesley said.

"Unless her revenge is to turn us against each other," Allie countered, her head tilted back against the wall like she was trying to stem a nosebleed.

Wesley ignored Allie.

"Dina, back me up," Wesley said. "You don't believe in ghosts, do you?"

"No," Dina said. "I like rational explanations. Hundreds of years, and scientists still haven't found credible evidence for the supernatural."

Wesley turned back to me, vindicated.

"Let's say for a second—and this is a huge assumption—your ghost is real. What would you have us do?"

This was a question I could answer.

"Stop playing," I said. "We can't control this anymore."

"And the money?"

I'd been preoccupied with the pot and what it could do for Coulter and me; a one-fifth share now seemed smaller than it had a week ago. I didn't know if it would cover the loan Coulter had taken out to keep the restaurant open. "What if we draw straws for it?"

Wesley barked with laughter.

"I'm not giving up my shot at the money because of a made-up ghost story," Wesley said. "This is so like you, Sara. Keeping us in the dark while we clean up your mess."

"Since you keep bringing it up, Wesley," I said, a hard edge to my voice, "let's get into it. What is it you think I did?"

Dina and Allie both avoided my gaze.

"Yeah, fine," Wesley said. "Let's talk about how we stuck our necks out for you. I'll admit that was a choice I made. But we have no idea what happened between you and Claudine in her room that night, do we? All we have to go on is the story we've been fed by the person who made it out alive. And now we have another roommate who's taken a bad fall. Maybe history does repeat itself."

"Wesley," Allie said sharply.

Wesley's accusation stung. How long had her suspicion been festering? Dina and Allie both started to speak; Dina relented, gesturing for Allie to go first.

"If we're going there, Wesley," Allie said, "it's only fair that we come clean too."

Wesley didn't agree, but neither did she object, so Allie covered her mouth with both hands, composing herself with a deep breath before speaking.

"After Claudine died," Allie said, "we felt like we had to do something when the investigation got serious. For your sake, for our sakes, I don't know. We kept Bee out of it, though. She was making the rounds to the deans, so she needed to have her conscience clear. The three of us decided that Dina and I would lean on the boys, get them to recant their story. Wesley would tell the cops she saw Claudine sitting on the ledge, losing her balance, you trying to save her. It didn't seem wrong at the time."

I was dumbfounded. All these years, they'd kept this secret. They had spared me the pain of a trial and the melee that would've followed, risking their own necks if they had been discovered. I had no idea how much I owed them.

Wesley snorted.

"What?" Allie asked defensively. "We were young and scared. We did the best we could."

"The best we could?" Wesley repeated, incensed. "We lied to the police, to the administration, even to Bee."

"I'm not proud of it," Allie said in a quiet voice, "but I'd do it again for Sara. For any of you."

Wesley cut in before I could say anything.

"I sure as hell wouldn't," Wesley said.

"None of it was a lie," I said, and Wesley shrugged, but what worried me was how quickly Allie looked away.

"Can we focus?" Dina asked impatiently. "We don't have much time. Let's go back to where everyone was earlier." When no one objected, she said, "I was meeting with an old colleague from Columbia up on 110th."

"Can we verify that?" Wesley asked, and Dina's nod seemed to satisfy her.

"I was with Nick," Wesley said then, to no one in particular. "Ask him yourself."

Neither Allie nor I jumped at the chance to go next. Did I see a glimmer of panic in her eyes? And did she see the same in mine?

"I was running errands downtown," Allie said feebly, but I was too preoccupied with my own predicament to doubt her.

"I was uptown," I said, bracing for imminent blowback. "At Chloe's music school."

Allie locked onto me with a wide-eyed fury, her mouth a thin line. She looked poised to unleash a wild tirade, so I rushed to explain that I was never going to bother Chloe, and I could see how wrong it was to involve her. Allie opened her mouth, but she was so angry the words didn't come. Her gaze flew around the waiting room, searching for a place to put her anger.

"I should never have agreed to this," Allie said, reaching for the clasp behind her neck. "At least I tried to warn you."

She pulled her necklace off, flung it at Dina, and stormed out. A hush settled over the waiting room, all of us feeling raw. Wesley wandered over to the vending machines at the far end of the room. Dina dropped into one of the brown chairs. I took a seat farther down, at a distance.

We sat like this, each of us deep in our own thoughts but acutely aware of the others, until Wesley turned her back to us, mulling over drink options, and in a second Dina was by my side. She gestured for my hand, placing a tangled chain in my outstretched palm.

"I remembered something," Dina whispered. "About Claudine."

"What about her?" I asked as I looked down at the medallion in my hand, unsure why Dina was giving me Allie's medallion now.

Wesley turned around suddenly, her eyes narrowed at us, causing me to forget about whatever it was that Dina had remembered. I stuffed the medallion hurriedly into my pocket, guessing Dina was following the old rule: whoever dropped out passed their medallion on to the person assigned to eliminate them. Dina settled into her chair and was working a thin woven bamboo tube—a finger trap, a children's toy—painted a garish shade of orange between her palms, a tchotchke that helped her focus.

Wesley marched over and it occurred to me that the two of them could've scattered to the far corners of the hospital, but they hadn't. Their presence struck me as a show of solidarity, however lukewarm, or at least a shared commitment to doing whatever we could for Bee. We owed Bee that much.

"Dina's right," I said. "We need to figure out who did this."

"What do you have in mind?" Wesley asked.

Dina was spinning the orange tube around in one hand at a frenetic pace.

"Pretend the Circus is still on," I said. "Draw them out."

Wesley grabbed the tube out of Dina's hand and hurled it at me; I caught it on the cheek.

"We don't have to pretend," Wesley said. "I'm still playing."

"Are you serious?" I asked. "We're in a hospital. Bee's in surgery."

Wesley was shaking her head.

"We made a deal. Bee would want us to keep going."

I couldn't believe what I was hearing.

"You should be thrilled," Wesley said, pointing at my back pocket. "You're up two to one."

"Wesley, there's more to this than money," I said, hearing the desperation in my voice. I turned to Dina. "The Middlesex County DA is reopening Claudine's case."

I wasn't lying, but I also wasn't telling the whole truth. The case was further along than I was letting on. In addition to the voicemail on my phone from a cop assigned to the Cold Case Unit, I'd gotten a DM from a college classmate named Lynn—a friend I hadn't spoken to in a few years who now lived outside of Boston—about an investigator asking about me, my roommates, then Claudine and the circumstances around her death. This person wanted to know if we'd fought often. Had there been a falling-out? Any signs of depression, disordered behavior, physical violence? I assured Lynn she didn't need to worry. I made up a story about a job I'd applied to that required security clearance. Everything was fine, even though it obviously wasn't.

"We should stop playing, don't you think?" I asked Dina.

I expected her to offer up some common sense. Surely she didn't think keeping the Circus going was a good idea.

"It's over and done with tomorrow," Dina said. "I don't see how one more day is going to make much of a difference. And we did agree we'd go along with the vote."

I couldn't understand how we had ended up here: Wesley and Dina allied in their determination to keep playing, the cops breathing down our necks, and everything we had worked for—careers, reputations, relationships—on the verge of being blown to pieces when we were eventually, inevitably, exposed.

"Well then, it sounds like intermission's over," Wesley said as she pulled on her jacket. Just before turning to leave, she added, "I guess it's game on."

16

I RETURNED from the hospital to find two cops sitting on the green couch in my living room. This should've been the thing that bothered me the most, but Coulter, kneeling by the coffee table in his old brown flannel, wouldn't turn around. On a different day, under different circumstances, he might've been entertaining two old friends. A jazzy hip-hop beat lilted softly. He had built a fire and was pouring coffee as he laughed about the weather's indecision: snow, rain, sun, then rain again. I willed him to look at me—a glimpse of his face would've told me what I needed to know—but he didn't turn around.

When I cleared my throat, the cops—shiny blue jackets, close-cropped dark hair—leapt to their feet. I'm sure they were more distinct than that, but I was too frazzled to register much more than their holstered guns. Were these the same two cops lurking around the hospital? Or were they following up on the voicemail that I'd been ignoring—a team sent to figure out what happened the night of Claudine's death? Either way, Wesley was right. We should've gotten our story straight when we had the chance.

"Sorry to bother you at home, Mrs. Simons," the taller cop said. "We have some questions about Barbara Colasanti."

I had to remind myself that he was speaking to me. I didn't change my last name when Coulter and I got married; I didn't think of myself as Mrs. Simons. Coulter didn't even identify with his own last name. He was constantly toying with changing his to Russo, his mother's surname.

"Happy to help," I said as I stepped into the living room, desperate to get a read on what they wanted. Did they think I was responsible for Bee's accident? I donned what I hoped was an accommodating smile as a bloom of heat fired across my cheeks and down my neck.

The four of us stood awkwardly together in our petite living room, unsure how to organize ourselves. Without Coulter's reading chair, the couch was the only alternative to the floor. The shorter cop—broad-faced, with a gentler demeanor—encouraged Coulter and me to sit. I reached a hand up to take my jacket off, only to realize I had hung it on the rack on the way in.

"It's been a long day," Coulter said, eyeing me. "Can I have a second with my wife?"

"I don't think that's—" the taller one started to say.

"We'll give you a minute," the shorter one cut in, and they exchanged a look I couldn't decipher before filing out into the hallway, out of sight but not out of earshot. Thankfully, Coulter was one step ahead. He tapped his phone a few times and the room hummed with the woozy Frank Ocean track he'd been playing on repeat. We huddled in the far corner of the room, past the couch, where we had the best chance of not being overheard.

"Were you at the hospital?" Coulter asked in a strained voice. "How is Bee?"

He was standing too close, crowding me.

"Sara?"

Dizzy, I braced myself against the wall. There were pills I could take, an orange bottle hidden away at the back of my bathroom drawer, given to me by Wesley for panic attacks that subsided a year ago. It seemed the attacks had returned.

"Is she okay?" he asked again, his voice strained.

"I don't know," I said, trying to clear the fog that had enveloped me. "She was in surgery. Unconscious."

"What do they think happened?" he asked, genuinely distraught. I described Bee's fall onto the tracks in the Times Square station, how the police were searching for witnesses, videos, anything. I didn't mention the threatening notes or Wesley's insistence that someone had pushed Bee deliberately, nor did I feel a need to bring up my earlier run-in with the cops. I was used to talking around my roommates and the Circus, offering up alternative explanations that deflected attention and blame.

"But this was an accident, right?"

"We don't know," I said, then nodded toward the hallway. "What do they want?"

"I told them it wasn't a good time, but they were hell-bent on talking to you."

A log fell off the grate in a plume of ash and spark, startling us both.

"Whatever you do, don't tell them about the Circus," he said.

"What if they ask?"

"It won't look good for any of you."

"Mr. Simons?" a voice called out from the hallway.

"Be right there," he called back, then motioned to the medallion around my neck. "Leave that in case they drag you down to the station."

It hadn't occurred to me that the cops might take me in, and the thought terrified me. I remembered Allie's medallion in my pocket.

"Buy me some time," I whispered, and he nodded.

As he headed into the hallway, I rushed to the couch, fumbling with the clasp on my necklace. I had tucked the two medallions under the seat cushions and barely taken a seat when the three of them filed in.

Coulter joined me on the couch, shifting around so anxiously he didn't notice I was trembling. The cops stood over us; the room felt like a packed subway car in a July heat wave.

"Mrs. Simons," the shorter cop said, "I know it's late, so thank you for your cooperation in answering a few questions."

His voice, their faces, the shelves flanking the fireplace that held my books—everything had taken on a blurry sheen, like I was bobbing underwater. I needed to get ahold of myself, if not for my own sake, then for Bee's. This conversation was no different from a lifetime of interviews, auditions, and cocktail parties, I told myself, where I'd honed my ability to say what people wanted to hear.

"Can you tell us how you know Barbara Colasanti?"

I was surprised the cops were going this far back—did they actually know so little about us, or was this a warm-up? I explained how Bee and I were old friends. College roommates, in fact, but she'd been so busy with work and the campaign that we didn't see each other as often as we'd like.

"Would you say you're on good terms?" the shorter cop asked. The taller cop had a notebook in hand. He hadn't written anything down yet, which I took as a good sign.

"Yes, definitely."

Coulter was fidgeting with the cuff on his flannel. I launched into an explanation of how the four of us rushed to the hospital the minute we heard, how none of us saw Bee because she was in surgery, how I was eager to rejoin the others in case there was any news. I was rambling, breaking Bee's cardinal rule of interrogation: never offer up information without being asked.

"How often would you say Ms. Colasanti takes public transportation?" the taller cop asked.

"She tries to take the subway as much as she can. She doesn't want to be one of those officials who rides around in a town car all day. She likes talking to people, asking their opinions."

The taller cop scribbled a note, which seemed like a failing on my part.

"And where were you earlier tonight, around five or six?" the shorter cop asked.

"Seeing a friend. Uptown."

I started to explain, but I held myself back, remembering Bee's rule.

"Whole lotta city uptown from here. Can you be more specific?"

"Morningside Heights."

I knew what Coulter was thinking: I didn't have any friends in that neighborhood.

"Could that friend confirm you were together?"

"Yes," I said, praying it wouldn't come to that. Given the hole that I'd dug for myself with Allie, the last thing I wanted to do was ask Chloe to talk to the cops.

"And what's your friend's name?"

"Um, Allie—Alison—Kohlstedt."

"Alison Kohlstedt," the shorter cop said, and it rolled off his tongue a little too easily—like it was a name he knew. "She was your college roommate too?"

"Yes." How did he know this?

"So what you're saying is that she was with you earlier tonight in Morningside Heights?"

I panicked—should I tell the truth? I was struck by a harrowing thought: What if the cops were making the rounds, talking to my roommates? I wasn't worried about Wesley, who would play dumb, or Dina, who would figure out what had already been said, but Allie would tell the truth no matter what. If they sought her out, it was only a matter of time before they figured out the rest of us were lying.

"Um, no, not exactly. I was waiting for her, but we got our signals crossed. She didn't show."

"Did you talk to her then? Or see her later?"

I felt as if I was burning up, armpits damp, the back of my shirt sticky.

"She was the one who called me from the hospital."

"But you didn't see her before that?"

"No," I said, feeling as if I were traversing a narrow ledge. I could feel both of the cops sizing me up.

"We have reason to believe Mrs. Kohlstedt was at the Times Square station around the time of Ms. Colasanti's incident," the taller cop said. "Any idea why she'd be there?"

Allie was at the station?

"No," I said quietly, and we sat in an interminable silence. I had no idea how to spin this.

Coulter stood then, reminding the cops it was late. I jumped up, too, not wanting them to leave here thinking Allie was responsible for Bee's fall.

"Actually, yes, come to think of it," I said. "Allie picks up her daughter on Thursdays from music school. She works in the financial district, so she was changing trains, headed uptown."

The taller cop scribbled this down. I hoped my explanation sounded plausible enough, but something Allie once told me dropped into my head: people lie ten times a day, college kids double or triple that, and they get away with it at least half the time. I'd never seen myself in these statistics, but now the numbers seemed about right.

"One more thing, Mrs. Simons," the taller cop said from the hallway. "Any idea why Ms. Colasanti was asking for you when they brought her in?"

The punch landed. Why would Bee ask for me? Except, of course, if she was pointing a finger at the person who had pushed her.

"Like I said, we're old friends," I said with as much conviction as I could muster. "I really should get back to the hospital."

"Of course," the shorter cop said, dropping his business card on the coffee table. "If you think of anything else, you got our number."

When the front door shut behind them, my hands flew to my head. It was nearly one in the morning, and I was stunned by the realization that I had become the kind of person who lies to cops. I was hoping for reassurance, maybe even a stiff drink, so when Coulter disappeared into the kitchen to whip up an omelet for himself, I stared him down from the doorway, unable to hide my irritation.

"Why did you let them in?" I asked.

He whisked the eggs with a simmering ferocity.

"It's not every day I have two cops knocking down my door," he said.

The oil in the pan sizzled; he turned the flame down.

"You could've told them it wasn't a good time instead of inviting them in for a coffee chat."

"And you could've warned me that you were in over your head," he said. "Allie was at the station when Bee was pushed? Bee was asking for you when they brought her in? I thought you guys were smarter than this."

"You think we planned this? You think we want the cops sniffing around?"

He poured the eggs into the pan, his spatula poised to intervene at precisely the right moment.

"We both know what's really bothering you," I said. "You've always resented my roommates because they're successful."

"And I'm not?"

"That's not what I said."

"It's what you meant."

"And it's always a comparison with you. Why can't women be successful, period? Why does their success have to diminish yours?"

He sprinkled ham onto the setting eggs, then flipped and folded the whole thing over with a flick of his wrist.

"Sara, I can't help you if you keep me in the dark."

He slid the omelet onto a plate and cut the flame. Leaning against the counter, he took small bites, but I could tell he was going through the motions, waiting for me to back down. I was furious at him for claiming the high ground when I needed him on my side, but right now he was the only person I could trust.

"The whole thing's a mess," I said. "Allie wants nothing to do with us, and Wesley and Dina are hell-bent on playing until the bitter end."

"Bee's in the hospital. Why would they keep playing?"

I realized he had missed an important piece of the story.

"When we were starting out, we put aside a little money as a reward for the winner of the last round. Wesley invested it with a friend."

"Steve Camerino," he said, and I nodded.

"Turns out the prize is almost a million dollars," I said.

His fork hung in midair.

"I know," I said. "It's a lot of money."

"And how do you get it?"

"First one to walk five medallions into Hugo's diner by tomorrow at nine."

He set his plate and fork down in the sink.

"And you think because there's so much money in play, Bee's fall wasn't an accident."

"I don't know what to think."

"But you suspect one of your roommates."

"I don't know. Maybe. Allie's the most likely, but she's also the most unlikely."

The mounting evidence against Allie was hard to ignore. She'd been at the restaurant and could've left the note for Bee. Now we also knew she was at the Times Square station when Bee fell.

"How's that?"

"Bee was her target, so it would make sense that she was going after Bee earlier today. And she's been acting strangely. She moved without saying a word. I know she's worked up about Chloe heading off to school. The pot would cover college tuition for all three kids and then some."

"But?"

"There's no way Allie would intentionally hurt Bee," I said.

He shrugged as if to say people could disappoint you.

"Is there a chance Wesley did it?" he asked.

No one made us laugh like Wesley did, but she was also famous for taking things a step too far. I thought of the time she read Mr. Byrd's letter aloud, and the way she mocked Dina at the kickoff dinner. But Wesley was cleaning herself up, putting her skills to good use. Still, maybe feeling strapped for the first time in her life had made her more reckless than usual. We all knew that when Wesley felt cornered, she wouldn't think twice about burning everything down.

"She was pretty hot and cold at the hospital."

"When has she not been hot and cold?"

"She's terrified her dad will cut her off," I said.

"Can't say that's new either," Coulter said.

He stuck his hands in his jean pockets and leaned against the kitchen counter, close enough that I could reach out and touch him. When he spoke next, his voice had softened. "Look, Sara, the cops are circling. The way I see it, we need to throw them a bone."

"I'm not ratting Allie or Wesley out. I don't even know if they've done anything wrong."

"I'm not talking about them."

I understood then what he was proposing.

"You know it's not just about the money for Dina," Coulter said. "Winning would be the ultimate vindication—she's seen herself as an underdog her whole life."

He loved to portray Dina as a nutcase, a ticking bomb. Usually, I had no patience for his tired theories, but Bee's accident had shaken something in me. I could see how Dina became a different person when her ambition reared its head, how being told she was smarter than everyone else had made her uncompromising in the pursuit of her goals. Hadn't she told me on the sidewalk outside my building that she could use this win? As soon as she heard about the pot, she would've started planning, calculating probabilities, mapping out moves to put herself two steps ahead. The money would free her from student loans and buy an apartment for the aunt who'd raised her.

The clock over the kitchen doorway had ticked past one. My thoughts shifted to Bee. The surgery had to be over by now. Was she awake? Did she remember what happened?

"I'm going back to the hospital," I said, patting my pockets until I felt my house key.

"Wait until morning," Coulter said. "I'll drop you off on the way to work. Doye's with Bee. There's nothing you can do now."

"No, I need to talk to her," I insisted.

"Sara," he said firmly. "It's late. You're tired."

He looked at me sternly—as if to say his decision was final—before brushing past me. I heard the clink of coffee cups in the living room. He returned and began to rinse the dishes in the sink.

"Go to bed," he said. "I'll finish up here."

He was right—I was exhausted—but I didn't appreciate being spoken to like a child. I thanked him for cleaning up and pretended to drag myself to bed. Instead of heading to the bedroom, I paused in the hallway until I heard the fridge open. The door blocked Coulter's view of me, and I slipped past him. He yelled my name as I was pulling the front door shut behind me, but I was gone before he could stop me.

I was on the street when my phone vibrated in my pocket. I expected an admonishment from Coulter, but I stopped short at the sight of a text from Wesley that read: We need to talk now.

17

I WASN'T expecting a warm welcome when Wesley buzzed me in, and my nerves were brittle when I reached the third floor. She was standing in her doorway, barefoot in a wash-worn blue sweatshirt we had bought together at the Urban Outfitters in Harvard Square. The tan she was sporting a week ago had faded, and she looked pale, but it could've been the hallway lighting. Someone neglecting to put in the warm-toned bulbs.

"How's Bee?" I asked.

Wesley leaned against the doorjamb, hands tucked into the pockets of gray sweatpants. I propped myself against the opposite wall, catching my breath.

"They stopped the bleeding, but they're watching her closely."

"That's good. About the bleeding, I mean."

Wesley eyed the black leather jacket and dark jeans I'd been wearing for the last four days. I tried not to think about how ragged I must look with my bare face and scraggly ponytail.

"Wesley, the cops were at my place asking questions. Did you know they were coming?"

"You didn't say anything about the Circus, did you?" Wesley asked.

"Of course not."

"The nurse told me Bee was asking for you when they brought her in. What the hell did you do?"

Bad news travels fast, I thought.

"She was probably asking for me because I pick up when she calls," I said firmly. "I don't disappear, then pretend like I haven't been MIA for weeks."

Wesley looked down at her toenails, painted cornflower blue. I had hurt her, just as she had hurt me. I couldn't see how we'd work our way back from this.

"I can't do this right now," I said, and turned to go.

"Sara, wait," she said, her tone softening enough for me to hear her out.

I crossed my arms over my chest.

"How much do you talk to Dina these days?" she asked.

"Once a month. More or less."

"Has she said anything about tenure?"

"Not much. The committee's supposed to be meeting any day now."

Dina was a sandbagger. Always had been. Not because she was trying to mislead anyone, but because she was too tough on herself. That was the awful thing about perfectionism. The more you doubted yourself, the more desperately you had to push toward flawlessness, to fill the crevices where criticism could take hold.

Wesley looked troubled, then apologetic.

"Wes, just say whatever you're gonna say."

She sighed, as if she couldn't believe what she was about to tell me.

"She's getting passed over."

"That's impossible," I said. "She did everything they asked and more. They'd be idiots not to give her tenure."

I expected Wesley to push back. Instead, she fiddled with the gold signet ring she wore on her pinkie that she'd inherited from her grandmother.

"Where did you hear this?" I asked.

"Marjorie McDiarmid."

The name meant nothing.

"Head of the Harvard philosophy department. She and my mom are friends."

I remembered the semester two years ago when Dina lectured at Columbia. We spent more time together than we had in years, venturing to far-flung corners of the city in search of the most authentic ramen and the tangiest Korean barbecue. She was energized by the city after the quiet intellectualism of Cambridge, befriending faculty outspoken about racial injustice, questioning her own identity as a Japanese American. For a time, she was incensed at her mother for running off with a Brazilian dentist, her father for deserting before she was born, at anyone stupid enough to ask *Where are you from? No, where are you really from?* And at herself, for feeling like she was never enough of one thing or the other. Upon returning to Cambridge, she told me she was asked to tone down her rhetoric. Though she took the demand as a personal affront, she decided to bury her outrage, to sacrifice a part of herself for the sake of her career.

"What happened?"

"It's a fucked-up process," Wesley said, shaking her head. "The department chair, Marjorie, puts you forward, but it's not only up to her. You need letters of support from the department, but people won't stick their neck out if they don't think your file is strong enough. They put out a call for peer reviews, but it's all about who they ask. And after they boil down the papers you've published, the classes you've taught, the hours you've spent in boring committee meetings, all you get back is a yes or no."

"So her file wasn't strong enough?"

"Sometimes they want a published book."

"Wait. Did Princeton back out?"

"That's what I heard."

"And that sank her?"

Wesley shrugged.

"She's published in journals—prestigious ones," Wesley said. "I heard it was a letter. Anonymous. Claiming she plagiarized some paper. They looked into it—didn't find much—but the taint is there. If you ask me, this was some Machiavellian bullshit."

Dina had never been one to politick. Had she rubbed a colleague the wrong way? Even so, the process couldn't be so flimsy as to turn on a single letter. What about the years Dina had given over to teaching, to the detriment of everything else?

I thought of the time Dina was hospitalized after getting passed over for a fellowship. She wouldn't let me visit, but I saw her the day after she was discharged—she looked like hell. Skinny and pale, depressed and obviously suffering. It took her a few months to get back on her feet. She never let me bring it up again.

"We both know she can be a little off sometimes," Wesley said.

"Off?"

Wesley furrowed her brow like she knew she could do better.

"For people with Dina's profile, a precipitating event can trigger a break. They lose touch with reality. They have delusions."

"So now you're a psychiatrist?"

"No, this is basic Intro to Psych stuff."

"I took Intro to Psych. I have no idea what a precipitating event is."

"An event that's sudden. Emotionally traumatic."

"Yeah, I got that much. You mean Bee almost getting hit by a train?"

"That could be a trigger, but I meant not getting tenure," she said, throwing up her hands. "Come on, Sara. You can't tell me Dina hasn't been withdrawn. More agitated than usual. Paranoid even."

"Wesley, we're in the middle of the Circus. What do you expect? You're the one who ransacked your own apartment three years ago because you were convinced Dina had wired the place with hidden cameras."

She waved the memory away as if to say that was ancient history.

"This is different. Dina's wound pretty tightly. A blow like this could make her—I don't know—explode into violence."

"She's no more violent than any of us," I said. "Besides, Allie was the one at the station, not Dina."

"Yeah, but we both know Allie wouldn't lay a finger on Bee."

Wesley shifted around, frustrated.

"Sara, I'm just telling you what I know. The thing that really sucks is the timing."

"Why? How long has she known?"

Wesley grimaced.

"Marjorie told her on the twenty-seventh of December."

My stomach turned. This explained why Dina was late to our kickoff dinner. She had come straight to us on the heels of receiving this awful blow, only to walk in on Wesley mocking her. I'd made her suffer through my awful toast. What fine friends we were.

"Do you remember the screw-your-roommate dance junior year?" Wesley asked, and she could tell I wasn't interested. She held up a hand, imploring me to listen. "The one where we set Claudine up with Trevor?"

"What does it matter?" I asked.

"Remember how we spent hours in Claudine's room getting Dina to try on Claudine's dresses?" she asked.

It was easy to picture us sprawled on Claudine's shaggy white rug as Dina slipped in and out of an endless parade of minidresses Claudine foraged from her closet. Claudine and Dina couldn't have been more different in taste and style, but they were exactly the same size. We were surprised to find that every one of those dresses fit Dina perfectly, even if getting her to wear an outfit that was short and revealing took another hour of cajoling.

"What's your point?" I asked.

"When you said you've been seeing Claudine—like really seeing her—it came to me. Yeah, the dance was years ago, but Dina hasn't changed. She's probably still the same size as Claudine."

Now I saw where this was going.

"You think Dina dressed up like Claudine to spook me."

"And sneak up on Bee. Grab her medallion. It's smart—I'll admit it."

"Why is everyone trying to pin this on Dina? You think she's so depraved that she'd shove Bee onto the tracks to get closer to the money?"

"Look, we're all really fucking good at coming up with new angles when it comes to the Circus."

"No," I said, shaking my head. "We have boundaries."

"Do we?" she asked, and we both knew she was talking about my stunt at Chloe's school. She took advantage of my mortified silence to press her case. "Why do you feel like you have to protect her all the time? Dina is a grown woman. Smart too. She can take care of herself."

I couldn't stop the words from tumbling out.

"I don't get why you're so threatened by her," I said. "You always have to knock her down like a high school mean girl. You really have some nerve going after Allie, then me, and now Dina. All that tells me is that you're probably the one screwing us all."

Wesley squeezed her eyes shut, and when they reopened, I could tell she was far away.

"Sara, you're not doing Bee any favors by pretending this isn't happening."

"This?" I said, my anger roiling. "If by *this,* you mean pinning what happened to Bee on Dina, then no. *This* isn't happening."

She crossed her arms over her chest—a signal our conversation was over.

"Well then, you should watch out," Wesley said.

"So now you're threatening me?"

She shook her head. The fervor had subsided, leaving only a weary regret behind.

"Not at all," Wesley said. "But you should be ready. Dina's coming for us next."

18

In the small hours of Friday morning, I stood on the sidewalk in front of the hospital, grindng apart shards of ice with my heel. Wesley had fanned a spark of uncertainty into full-blown doubt. Perhaps I'd always known Dina was capable of a quiet, controlled violence. She grew up near the Bowery back when New York was gritty, lawless, and tough, and she still carried a butterfly knife when she planned to stay out late. I wondered how well you could keep knowing a person over intermittent snatches of time. I once thought history was enough—now I wasn't so sure.

Dragging myself inside, I hoped Bee or the hospital staff who admitted her could give me the answers I needed. Surprised to find there was no nighttime security, I stole through the lobby. As I made my way down the dimmed corridor toward Bee's room, a text from Coulter popped up on my phone: did you see Bee? I didn't respond, and he let it go.

I was passing the staff lounge—sturdy oak tables, a muted Oprah playing on a TV mounted in the corner—when the bitter, sweet smell of coffee pulled me in. A handwritten note next to an old coffee urn suggested a fifty-cent contribution, and I left my last dollar. Cradling the cup between my hands, the scorching heat a welcome penance, I drifted toward yellowing pictures of the hospital prerenovation on the far wall. As I drew closer, a shimmer in the glass revealed the room extended into an L shape; I wasn't alone. I could still slink off without being seen, but the sight of a hunched woman sitting in the alcove, her face propped heavily on one hand, telegraphing a miserable weight, cratered me.

Allie startled when she saw me, flattening both hands on her chest.

"Jesus, Sara, you're like the grim reaper."

She wasn't pleased to see me, but she didn't storm off either. I glanced at the book on the table: a Cyrillic title. Allie had taken up Russian sophomore year, when an old lefty professor waxed on about the wonderful, life-changing years he spent teaching English in St. Petersburg. I was impressed she still found time to keep her studies up.

"Okay if I sit?"

I set my coffee down and pointed at the chair where her trench coat hung. She shrugged, and I wrangled the chair around to face her. I wondered how far my transgression with Chloe had set us back; I didn't know if we were starting from scratch.

"Any news?"

Allie shook her head: "Doye's here. You should go home."

I couldn't tell if her tight-lipped answer was a dismissal or a warning that I wasn't welcome. Either way, I knew I had squashed any chance of us feeling our way through this together.

My roommates and I had known each other for more than half of our lives. I'd always assumed our friendship was impervious to shifting winds, steadfast enough to allow for second chances. The proof was in the way we'd held on to one another all these years, beating back life's repeated attempts to cleave us apart. But now I was waking up to the possibility that without patience and dogged persistence, these relationships, like many others in my life, could be neglected, outgrown, and lost forever.

"Allie, I screwed up," I said. "I shouldn't have gone anywhere near Chloe. It was stupid. I wasn't thinking. I'm sorry."

Allie picked at the corner of her book, her gaze fuzzy. I expected her to say something in return. An admission or an apology of her own.

When the silence became uncomfortable, I asked, "Is everything okay?"

Allie's head jerked up, her expression indignant.

"Why? What did Wesley say?"

"Nothing—it was only a question," I said, unsure how to tell her that I wanted to feel connected to her again.

"Did you know Wesley was in rehab for three weeks in July? I guess Bee was the only one she told."

I didn't know, but it made sense given Wesley's skittishness about the birthday photo. We'd never been good at copping to our struggles.

"I never should've agreed to play," Allie said, slamming a fist down on the table. "I knew it was a terrible idea. How could I be so fucking stupid?"

In the quarter century I'd known her, I couldn't remember ever hearing Allie say the word *fuck*. I thought of what Chloe had said about her mother acting strangely, even for January.

"Allie, this isn't on you," I said. "We made the decision together. And we don't know for sure that Bee's fall had anything to do with us."

Allie glared at me like I'd completely lost it.

"You still don't get it, do you? It's all related. None of this would've happened if we hadn't agreed to play. And we only let ourselves play because we feel this bottomless guilt over what happened to Claudine. It's ironic, don't you think? The guilt we're carrying around is toxic. It's literally killing us."

She wore a tormented expression.

"Allie," I said tentatively. "What's going on?"

When she realized I wasn't going to let this go, she sat back in her chair. We waited for a pair of nurses to fill their coffee mugs.

"I haven't been honest with you either," she said when we were alone again. I braced for whatever she was about to say: a confession that greed had gotten the better of her or that she had done things she shouldn't have.

Allie began by telling me she had found out earlier in the week that Bee was speaking at the Nederlander Theatre Thursday afternoon before dashing over to the Guggenheim for a donor meet and greet. She knew Bee would take the subway. Not just because it would be faster in weekday traffic, but because riding public transportation gave Bee the chance to be seen and photographed, an imperative during campaign season.

"I followed her down into the station," Allie said. "I was so close I had my gun out. I had the shot, but she must've seen me. She started running. I lost her."

I shifted uneasily in my chair.

"I was coming down the stairs when I heard the shouting. A commotion up ahead on the platform. I ran toward it—as fast as I could. Even before I pushed through the crowd, I knew it was Bee on the tracks. I did. And then the rattling started. The train was bearing down, shaking the whole station. Sounded like it was coming in at a hundred miles an hour. People were freaking out. And I froze."

Allie started to cry. I studied the greenish-blue veins bulging across the back of my hand, feeling stupidly emotional.

"Thank god some Good Samaritan pulled her up, because I don't know what happened. I stood there like an idiot. Bee could've died."

"Allie," I said softly. "This isn't your fault."

A memory flooded me: Allie saying the same thing in the hours after Claudine's fall. I'd hung on to those words for weeks, even months, afterward; I hoped they would be the same salve for her now.

"I could've helped, and I didn't," she said. "And now it's over for Bee. What kind of friend am I?"

"No," I said, panic overtaking me. "Wesley said they stopped the bleeding. She's going to be okay, isn't she?"

"I mean the mayor's race. The party is withdrawing its support. They're giving the nod to someone else."

"Oh," I said, sitting back in my chair. Still, we all knew Bee's career was everything to her; how stupid we were to put her dream at risk. I felt heartbroken for her, and for my other roommates too. Bee wanted so badly to be mayor. Dina gave up everything for a shot at tenure. Allie hoped to teach. Wesley wanted to be free of her father's manipulations. And I wanted to feel like my work mattered. Maybe our desperation to play one more time was bound up as much with our awareness of time passing too quickly as it was with the knowledge that the brass rings we'd been chasing all these years were slipping out of our reach.

Allie wiped her eyes on her sleeve. Sitting with her reminded me of the day she came back to school after winter break freshman year with her jaw wired shut. I never quite understood why this cruelty should have been inflicted upon her, but she was miserable, and for a month she drank her meals through a straw and refused to leave our room except for class, where she sat in the back with her eyes cast downward. Mostly, she lay on the common room couch, working through *Anna Karenina* while the rest of us ferried smoothies from the dining hall, feeling utterly helpless.

"I heard you went to our house," she said finally, and while I figured we'd get around to this eventually, I didn't think it would be so soon.

"I was lucky to get out alive."

She laughed.

"I take it you guys moved?" I asked.

"South Orange."

I leaned back in my chair, trying to hide my amazement at how well she'd covered her tracks.

"It's funny. I never thought I'd live in a place where the neighbors chat over the backyard fence, but everyone's so normal." Allie smiled. Not at me. More at the surprise of finding herself here. "One neighbor brought over banana bread the day we moved in. That never happened in Short Hills."

I was reminded of the Japanese word Dina used to describe Allie: *majime*. An earnest, reliable person who got things done without drama.

"I camped out in front of your office for two days," I said. "I know how hard you work, but your hours are even longer than I thought. I don't know how you do it. The job, three kids, the commute."

I meant it as a compliment, but she grimaced. Clearly, I'd offended her.

"I mean you—"

"I know what you mean," she said, but she wasn't miffed. "I haven't been going to the office."

Allie sighed as if to say there was no point in hiding the truth anymore.

"They laid me off."

I was appalled.

"Twenty years," she said, but there was no anger in her voice—only a vague, regretful longing.

I knew it wasn't normal to carry around a secret this big, this important, but we weren't like other people.

"Brad doesn't know?" I asked.

She seemed impressed that I had caught on.

"I needed a second. Okay, a month."

"Yeah, of course," I said amiably. "You were busy with the move."

"No, not exactly," she said. "We moved before Thanksgiving. I don't know why I felt like I needed to hide this, but we've never owned our house. We've always rented. I'm weird about debt—got that from my dad. Anyway, when our landlord decided to sell the house, our agent found the place in South Orange. The schools are really good, and we're paying a lot less. I think deep down I knew a reorganization was coming at work. Practical to the bitter end."

"Don't say that," I snapped, and she laughed it off. "Hopefully you had some fun with your free time?"

"I got my nails done," she said with delight, holding up a perfect French manicure. "I haven't done that since, I don't know, Chloe was little? Lots of window-shopping. Wandering through the museums I never have time to see. The audio tour at MoMA is amazing, by the way. Mostly, I walked. Is that weird?"

Her expression was earnest.

"You know what I'm saying," Allie said. "I needed space. Without kids hanging on me, without a husband asking what we're doing for dinner the minute I walk through the door after a twelve-hour day. Have I completely lost it?" She sat back, both hands on her forehead. "The other day Brad and the kids drove down to Philly to see his parents. I made up an excuse about a partnership blowing up, and do you know what I did? I got on my regular train, and one stop later I got off, crossed the platform, and took the next train home. I spent the whole day bingeing *Sex and the City* and eating pad thai. It was bliss."

I wanted to tell her she deserved every second of that bliss.

"I needed things to stay the way they were a little longer—Brad, the girls, all of us together, this moment in time. Is that so terrible? Because I have no idea what happens next."

A fat tear rolled down her cheek. My heart ached; I wished I had an answer for her.

"I worked more hours last year and hit bigger customer acquisition targets than any of the guys on my team. I took more shit than I should have. I only cried once at work. I made it to every parent-teacher conference and sewed a Halloween costume for Carin that won best costume last year. I leaned all the fucking way in."

She was straining so hard her voice cracked. The idea that all of this could fit on her shoulders was so absurd to me that the tiniest laugh slipped out. I clapped a hand over my mouth; she narrowed her eyes at me like I was mental, then started laughing too. Soon we were bent over with tears in our eyes.

"God, you must think I'm pathetic," she said when we had settled down.

"The opposite, actually."

She cocked her head like she didn't believe me, then pressed on.

"The thing that really gets me? Brad and I are so responsible. We don't do fancy dinners or crazy vacations. We order one venti at Starbucks and ask for two cups." She laughed a staccato *ha!* then lowered her eyes. "I thought a Harvard degree was a guarantee against all this."

Her words gutted me.

When people heard where I'd gone to school, they were quick to make assumptions about my level of privilege or wealth. Four years in Cambridge had given us so many gifts—a road map for how to think, an understanding that people were complex but generally good-natured, and friends we treasured—but after everything that had happened with Claudine, after the hole that she opened up, we mistook our dedication to the Circus for loyalty to one another. I can see now that the Circus would never have filled the void within us. We simply needed to cast off our facades and embrace one another for who we were: imperfect women trying to do our best.

Allie had always been the steady one. Now her anguish steeped me in a mix of frustration and anger, sorrow and loss. She never pretended that juggling work and family was easy, but somehow I dismissed her minimizing as a thing badass women did to make the rest of us feel better about ourselves. She had secretly convinced me that you *could* do it all, if you were as well-adjusted and capable as Allie. A part of me had hoped she was immune to the way life thickened our calluses and salted our sores. Now I admired her more because she wasn't.

"Why didn't you tell me?" I asked.

"You think it's easy being the loser in the group?" Allie asked, incredulous. "Dina's the soon-to-be-tenured professor, and you're the artsy photographer married to the cool restaurant guy. Bee's the hotshot DA, and Wesley, well, she's Wesley. She's never had to worry about anything."

It shocked me that Allie saw herself this way. I'd thought I had claimed the loser title.

"And believe me," she said, holding out a hand, "I tried."

When I gave her a puzzled look, she lowered her voice.

"I asked you for help, remember? Maybe you were too busy. Or maybe you didn't think I was up to the job."

Allie first floated the idea of leaving Amex last spring. Come summer, when Coulter's buddy Tad had an opening for a head of marketing, Allie asked me to pass her résumé on. She must've asked two or three times, and every time I said I would do it. I didn't. I was too consumed with my own problems. I'd been rejected from the last gallery on my list, and Coulter and I had hit a rough patch; he was struggling to get a loan to keep the restaurant afloat.

How was I so inept at friendship? How had I missed learning something so fundamental? I'd made so many mistakes—shying away from difficult conversations, not showing up when I was needed, refusing to trust—all of which I'd rationalized, convinced that toughing it out on my own was a sign of strength.

I thought back to a question Claudine had posed to me as part of the either/or game she liked to play: Would I choose career success or real friendship? I hadn't needed to think that much. At the time, I'd considered myself fiercely independent and decently well-liked, so I'd chosen success. Now, given all that Allie and I had been through together and how essential she was to my understanding of myself, I could see how wrong my earlier answer had been.

"Allie, I'm so sorry."

She stood, gathering up her book.

"What if there's a silver lining here?" I blurted out, grabbing her coat off the back of my chair, holding it hostage. Wesley liked to say, when Allie was within earshot, that she wouldn't be nearly as messed up if she'd had a teacher like Allie when she was a kid. "What if, after all this, you finally get to teach?"

"My kids still need to eat."

"What about a private school?" I asked. "Isn't the pay better?"

I could think of a thousand reasons why Allie deserved this, but the fight had drained from her face.

"I've asked myself that a million times. If I really wanted to teach, why haven't I done it already? I guess I have this stupid idea stuck in my head about who I'm supposed to be. It comes up every time I hand out my business card. People are impressed by my title. They think I'm worth something. I shouldn't care what they think, but I guess I do."

I relinquished her coat. Once she had it on, Allie turned back to me, her shoulders hunching forward.

"We should've known," she said.

"What?" I asked.

"That this would end badly," she said, her eyes wide with fear. "What the hell have we done?"

19

I WASN'T prepared for the sight of Bee lying in bed, injured and alone. White gauze wound around her head and snaked over her right eye. One hand was bandaged to the size of an oven mitt. A thin knit blanket was pulled up around her shoulders, and she seemed to be sleeping, or at least her good eye was closed.

The woman in front of me bore little resemblance to the Bee I knew: larger than life, always in motion, filling the room. Bee's star had been rising since the day we stepped through the gates of Harvard Yard, and she was supposed to keep climbing. For the Bees of the world, there were no upper bounds, which made this Bee seem all the more vulnerable. Fragile. Human.

I stepped lightly inside and whispered Bee's name; she didn't move.

Bee's quarters had the same ascetic feel as the rooms my mother had moved in and out of toward the end of her life, but they were unexpectedly humble for someone of Bee's stature. A folding chair was squeezed between the bed and the left wall and a white hanging curtain divided us from an unseen patient with a dry, rattling cough.

I had run into Doye in the lobby on his way to the cafeteria, an anxious, dulled version of his usual sharp, composed self. He regarded me warily, then suddenly lashed out, "Didn't any of you think about the consequences?" I was stunned into silence. Before I could say anything, he was apologizing for his outburst, waving my contrition away. After texting the guard stationed outside Bee's room to let me through, he told me he was going to get something to eat and it would be better if I was gone when he returned.

Bee and I didn't see much of each other these days—a couple of times a year at most. I remembered vividly a weekend three or four years ago when we found ourselves at the same wedding in the Poconos. A small affair, no kids, with everyone packed into a cozy mountain resort. I didn't remember who suggested tennis—I didn't even know Bee played—but we knocked the ball around for an hour after breakfast. We were both surprised to find how evenly matched we were—once-decent players, now sorely out of practice and shape, but none of that stood in the way of our good time. Afterward, we shook hands across the net and for the rest of the weekend Bee wondered out loud why we'd never played before. We hadn't played since, but it stuck with me: the idea that you could discover something so unexpected about a person you thought you knew.

I whispered Bee's name again, and her right arm twitched under the blanket. Perched on the chair next to her bed, I searched the creases around her mouth and the fine lines radiating from the corner of her unscathed eye for answers. There was so much I wanted to say: how I admired her fearlessness, how she figured so often in my thoughts, pushing me at every turn to step outside myself, to do things that scared me. Most of all, I wanted to tell her how much I loved being her friend.

And yet I was keenly aware of the chasm between us, which I could see clearly now was the product of my own self-doubt. All the times I should've reached out, but worried too much about how I'd be perceived, or even convinced myself my contribution wouldn't matter. I could've bared more of myself, but shied away from letting people see all of me, fearful they wouldn't like what they found.

"I wish we had cut the bullshit earlier," I said, the words slipping out.

I laid a hand on Bee's arm, and the warmth emanating from under the blanket surprised me. It was an uncomfortable gesture, one I wouldn't have dared at any other time, but in this moment it felt necessary.

A nurse charged into the room. I jerked my hand away and leapt to my feet.

"Can I help you?" she asked sternly.

"I'm a friend of Bee's," I said stupidly, pointing at Bee as if her identity was in question, then I remembered that no one called her Bee except us. "Barbara, I mean. I came to see how she's doing. Doye said it would be all right."

The nurse grabbed a clipboard from a plastic holder next to the door and looked me over.

"Unless you're immediate family, visiting hours are from ten to five. They didn't tell you that in the lobby?"

She perused Bee's chart and muttered under her breath.

"I won't be long," I said. "I—how is she?"

I glanced over at Bee, reassured to see her chest rise and fall with a slow, smooth cadence.

"I'm not at liberty to discuss patients. Am I gonna have to call security?"

"No, no, definitely not. I really am a friend of Bee's—Barbara's. I'm worried. That's all."

She sized me up again.

"They patched her up pretty good, but you still gotta worry about a brain bleed. If that happens, the doctor's gonna have to go in again. The recovery will take time."

"Like a few weeks?"

She laughed like I'd said something cute, then rounded to the other side of the bed and peeked under the blanket.

"Honey, people around here have colds longer than that. This woman fell on her head and nearly got hit by a train. Probably a good thing she doesn't remember."

She put the clipboard down on the bed—on top of Bee's legs— and checked that the tubes running in and out were intact.

"Sorry, one last question. Were you here when they brought her in?"

"Yeah, I was here," she said, peering at the bedside monitor.

"How did she seem? Was she asking for anyone?"

"That's three questions," the nurse said.

"I heard she was asking for me," I said. "I need to know why."

The nurse side-eyed me warily.

"You're Sara," she said, and I nodded.

She docked the clipboard in its holder and regarded Bee with a sober expression.

"She was pretty out of it. Worked up like nobody's business. Spouting all kinds of crazy."

"What do you mean by *crazy*?"

The nurse raised her eyebrows like she wasn't sure she should repeat whatever was said.

"Tell me and I'll get out of your hair," I said, taking a step toward the door as proof of my good intentions.

"You drive a hard bargain," the nurse said with a wink. "Well, she was talking real fast. Mostly, the same thing over and over. I had to tell her to give it a rest so we could hear ourselves think."

"What was it?" I asked. "What was she saying?"

The nurse clicked her tongue against her cheek.

"She was swearing up and down that just before her life flashed before her, she saw a goddamned ghost."

20

AFTER leaving Bee's room in a hurry, I found myself at Fabby's studio in Brooklyn with no memory of the subway ride or the walk over. I was still reeling from what the nurse had revealed. Had Bee seen Claudine too? Was the sight of our dead roommate what caused her to stumble and fall onto the tracks? Was this why Bee was asking for me when they brought her in?

"Talk to me, Claudine," I muttered as I studied the photo I had taken of Claudine on the street, searching for any sign of Dina lurking beneath its blurry facade.

When I started as Fabby's assistant a year ago, she paid me a full week's wages to learn the editing software she used to sharpen her photos. She'd been shooting more in the field, where wind and light didn't always bend to her will, so I was well-versed in the slow, painstaking steps—selecting, layering, masking—needed to make neon words pop against a leafy rainforest or a parched desert landscape. Now I was working in reverse—stripping, shaving, dismantling—hoping the image would reveal its secrets.

A hazy morning light filtered through the three skylights dotting the studio's lofty ceiling, a reminder that the last day of the Circus had begun. I leaned in closer, unable to shake the feeling that this photo was somehow the key to getting through the final hours of our game unscathed.

When the studio doorbell rang, I jumped. I raced back to my desk after buzzing Coulter in, hitting a key that put my screen to sleep. The studio was a twenty-five-minute walk from the restaurant, and he dropped in to see me now and then when the restaurant was slow, but he hadn't come around in a few weeks.

"Bones," Coulter called out as he strode into the studio holding two cups of coffee. He turned to show me the brown paper bag tucked under his arm. "Thought you could use an early-morning pick-me-up."

His voice echoed through the cavernous space, which still resembled the auto shop it had once been: paint-splattered cement floors, silver ducts that were more decorative than functional snaking across the ceiling, and cloudy mullioned windows that sat high above the street. Two stainless steel tables occupied the middle of the studio—laid with proofs from Fabby's last show. The rest of the space was taken up with backdrops and portable lighting, which Fabby and her other assistants were using to plan out specific shots before they headed into the field.

Coulter set the cups down on the desk, where my name was scrawled in purple Sharpie—Fabby's way of warning other assistants to stay away, since I was the one slogging through her jammed inbox. She wouldn't stand for me cracking another laptop by working with it propped on my knees, where it could slide off and crash to the floor.

"You took off so suddenly last night," he said, running a hand through his hair. He seemed preoccupied, anxious even. More likely, I was projecting what I was feeling onto him. "Did you get any sleep?"

"Not much," I said absently.

"Any news?"

"No," I said.

He looked at me sideways; he could tell I was holding out on him.

"All right, then—I guess I'll head to work," he said, pulling himself off the wall and pretending to take the brown bag with him. I leapt off my stool, lunging for the bag, which I knew held a ham-and-cheese croissant from the best bakery in Brooklyn, but he sidestepped nimbly out of reach. Defeated, I raised my coffee to him in a show of gratitude, and he handed the bag to me with a grin. Pulling the warm pastry out, I popped a piece in my mouth. The rest disappeared in seconds.

I appreciated Coulter for taking a chunk out of his morning to do this favor for me, but I was eager to get back to work. He was leaning against the wall with his hands on his thighs, his head tilted slightly, watching me. Settling back onto my stool, I didn't have the energy to tell him about the infighting among my roommates or to explain that Bee had also seen my ghost, but he deserved an update on the looming investigation, especially since the cost would cripple us.

"I forwarded you a list of lawyers that Bee sent over on Tuesday," I said. "She thinks defending a case like this could cost anywhere from ten to fifty thousand dollars."

His mouth hung open for a second, but he recovered quickly.

"We can take out a second mortgage," I started to say. Usually, I'd ramble on, batting around solutions or at least steps we could take to figure a way out, but the gravity of our situation was sinking in. I turned to my darkened screen, frustrated by my inability to keep my history in the past.

He pulled himself off the wall and crouched down beside me.

"Sara, what are you not telling me?" he asked.

"I saw Claudine," I said. "I mean, I've *been* seeing her. The first time was the night of Fabby's opening. I thought I was imagining it, but she was real."

I expected him to write this off as a sign I was too stressed, too sleep-deprived, or too guilt-ridden. Instead, he asked, "What do you mean 'the first time'?"

"I thought I saw her again two days ago, but it felt completely different. The first time, she was watching me. This time, it was like she wanted something from me."

"Sara, whatever you saw can't be real—"

"I know, I know, but after everything that's happened—"

"What else besides Bee?" he asked.

It was time to break our silence. We could no longer afford to have the Circus hanging over us like a dark cloud.

"I didn't want you to worry. Bee found a note at her seat during our lunch from someone threatening to expose her if she didn't stop playing. That same night, Wesley got an email saying they'd send her dad a compromising photo if she didn't drop out."

He started to interrupt; I cut him off.

"I know how crazy this sounds, but I swear there's a connection between Claudine and Bee's accident—I can't figure out what it is, and it's driving me crazy."

Coulter started to pace in a tight circle.

"Did you talk to Bee last night?" he asked. "Did she tell you anything?"

I straightened my laptop so that its long edge was aligned with the base of the monitor.

"The nurse said she doesn't remember the fall."

"What about before that?" he asked, his voice tight. "Did she see anyone?"

I started in on the mouse pad, lining it up with my laptop. Coulter grabbed my wrist.

"Sara, this is important," he said.

I nodded, and he let go. I trapped my hands underneath my thighs.

"Why am I seeing Claudine?" I asked, but he wasn't listening.

"You said Bee and Wesley both got these anonymous letters. What about Allie and Dina? Did anyone threaten them?"

I shook my head.

"But someone's been targeting you, too, haven't they?" he asked.

I wasn't following.

"Think about it. If the goal was to drive Bee and Wesley out of the Circus, then isn't seeing Claudine the same thing? Someone's using her to get you to stop playing too."

He had a point; I hadn't thought of it this way.

"Look," he said, "Dina's always been jealous of your roommates.

Their money, their success. I've let this go on long enough, but she needs to be stopped before someone else—probably you—gets hurt."

I noticed he didn't say that Dina was envious of my success, and I was reminded of how insecure I'd felt when I was younger. I arrived at school to find that one of the kids in our freshman entryway had discovered a gene in high school and another had won gold at IMO, which Allie explained was the geek Olympics—like the real Olympics but for math. At times, I felt hopelessly out of my league, left to wonder if my college acceptance had been a mistake. It was only when I got to know Claudine that I realized my fears weren't unique. She was already a proficient artist, but she swore she felt as much a pretender as I did. Claudine assured me it was a phase, a temporary crisis of faith we would overcome together, and suddenly everything seemed a little brighter.

I knew the same doubt lived on in Dina, but I didn't think her wounds would be this deep or this long-lasting. She carried a dark, closed-off place within her, and not even I knew its depth or dimensions. Maybe the money was too tempting; a win would be retribution against the colleagues who had voted and found her lacking. A fix for her wounded pride.

If Wesley was right that she had been denied tenure, Dina had nothing to lose.

"Sara, I know this is tough. You've been a good friend all these years, but she's obviously snapped. We need to get to her before she creates more problems. Do you know where she is?"

"No," I said forcefully. "But I can find her. I'll talk to her."

I had no idea how to find Dina or what I could say to her, but the prospect of Coulter charging after her seemed far worse.

"The only way to stop this craziness is to take her medallion. Eliminate her from the game. But be careful. We know what she's capable of."

He leaned over, his hair flopping across the top of his right eye, to wrap me in his arms. I grabbed onto his brown flannel shirt and breathed in his briny, citrusy smell, reassured that I wasn't alone. He nuzzled my neck, and I laughed, tipping us to one side. I put a hand out to steady myself, accidentally hitting my keyboard. The picture of Claudine sprang to life.

He pulled away and nodded at my screen.

"Is this what were you working on when I came in?"

"Yeah, but I can't get it any clearer," I said, leaning back on my stool to make room for him.

He leaned in with his hands on his thighs. Transfixed by the image of her.

"What is this?" he asked.

Wasn't it obvious? This was proof I wasn't crazy.

"I took this on the sidewalk near Fabby's gallery," I said.

"No, I mean who is this supposed to be?"

"It's her. It's Claudine."

He muttered something indecipherable.

"Coulter?"

He shook off whatever had come over him as soon as I said his name.

"Sorry," he stammered, bolting upright. "I just remembered. I forgot to put in an important order for the restaurant. Bad timing, I know."

He tossed out a hurried goodbye and slammed the studio door behind him. I wasn't sure what to make of his sudden departure; I figured he was overwhelmed by everything I'd unloaded on him. And I didn't blame him. I, too, felt like I was driving a car through a thick fog that obscured everything outside my narrow field of vision, unaware of the dangers waiting for me on the road ahead. I swept the crumbs from my lap and shut down my computer, hesitant to leave the safety of the studio, but I had too many questions for Dina. And if twenty years of playing against her was any guide, I knew that I needed to find Dina before she found me.

21

It was midafternoon on Friday when I finally found Dina's building, a hulking brick property a three-minute walk from Columbia's main quad. It did strike me as strange that I'd never been to her apartment here or in Cambridge; Dina always insisted we meet at a bar, a new ramen spot, or for drinks at the Harvard Club due to the generous faculty discount. I assumed this was because she didn't want me to see what she thought was a modest apartment, and after a while I stopped pressing, but now and then her wariness had made me wonder if our bond was more tenuous than I'd thought.

Finding Dina's apartment was a lucky break, especially since the Circus was ending in a matter of hours. Only after striking out at her known neighborhood haunts—a classical record shop, a dusty used bookstore, a hip dumpling place—did I remember a throwaway comment from a few months ago: Dina complaining about the guys in the barbershop downstairs smoking weed all day long, the fumes making it impossible for her to work. I would've forgotten it entirely if Dina hadn't been so stubborn in her refusal to see the humor in her getting high against her will. A search on my phone of the neighborhood around Columbia revealed a handful of barbershops, and only one had been getting two-star reviews online due to how the place reeked, which I assumed had been posted by a disgruntled neighbor.

If Wesley's building was a sleek downtown socialite, Dina's old brick behemoth was a fallen grande dame who had to hustle for a living. The stone cornices had chipped away, the grimy storefronts didn't line up with the apartment windows above, and the letters on the barbershop sign hung askew. The building took up half the block, which worked in my favor; it was big enough that a tenant barreled in or out every few minutes. Before long, I was tailing a twentysomething buried in her phone through the glass doors.

I climbed the carpeted stairs to the second floor and headed down a dingy hallway, the walls muddy brown and badly patched. I was trying to gauge which apartments sat above the barbershop when a thick orchestral dirge kicked on. A door farther down the hall cracked open, the brass drowning everything out. A bearded guy in a burgundy velour robe dropped a tied-up plastic bag in the hallway, startling at the sight of me.

He disappeared inside, and a few seconds later, the music cut out. I was craning around for the nearest exit in case I needed a quick escape when he poked his head back into the hallway.

"You the new tenant?"

Up close I could see he was younger than I had thought—midtwenties perhaps. His beard was more mountain man than hipster—shaggy, thin, a little unkempt. He had the pallor of a man who hadn't been outside in weeks.

"I'm looking for a friend. Dina. Dina Aoki."

"Sorry—don't know her," he said quickly and began to retreat.

"You like Mahler?" I called out. "That's what you were playing just now, wasn't it?"

The guy bounded out of his apartment, barefoot and unabashed in his velour robe.

"You a fellow disciple?"

I moved in closer.

"Not like Dina. She knows everything about Mahler."

The guy harrumphed.

"Anyone who thinks the Cooke version of the Tenth worthy of the canon is seriously misinformed."

"So you do know Dina."

He shifted around, annoyed he'd been duped so easily.

"We're old friends," I told him. "Something's come up, and I need to find her. It's kind of urgent."

"I don't know anything."

"Okay, well, do you know where her place is?"

He pointed at the apartment two doors down.

"Not for long, though. She's moving out," he said in a thin voice that hinted at hurt feelings. I assumed this meant Dina was upgrading, banking on a win.

"Any idea where she's headed?" I asked, even though we both knew it was a question a good friend wouldn't have to ask a stranger.

"Sorry, ma'am, simulcast's about to start," he said, pointing over his shoulder. "Mahler's Eighth."

He ducked inside, marooning me in the hallway, so I headed over to Dina's. I knocked lightly, suddenly hoping she wasn't home. When there was no answer, I tried the handle. Locked, of course. My immediate thought was that Dina could pick it in a second with the kit she had bought off the internet—and then the terrible irony of wanting her help to break into her own apartment made me feel awful about the conversation we needed to have.

Friendship was easier when we were young. The rules were clear: you didn't bad-mouth a friend when her back was turned, and you made sure no one got left behind. In return, you felt like you belonged, or at least you knew someone was watching out for you. Since then, the waters had muddied. The rules weren't clear—and hadn't been for a long time. Friendship was a fluid, shifting thing, and everyone had their own understanding of what was required. Allie hewed closest to the old bargain with a steadfast belief in honesty and loyalty; there wasn't much room for misinterpretation, and her ire was generally deserved. Wesley was indiscriminately generous, but unpredictable. She disappeared for weeks at a time, not bothering to return calls or texts, and when she did reach out, she was unapologetic. Yet in her company, you felt like you mattered. She had that kind of power.

Dina was another story. Loyal and smart, but sensitive to the smallest slight. Prone to dark moods. Always withholding. In certain ways, Dina and I were two halves of a self. Not just in our shared obsession with homemade mint chip ice cream, untranslatable words, and Miyazaki movies, but in the way we viewed the world, craving things we'd never had. We loathed feeling uncomfortable, balling up and burying our emotions so that explosions were rare, but enormous and inevitable when our feelings escaped to the surface. We shied away from people who sucked the air out of the room, from activities that required being onstage, and from anything that rooted too deeply in the muddied waters of our pasts. This is what had hewed us together—an unspoken assurance that the other would not probe. Now I wondered if that courtesy had been a disservice to us both. I was clearly no expert at friendship, but I knew it wasn't a circumspect thing, with predetermined boundaries to keep discomfort at bay. Could real friendship exist between two people who withheld so much of themselves?

I turned to find Dina standing in the hallway, her backpack hanging from one shoulder. She was still in the clothes she'd worn at the hospital—dark jeans and a blue peacoat. She looked as haggard as I felt.

"Can we talk?" I asked.

Her studio was barely larger than a suburban walk-in closet, but what stunned me was its asceticism. A sink, a two-burner stove, and a minifridge lined the left wall. A puffy blue sleeping bag and a twin mattress lay on the floor to my right. The rest of the room was taken up by a cheap folding table and chair. Shoulder-high stacks of books framed the window overlooking the street. The room smelled artificially sweet, which I guessed was a combination of the pot from downstairs and the air freshener plugged in next to the stove. Dina was the practical type, but there was nothing about this place—bare walls, table, and counters—that felt like a home. I was crushed; this was how Dina lived, and I'd had no idea.

She busied herself with filling a kettle, setting it on the stove, and standing guard over it with her back to me.

"Dina—"

She reached into the fridge for a carton of milk, opening the door just enough to squeeze her arm through. I happened to be standing next to the card table at exactly the right angle to win a glimpse inside. Every inch of the refrigerator was jammed with jars of baby food. Dina caught me staring and slammed it shut.

I considered the heartache she must have felt: the unpublished book, the anonymous letter calling her a cheat, the knowledge that a colleague, maybe even someone she considered a friend, had tried to sabotage her. If the pressure to outshine brilliant minds and produce novel work had driven a grown woman to eat baby food, what damage would a firm rejection from the tenure committee do? I pictured the destruction that must've ensued when Dina received the news: shattered mugs, smashed pictures, ripped books. Later, a spare apartment cleaned up and left even more bare.

The kettle began to whistle sweetly, then climbed to an urgent shrill.

"Go ahead," she said as she silenced the kettle. "Ask me whatever you want."

Dina and I had lived together for two years, decades ago. Since then, we'd seen each other once a month at best. We made an effort to stay in touch, but phone calls felt stilted and emails fell flat. We were better in person, eye to eye, where I could glean more from the way Dina danced around certain topics, swinging her glasses around, than anything she actually said, but this was new territory for us both.

"Is it you?" I asked.

She filled a mug with hot water and sank a tea bag into it. I was braced for anger or a smart, biting comeback. I wasn't expecting her to turn and slump against the cabinet, her shoulders folded forward with disappointment.

"It was a week before the spring holiday," Dina said, cradling the mug with both hands. "A Tuesday, which I only remember because it was the one morning I didn't have early classes and everyone else was gone. I usually got a lot of work done then."

She pulled the tea bag out and dribbled in a little milk. I wasn't sure where this was going, if we were talking about a few years or a few decades ago.

"No one told me they were coming," she said ruefully. "So I spent the whole free block making small talk while we sorted through Claudine's stuff."

At the mention of Claudine, I realized I'd missed an important part of the story.

"Wait—who are we talking about?"

"Claudine's father," she said as if this was obvious. Claudine's parents never came to Winthrop after her accident, which we all thought was strange, especially after Bee spotted them outside the university president's office a few days after Claudine's death. We held our breath after that, thinking they'd turn up at our door any second, but the days passed and we never saw them.

"Claudine's father came to Winthrop?"

"Yes," she said. "All of you were out, so I had to sit with them. He went on about the storms they'd been having in Charleston. Asked what growing up in New York City had been like. I remember thinking he was a decent man. Good listener too."

I was perched on the folding table, swinging one foot nervously. None of this lined up with what I'd heard from Claudine about her father.

"He'd brought a duffel bag, but it was way too small. Claudine had a suitcase in the closet, so we filled that with the stuff he thought her mother would want. Jewelry, a frilly dress she would never have been caught dead wearing. Her Clemson sweatshirt. He didn't take any of the stuff she actually wore, like the black jeans with the hole in the knee—"

"Or the Thrasher sweatshirt," I said.

"And definitely not the white shirt she always knotted at the waist," Dina added with a fleeting smile.

"Her going-out shirt," I said, remembering a night sophomore year when Claudine came out of the bathroom wearing that shirt. She took one look at me—ratty wool sweater, baggy jeans, combat boots—and insisted on dressing me up in a cropped tee and corduroy micro-mini. I fidgeted with the T-shirt the whole night, but I was secretly grateful.

"He didn't know her," Dina said, and we each mulled this over, reassuring ourselves that we did. We knew her.

"Do you remember her closet?" Dina asked abruptly, and I thought it was a strange thing to ask.

"The giant pile of shoes," I said.

We were always waiting for Claudine on nights we went out. She had a habit of throwing her shoes onto the enormous heap at the back of her closet—she must've had thirty pairs back there, nearly all of them black, and it would take her forever to find a matching set.

"What you said at the gallery about seeing Claudine—I couldn't stop thinking about it. I knew there had to be a logical explanation. It came to me the other day. I don't know why I didn't think of it before, but that day—when her father came—we got hung up on the shoes because she wanted to try on every last pair."

"Who?"

"I had forgotten that Claudine's father came with a little girl. She couldn't have been more than three or four. She was so quiet, following him around like a duckling, barely saying a word except when she found the shoes. Jumped on top like it was a pile of leaves. Neither of us were paying her much attention; we were both so broken up by what happened."

It took me a second to piece together what she was saying.

"Claudine had a younger sister?"

"Still has, probably."

"Are you sure? She never mentioned a sister. I think she would've told me something like that."

"They were half sisters. And the man I thought was her father was actually her stepfather. I asked him how Claudine got that burn on the back of her hand and he didn't know. He married Claudine's mom right before Claudine left for school. Claudine had two feet out the door by the time he came on the scene, he told me."

"Why didn't you say anything before?" I asked.

"I tried to—in the hospital," she said, and I knew what had happened. We had been arguing in the waiting room and Wesley had cut us off.

I tried to remember what else I knew about Claudine's family. Apart from what she had told me about her mother and the shouting matches she had now and then with her mother on the phone, Claudine rarely talked about them, and she was good at deflecting anytime we veered close to the subject. I would've sworn she was an only child because she seemed so alone in the world. She always turned up to school alone, lugging two huge suitcases all the way from the airport and up the stairs to our rooms by herself. We knew it wasn't the cost of plane tickets and hotels that kept her parents away because her mother was constantly sending Claudine floaty floral dresses and Italian leather headbands. We figured instead that her mother couldn't be bothered to miss a meeting at the garden club or historical society, which was heartbreaking.

"Let's say her sister was three or four at the time," Dina was saying. "Seventeen or eighteen years younger than we were when Claudine died. That would put her in her mid-twenties now."

Dina didn't need to say what we were both thinking: that her sister would be only a year or two older than Claudine had been when she died.

Was it possible her sister was here in New York? Had she been following me? Was she making a play for the money, or was she determined to avenge her sister's death?

"It makes sense," I said to Dina. "That's who Bee saw in the subway."

Dina's eyebrows shot up, and I realized I'd skipped a few steps. I told her about the cops and how Bee must've thought she was seeing Claudine too. I didn't need to explain that Claudine's sister must've taken Bee's medallion.

Dina pulled out her laptop and got to work at the table.

"Search Claudine's name, Charleston, Harvard. Look for an obituary, a graduation or wedding announcement—any article that mentions her family. We need a name." Dina's eyes were glued to her screen. "I'll work on her parents. Her mom remarried but didn't change her last name—"

"So her half sister may not be an Abernathy," I said, completing Dina's thought.

Hopping up, I pulled out my phone and began to search, scrolling through pages of results until I stumbled onto a screenshot of an old obituary for Claudine from a Charleston paper. It was a paragraph long and didn't say much, except announce her death and that a memorial service would be held in the future. And then one final sentence: Claudine was survived by her parents and her sister. Unnamed, but right there in black print. Why hadn't I seen this before?

I paced the room, searching various combinations of *Claudine Abernathy, sister, sibling, Charleston*—but the internet was strangely silent.

"Claudine was from Charleston," Dina said without looking up. "Where was their house exactly?"

"I don't remember, but I know the house had history. I think it was handed down on her mother's side. It had a big yard, which was unusual because it was right in town."

This seemed to confirm whatever Dina was seeing.

"Her parents sold that house in October," Dina said. "They moved to an assisted-living facility in Virginia Beach."

Impressed with her sleuthing, I scrolled more determinedly through pages of Charleston Abernathys, racing down offshoots and rabbit holes with no luck. I was searching for Claudine's grandparents when I remembered her grandfather passed away soon after we graduated. He was survived by his daughter, Judith Abernathy; her husband; and his granddaughter, Clementine Penelope Waring.

"Clementine," I said, feeling triumphant. "Her name is Clementine."

"Good. See if you can find a picture," Dina said, tapping frantically on her keyboard, but I didn't need to look far. I pulled up the photo I had been working on earlier and showed it to Dina. She pinched two fingers together to enlarge it, studying it from different angles.

"Wow. The blue eyes and the nose are the same. Definitely not Claudine, though."

She handed the phone back.

"How can you tell?"

"No freckles," she said.

I couldn't believe I'd missed what was so obvious. When I peered closer, I could see she was right.

"So why show up here?" I asked. "Why now?"

Dina sat back in her chair and mulled this over.

"When did Claudine's mother fund that smear campaign against Bee?"

"The election was two years ago last November," I said.

"So two years ago her mother was still holding on to the theory that we killed her daughter and covered it up."

It was an accusation I'd heard many times, but it still stung.

"Clementine was probably raised to think Claudine was murdered," Dina said. "Now her parents are getting older, moving to an assisted-living facility."

"So Clementine is carrying the torch."

"It's possible," Dina said. "Maybe she's been goading the Middlesex County DA to reopen her sister's case, but he's not moving fast enough. Or the legal route was too much of a long shot, so she has to take matters into her own hands."

It was a staggering theory, and it almost made sense.

"One thing doesn't add up," I said. "She's been following me around for the last few weeks, so why go after Bee? Why not me?"

"Bee got the university to drop the case," Dina said matter-of-factly. "So in a sense, she's as responsible as, or even more responsible than, you are."

"Yeah, okay."

"Only one way to know for sure," Dina said, turning her computer so I could see the screen.

It was a byline. Clementine Waring, in *The Atlanta Journal-Constitution*. Dina put the call through from her computer.

"Accounting," Dina whispered as it rang. "Easiest way in."

When a woman answered, Dina said in a bouncy voice, "Hi, this is Clementine Waring. I'm not sure if I have the right department, but I changed my address to New York while I'm working here on assignment, and I haven't received my last paycheck. Can I see if you have the right address for me?"

I heard the *click-clack* of a keyboard as the woman pulled up Clementine's account. Dina pointed at a drawer next to the stove, and I pulled out a notepad and pencil. The woman recited an address that Dina jotted down. "Hmm. That's so strange. That is the right address. Maybe it's held up in the mail? I'll give a call back if it doesn't show up in a few days. Thanks for your help."

Dina beamed as she stood up and tugged on her peacoat, ready to storm Clementine's apartment. She stopped short when she noticed I hadn't moved.

"Wesley's in surgery tonight until eight," I said. "No one will look at you twice if you're in scrubs and a mask."

"No, we should go together," Dina said, ripping the top sheet off her notepad and holding up Clementine's address. "You don't know what you're walking into."

"There's no time," I said, shaking my head. We both knew the Circus was ending in four hours. "We have to split up. You have a shot at winning this."

"Sara, she could be dangerous."

"Look, thanks to you I have Allie's medallion and my own stashed away at my place. I can get them to you in time. And if my hunch is right," I said, pointing at the address in Dina's hand, "I might be able to get Bee's for you too."

I watched her resolve soften as she realized how much I wanted her to have the money. She looked dubious, but I knew what the windfall could do for her. I couldn't remember feeling as sure about a decision as I felt about this one.

"You're assuming I can take Wesley."

"I've never known you to back down from a fight with her."

She put the address in my hand and pretended to busy herself with the kettle, but as I closed the apartment door behind me, I heard her whisper "thank you."

22

THE Circus had made us into good liars, so it didn't take long for me to steal my way into Clementine's building and up to her apartment. I pounded on her door, intent on making her answer for what she'd done to Wesley and Bee, not to mention the trouble she had stirred up for me with the DA. When she didn't answer after the third knock, I tried the knob, and the door swung open with a stuttering creak.

The place smelled faintly of rotting bananas. A narrow hallway fronted a tiny kitchen with Formica countertops and dark ceiling-hung cabinets. I listened for Clementine, but apart from the hammer of a radiator, the only other sound was the rush of water running through pipes in the walls.

Braced for whatever surprises I might encounter, I crept past the kitchen to a modest living room, decorated in late-nineties bachelor style—black leather sofa and hulking TV on a squat rolling stand—and dimly illuminated by a small window that was mostly blocked by the scaffolding outside. The bedroom lay to my left and was barely large enough to hold an unmade queen bed and an old wooden nightstand in the narrow gap. The closet to the right of the bed had been cleaned out, except for a few empty boxes on a high shelf. I nearly missed the suitcase under the foot of the bed, clamshelled open to reveal pink flannel pajamas, a Fair Isle sweater, and a pile of crumpled underwear. Clementine's things were here, but where was she?

I wasted no time rummaging through her suitcase, checking under the sofa cushions, and rifling through kitchen drawers in search of Bee's medallion. A stack of letters on the kitchen counter were all addressed to a guy named Joel, who had to be the apartment's absentee owner. Whether he was a friend or a landlord to Clementine I didn't know, but the earliest postmark was from late October, which suggested Clementine had arrived here two months ago.

I'd searched the whole apartment with no sign of the medallion when I realized I hadn't seen a bathroom. I found a door on the other side of the living room that had been painted to blend in with the wall. Yanking the door open, I caught a flicker of movement in the darkness and jumped back. Realizing it was only my own reflection in the bathroom mirror, I flipped on the lights, then screamed at the sight of a body on the floor.

It was Clementine.

She was slumped next to the toilet, leaning against the bathtub at an odd angle, as if her head was so heavy her torso couldn't bear its weight. Her face was puffy, her eyes swollen, her hair matted. I reached for her hand—cool and limp—and pressed two fingers to her neck. Did I feel the faint flick of a pulse? I wanted to run, but despite everything Clementine had done, she was still Claudine's half sister.

"Come on, Clementine," I said, taking her by the shoulders. I expected her to push back, but her head lolled to one side. I tugged at her legs—she had the same petite frame as Claudine, but was an inch or two taller—then rushed to cradle her head. I managed to pull her away from the tub so that she lay on the floor at only a slight angle in the cramped bathroom. I wedged myself in and pinched her nose. What was the right way to do this? Three breaths, three compressions—my faint recollection from the lifesaving course I'd taken at a YMCA camp the summer I turned ten. I pumped her chest with pancaked hands, puffing, compressing, puffing, compressing. Locked into an urgent, mechanical rhythm, I willed her to show me a sign, to sputter like people do on TV right before they come back to life.

I kept on like this, thinking I had a shot at saving her, until I noticed a black pouch—slightly larger than a pencil case—lying at the base of the toilet. I bent down and reached for what I thought might be an EpiPen; Wesley had carried one around in a similar bag with a white cross on it when we were in school. If this was an allergic reaction, my half-baked CPR wasn't going to save Clementine.

I unzipped the case; it was empty. I felt around the floor and behind the toilet, then scanned the counter, but there was no sign of an injector.

I fumbled for my phone. The reception in the bathroom was weak, so I retreated to the living room. 911 promised help. The pounding in my head was thick and heavy, and when I spun around too quickly, the strangest thing happened. I caught a familiar scent: the briny Mediterranean, the scorching sun, the delicate, sweet scent of lavender. Strange to find it lingering here.

I got back to work pressing on Clementine's chest, aware that my fingerprints were sprinkled throughout the apartment. It wasn't hard to imagine what the cops would think when they stitched together my involvement in the deaths of two sisters, but the harrowing knowledge that I'd failed Claudine again kept me going until the paramedics pulled me off and banished me to the bedroom, admonishing me to stay out of the way.

Perched on the edge of Clementine's bed with my hands over my mouth, I thought I might be sick. When the paramedics rushed through the living room with a stretcher, my gaze snagged on a grainy picture poking out of Clementine's suitcase. Allie, Bee, Wesley, Dina, Claudine, and me. We were dressed in shorts and T-shirts, arms linked in front of the tall black gates of Winthrop House, the sun-dappled river glittering in the background. How young we looked. And how happy.

Claudine's head was tilted sideways; I remembered that innocent expression so well. We were still close then, but on the verge of drifting apart. I should've fought harder for Claudine, but I was too steeped in a ridiculous fear of being replaced by Wesley. At the very least, I should've spoken up that spring or the following fall, when the biggest problem we had was Claudine's chain-smoking. Allie was always lecturing her about sitting on the windowsill—it wasn't safe; the pitch of the tiles under our dormer windows was precarious, the drop five stories down. Claudine placated Allie by rigging a rope from the leg of her bed, running it up and over the windowsill, knotted at regular intervals like the climbing ropes hanging from the rafters in a high school gym.

I'm embarrassed to say that I did my part in driving Claudine away. A few days before the Christmas break of our senior year, I announced to Bee and Allie at lunch that I wasn't going to play the Winthrop House game. It was an act of protest, a childish plea for attention. Bee looked aghast. Allie lectured me on how much the game meant to Claudine, on how important it was that we did this together, but I insisted the timing was inconvenient. I was staring down massive student loans, and every free minute was consumed by the work-study job I'd picked up in the alumni office and my desperate scrabbling for interviews so I wouldn't drown after graduation.

I wasn't lying, not exactly, but Bee and Allie saw through me. Word got back to Claudine that night. When we ran into each other in the bathroom the next day, she asked me what my problem was. I didn't have a good answer—how could I tell her I missed her, that I wanted things to go back to the way they were before, without sounding pathetic? She accused me of being closed-off, of not caring about anyone but myself. I was stunned. I ran back to my room and crumpled over my desk, sobbing as her words turned over in my head. The exchange devastated me because I felt the opposite of what she had described. Claudine played in my thoughts with such frequency, the world papered with books and songs I knew she would like, movies I'd hoped to see with her. Stories that I knew would make her laugh.

That Christmas break was a blur. I had taken up an offer from my mother's cousin to stay at her house in Akron, but it was an awkward setup, with me on the pullout in the den and her kids and their families knowing they needed to show kindness even if they didn't understand why. I couldn't sleep, thinking only of the horrible mess

I'd made of my relationship with Claudine and Wesley too. When we came back to school, I quietly reversed my decision and signed up to play. When the game finally started, I tore through my first two kills with ease, nabbing a junior coming out of class in Sever Hall and a sophomore in a corner of the Winthrop dining hall. When I turned over the white card that revealed the name of my third target, I laughed out loud. The universe had a twisted sense of humor: my third target was Claudine.

That night, I walked gingerly down to her room, gun in hand, hoping to corner her. As I slipped inside, I was met with a blast of frigid air, and I remember wrapping my arms around my chest to stay warm. Claudine was straddling the windowsill, tucked into her puffy green parka. The sight of her there, one leg out the window, made me nervous, but she didn't seem the least bit concerned. She puffed on her cigarette, not looking at me, but she knew why I had come.

"Before you kill me," she said sweetly, "you have to answer three questions."

It was just like her, turning everything into a game.

"New York or Santa Fe?"

I knew what she was asking: where she should go after graduation. I was fixed on New York, praying for an offer from one of the banks, but she'd been looking for work in both places. I couldn't say whether my trajectory figured into her thinking, and even if I hoped it would, the distance that had grown between us likely meant she was only considering New York because of its abundance of art galleries.

The question surprised me, though. Santa Fe was her dream. She was doing her senior honors project on Georgia O'Keeffe and fantasized about following in Georgia's footsteps, seeking inspiration in wide open spaces and comfort in the artistic community that had sprung up since the artist's death. The cost of living would be more manageable out west. And she could easily find a job to tide her over until she sold a few paintings. I worried the hustle of New York would sap her spirits, but I could easily see her being happy in a place like Santa Fe.

"Santa Fe," I said, and she seemed displeased by my answer, but moved on to the second question.

"Money or passion?"

This was the most Claudine question I could imagine, and it was a litmus test to check that I hadn't strayed too far from the person she knew. The right answer was obvious.

"Passion."

A drag on her cigarette seemed to signal approval, or perhaps she was fueling up for the next question.

"Dina or me?" she asked.

She wanted to put me in a corner, make me cast Dina aside. I was still angry that she'd chosen Wesley over me, so what right did she have to make me choose? What I couldn't see then was that this was an overture. An opening to talk about the wounds we'd both been nursing.

But we never got to any of that.

Claudine held her cigarette up, careful not to drop it, and swung her legs up so that she was curled in the window, knees to her chest, bare feet planted on the sill. A picture in its neat little frame, puffing with such sophistication.

"Can you come down from there?" I asked, noticing she hadn't tied the rope around her; it was draped over the sill for show, a prop in case Allie came barging in.

She took another drag.

"Claudine, I'm serious. I'm not answering until you get down."

She ashed out the window, but she must've leaned too far, because she started to fall. In a split second, as quickly as a cat, she managed to twist herself around, grabbing onto the rope. Her torso lay across the sill, her legs dangling outside. I rushed over, clutching her arm, wondering how I could tie the rope around her without letting go. She was kicking, trying to push herself up, but the slate tiles below her window were slick with ice, and the more she struggled for some kind of purchase, the more tenuous my hold became. "Stop,

stop, Claudine," I remember saying frantically. Whatever we had—whatever grip I had on her—wasn't enough.

"Help," I screamed over my shoulder, hoping Wesley wasn't blasting her eighties dance music, that Dina wasn't studying with her headphones on. "Help us!"

I wedged my feet into the corner below the window, leaning back as far as I could, an awkward angle, desperately holding on.

"Claudine," I cried, and she looked at me with a terrified expression—a look that haunts me to this day. My grip was slipping across the slick finish of her green parka, sliding down toward her wrist.

I screamed for help again, heard footsteps in the hall.

"It's okay," she said to me.

"No," I said, redoubling my efforts to pull her back in.

But it was no use. Claudine's hand fell away, and she was gone.

"Ma'am?" The cop's voice jolted me back to Clementine's apartment, to the unmade bed and the suitcase on the floor.

"You mind coming downstairs with me? We need a preliminary statement."

"Is she going to be okay?" I asked.

"I can't say, ma'am," he said, and I guessed this was his polite way of telling me Clementine wasn't going to make it.

"I'll be right there," I said, still holding the photo.

As I was nestling the picture back into the suitcase, my eyes landed on a green cloth-covered book tucked between its companions on the bedside table. I'd lived with that book, seeing it morning and night for two whole years. Running a hand over the fabric, I studied the initials carved into its cover. *Property of C.A.*

I bowed my head in a show of respect, then slipped the journal inside my jacket.

23

FRIDAY, the seventh of January, is a date that will always be etched in a dark corner of my mind. From time to time, a fragment will come racing back—the photo of us tucked away in Clementine's suitcase, her body on the bathroom floor, the brusque efficiency of the paramedics—but one image haunts me like an indelible blot on my conscience: residents milling around on the sidewalk, curious and surprised by the sudden celebrity of their building, until a body is rolled out on a stretcher.

After coming up with enough right answers to put the cops off for the moment, I stood on the curb across the street from Clementine's building, not knowing what to do with myself. Without Bee's medallion, I couldn't see any point in rushing my own medallions over to the diner. I felt awful that I had let Dina down. And even though I wanted her to have the money, maybe I had been holding on to a hope of my own; I felt like I, too, had suffered a terrible loss.

When the blare of a police horn rattled me, I realized that I was still clutching Claudine's journal. Her inky initials stared back at me from the green cover, and I flipped to the first page. This was another line I wouldn't have crossed before, but I needed to know if our ending could've been different.

The freshman year entries were bubbly and hopeful. I could hear how thrilled she was to put Charleston in her rearview mirror. When I came upon a page dated the third of March—the spring of our freshman year, the day Bee, Allie, and I first met Claudine—I was struck by how the same event can unfold so differently in other people's minds. We loved Claudine from the moment we met her over lunch in Annenberg, the freshman dining hall, but she seemed unsure, even a little standoffish, so I was surprised to read how enamored she was of us from that very first day. How intimidated she was by our swagger and our private jokes, both of which she mistook for preternatural confidence. We were such puddles of insecurity, but practiced in the art of dissembling. And when she moved in with us sophomore year, she instantly became one of us, hamming it up in our tapestry-laden common room, gossiping over long Sunday brunches in the dining hall, and dragging one another out of tight corners in final clubs around Harvard Square.

So many details I had forgotten: Bee, Wesley, Claudine, and I, united in our annoyance at Allie for having won the only single room in a coin toss. Parades through Harvard Square in fancy dresses, battles with overachievers to become the leaders of our various teams and clubs, the respect Claudine garnered from upperclassmen after placing fourth in the Winthrop House game on her first try. It occurred to me with a pang of melancholy that her shining account of those early days was like the opening to Shirley Jackson's famous story: the bright descriptions of richly green grass and the fresh warmth of a full-summer day false flags to disguise the horrors that would unfold later. The joy that I heard in Claudine's voice was made all the more gut-wrenching because of the darkness that I knew would follow.

I devoured her account of junior year, seeing so clearly what I couldn't back then: my friendship with Claudine was fracturing, and neither of us had any idea how to put it back together. Reading her journal made me realize that Claudine's life had become more complicated than the glassy perfection I saw from an increasing distance. She wrote about feeling boxed in by Wesley, who was already drinking herself into oblivion. To me, Claudine appeared to be on top of the world, so I was stunned when I came upon an entry three days before her death. She admitted to liking her newfound popularity, but missed the simple, easy relationship we'd had, the way I listened when she shared her secrets and feelings, and the either/or game we played. She hated the jealousy she felt over my relationship with Dina and regretted the petty ways in which she'd exclude Dina when I wasn't around. I was surprised to read her lamentation that I had moved on without her. She'd trade all the parties and the attention, she wrote, to go back to the way things were before. The last entry held a single resolution: Claudine was determined to tell me that she still needed me.

I closed the journal.

If I had been a bigger person, if I had believed a little more in myself, I might've found the courage to tell her how I felt. How important she was to me, how much I missed her. It was extravagant to think that this might've saved her, but deep down I knew it would've changed our trajectories, perhaps shifting hers just enough to bring her down off that narrow ledge. It occurred to me that this was why I had kept the Circus going all these years—a deep-seated desire to undo our terrible history, to keep her close to me in a way that I wasn't able to when I had the chance, to atone for my part in her death.

On the walk home, the thing that grabbed me most about Claudine's account was that she didn't accuse or lay blame. She portrayed us as kids fighting to be seen and heard, the heroes of our own myopic stories. We may have done our share of stupid things, but her words seemed to suggest that we would never have done anything to hurt one another.

I wondered what ran through Clementine's head as she read these pages. Was she surprised by what her sister had felt for us? Did these entries allow her to see us in a more sympathetic light?

A strange thought rippled along the edges of my mind. I tried to remember what the nurse said in Bee's room.

Before her life flashed before her, she saw a goddamned ghost.

Allie said Bee was on the tracks before they heard the train approaching. I was trying to imagine how terrified Bee must've been, listening to the train closing in, when it hit me. The ghost she saw appeared when Bee was already on the tracks, not when she was on the platform.

My understanding of Bee's accident had been completely backward.

I pulled out my phone; I wanted to tell someone, but who? It was then that I noticed a missed text from Allie: At the hospital. Cops say mugging.

The prospect that this was a mugging, a wrong-place-wrong-time kind of luck, should've been a relief.

Suspects? I wrote back.

I was wondering if Allie had told them about Bee's missing necklace when her response popped up.

B fought back and fell.

Three dots told me Allie was typing. They pulsed, then disappeared. A picture appeared on my screen.

The image was a grainy, low-res shot from a bird's-eye view of the platform. The crowd was thin for a weekday rush hour, making Bee easy to spot due to her height and straight black hair. She was turned toward the camera and away from the tracks, wearing the black overcoat Dina had laid out in the waiting room. Her hands were pushing against a hooded figure, who was lunging, reaching for Bee's throat, a few feet from the edge of the platform.

I zoomed in. It didn't matter that I couldn't see the mugger's face—I recognized that stance. The realization felt surreal, but the proof was right there on my phone, and I had been looking in the wrong direction the whole time.

24

THE sweet smell of freshly baked bread enveloped me as I let myself into the apartment. For a second, I was lulled into thinking it was Tuesday, the night Coulter always had off. We'd sip cocktails while he simmered osso buco and I stirred risotto, both of us cracking up over the antics of his most challenging customers. But the image of Clementine's limp body came rushing back, reminding me it was Friday night, the final stretch of the Circus, and the yeasty aroma made me gag.

The apartment had never been perfect for us, I thought as I hung my jacket in the entryway. We were five flights up, the bathroom was only accessible through our bedroom, and the place required never-ending repairs (the perpetually loose bathroom doorknob, and now the hole in the living room ceiling). It was the galley kitchen that had sold us, though, with enough counter space to lay out a real mise en place. As I came around the corner, this is where I found Coulter, crushing shallots with a stone mortar and pestle at his neatly laid station. The mixing bowl at his left elbow held capers, mustard, and egg yolks; the plate on his right was piled high with discarded bread crusts.

"Steak tartare," I said, curious why Coulter wasn't at work. Fridays were the restaurant's busiest night of the week.

"That's not all," he said brightly.

An orange and a peeler sat on the opposite counter, the garnish for an old-fashioned. The cocktails, the tartare, his mood—cheerful, buoyant even—suggested we were celebrating.

"What?" he asked, flashing a roguish smile. "Do I need a reason to make my girl a decent meal?"

"Tartare and old-fashioneds—that's more than a decent meal."

He chopped parsley at breakneck speed, looking up from his cutting board. I always worried his cavalier attitude would cost him a finger and usually told him so, but tonight I sensed he wouldn't be deterred.

My phone rang, giving me a start. The number was blocked.

"Go ahead, grab it," he said. "The steak needs to chill for a few more minutes."

Grateful for the excuse, I darted out of the kitchen.

"Hello," I said absently as I headed to the living room. In the slanting light, I could see that the beam in the ceiling had rotted through. It was a wonder it had held for so long.

"Sara?"

My throat went dry.

"This is Clementine," she said in a voice that was lower than I had expected, but also raspy and frail.

She was alive. How was that possible? Her chances had seemed slim on the bathroom floor, and the paramedics had worked on her for what seemed like an eternity.

"I know what you did," she said with a labored cadence, and my face grew suddenly hot. Before I could defend myself, she blindsided me.

"Thank you for staying with me," she said.

I wondered how she knew, but she was a reporter; she wouldn't have been shy about pressing the cops for specifics.

"I wanted to help," I said and was met with a faint wheezing.

"You took a risk," she said when she could get the words out.

"You did too," I said and then rushed to add, "You were the one who pulled Bee up from the tracks, weren't you? In the Times Square station?"

After replaying what the nurse had said in Bee's room, I felt sure that Bee had already been on the tracks when she thought she saw a ghost. Clementine hadn't pushed Bee. She had saved Bee.

A long pause. Then Clementine said, "It was lucky timing."

I heard a man's voice in the background, jovial but firm, and Clementine began to speak more quickly.

"I didn't grow up with Claudine," she said, "but she cast a long shadow. I came here to understand for myself who she was. And the truth about what happened to her."

I had no idea what to say next. There was so much to be accounted for, so much to explain. My college roommates and I weren't the horrible people her mother imagined—we weren't even the people in Claudine's journal, though I saw a likeness there to our younger selves.

"You have to be careful," she said, and the wheezing grew louder. The nurse came on to tell me Clementine needed her rest. I pleaded with him to give us a few more minutes—I needed to know what she meant. The nurse apologized and hung up.

I had to be careful. What had Clementine seen when she was following me?

I checked the time—nearly eight. Dina would have figured out how to get Wesley's medallion and would be racing to the diner to meet me and collect her prize. I was running out of time to find Bee's medallion.

Checking the doorway, I prayed I had a few more seconds before Coulter looked in on me and rushed to grab the two medallions I had secreted away under the sofa cushions. I reached under the left side, but they weren't where I had put them. I felt around on the right side and lifted up both cushions.

My medallions were gone.

In the kitchen, a tray of toasted croutons sat on top of the stove. Coulter was dragging the blade of his santoku across a whetstone; the scraping shivered down my spine. I stationed myself near the doorway, out of reach.

"Who was that?" he asked as he pulled a wrapped parcel from the fridge.

"Oh, a political poll," I said, wondering if I had misremembered where I'd put the medallions. I played back the cops' visit the night before. Had I tucked them away in another hiding spot of mine?

"Block them," Coulter said as he unfurled the butcher paper to reveal two rounds of pink flesh resembling human hearts. Examining the meat like a surgeon, he studied the lines, pressed the flesh to test its firmness, and carved thin slices. The steel glided smoothly as he pulled, then he began to dice, his right hand moving with furious speed, his left guiding. My pulse ticked up with each scissoring cut.

"Grab me the bitters, will you?" he asked.

I headed to the living room cabinet where Coulter kept his bar, still stunned by my conversation with Claudine. As I was grabbing the bitters, the image Allie had sent me of the mugger echoed in my head.

Coulter came running when he heard the crash.

"Sara?"

I stood over the sticky mess, feeling as if I were outside myself. Auburn liquid seeped into the living room rug. He brought paper towels, the dustpan, a brush. I swept while he collected triangles of broken glass.

"Where were we?" he asked with a veneer of sunniness when we returned to the kitchen.

"Bitters," I said stiffly.

"Yes," he said as he slid the meat into the fridge. "The Scheitelmans must have some. Be right back."

The second I heard the front door slam, I reached for Coulter's phone on the counter, desperate for proof that I had misread the situation. I tapped in his password and headed to his photos. By now, the Scheitelmans would have eaten and settled into their corduroy armchairs in front of the television, so they'd be eager to send Coulter on his way. I had a few minutes at most.

I scrolled nervously past shots of the Brooklyn Bridge, snaps of dishes he was testing and cocktails he was trying out, candids of the family that one of his nieces must've taken at Sunday lunch. Then I found what I'd hoped I wouldn't: a picture of Wesley kneeling in front of a glass coffee table, dazzling in a sparkling silver headband that spelled out "Happy Birthday," all smiles as she surveyed the line of coke laid out before her.

Coulter hadn't even been at that party.

Footsteps thumped in the hallway, and Coulter strode into the kitchen triumphantly, a bottle of bitters in one hand and whiskey in the other. When he saw my stilted expression, he froze, lightness draining away. He looked for his phone, which was sitting a few feet away from where he'd left it. He could tell I'd been up to no good, but he got to work mixing our drinks, muddling sweet and bitter.

I suspected Coulter first learned about the money the night he sat next to Steve Camerino at Tad's poker game. A guy like Steve would've been bragging about the returns he'd gotten for Wesley. How lucky she was to have invested with him. A few artful questions and Coulter would've tied that money to my roommates and to the Circus.

Coulter and I had an argument a week later, which I could see now was no coincidence, about my roommates and how I always put them first. He warned me with an unusually sharp edge that he would give me one final chance to indulge in our little game, but after that, he'd leave if I didn't put an end to the Circus. What I didn't realize then was that he was effectively urging me to play, betting based on everything he knew about me and my roommates that none of us would be able to resist playing one more time when we discovered the prize was a million dollars. And he would be ready too.

The night the cops visited our apartment, I filled in the blanks for him. He pretended not to know any of the details of the Circus or the prize money, and he was a much better actor than I'd realized. What I couldn't figure out was when he'd decided he deserved the money more than any of my roommates did. Did he intend to clear a path for the two of us, or had his goal always been to take the pot for himself?

"How did you do it?" I asked, and he paused before pulling the ice tray from the fridge. "A dab of peanut butter? Or did you slip a drug into her drink?"

The ice cracked as he dislodged the cubes from their mold.

"There's a saying in Italian," he said, an edge in his voice. "*Fare la gatta morta.*"

"Playing a dead cat," I said, piecing together the broken Italian I'd picked up from hanging out with his family all these years.

"Literally, yes," he said. "But really it means a woman with hidden intentions."

He garnished our drinks with orange peels and handed me a glass.

"It was strange that a woman with life-threatening food allergies was so desperate to work in the restaurant," he said. "She had zero experience but talked such a good game. She was new to the city, needed the money and all that. Once she started, I thought she might be, you know, the kind of person who doesn't pick up on social cues. She kept asking about you, did you really go to Harvard, what that was like. And your roommates. She was always asking about your roommates."

He sounded annoyed that anyone could find my roommates interesting.

"It never occurred to me she might be related to Claudine," he said. "But I knew when I saw the picture on your computer."

"Were you sleeping with her?"

"No, nothing like that."

"Then why did you do it?" I asked, pushing farther into the kitchen, driving him toward the kitchen table. "Why did you want to kill her?"

He ran a hand through his hair.

"Sara, she was going to drag you through the mud. Make you pay. She's been pushing Claudine's case. I'll bet you didn't even know the Middlesex County DA is her cousin."

Pay off the restaurant's loan. And we'll still have enough to set up in Indonesia or Vietnam. We won't have to worry about the DA coming after you. And we can focus on writing and photography, just like we promised."

I considered what life on the other side of the world might be like. Coulter pitching editors with the hope of turning one of his stories into a book, while I tried to sell photos to tourists to keep us bouncing along. I could picture happiness, or at least moments of peaceable contentment—but only if I could forget the lengths to which he'd gone.

And then it occurred to me that we'd talked about traveling across Asia, but never specifically about Indonesia or Vietnam. Only then did I wonder if he had singled out these two countries because they lacked an extradition treaty with the US. I couldn't be prosecuted there for a crime committed here.

I pictured Dina sitting at our corner table in Hugo's diner with her two medallions, confident I'd arrive any minute to make good on my end of our deal. The thought turned my stomach, especially after I'd doubted her. It was obvious now that Coulter had left that note for Bee at the luncheon and had emailed Wesley the picture from her birthday. He'd never felt animosity toward Allie, but he'd always seen Dina as a threat. What had he done in his desperation to drive her from the Circus?

When it hit me, I felt a boundless, feral rage. He must've sent the anonymous letter that sank Dina's tenure. A baseless claim of plagiarism that cast a shadow over decades of hard work. Her entire career, leveled by his greed.

"This was always about you," I said, "wasn't it?"

I grabbed the santoku. We stood facing each other in the kitchen.

"You might have three medallions," I said, "but you won't get the money without five."

He smiled at this.

"One thing I've always admired about your roommates is how

I was floored; how had I missed this? Then I remembered Cl[audine] dine saying she had relatives in Boston—her uncle's family, but th[ey] weren't close. Her mother and uncle hadn't spoken in years.

"I went to Clementine's place to tell her it was over. That she w[as] done with her con, with whatever she had on you. She stood the[re] with this stupid little smile, pretending she was so innocent."

His face was clenched with the hot-blooded anger I knew stil[l] lived within him, even if he had pretended to bury it. There was nothing Coulter despised more than disloyalty, especially from someone he felt he'd gone out of his way to help. He had no mercy for that kind of betrayal.

"But what you did to her—"

"Sara, do you really want to spend the rest of your life shooting ads for disposable razors?" he asked testily. "I can't do this anymore. You don't know what it feels like in the kitchen, always shorthanded, always playing catch-up. I'm constantly bending over to make the staff, the customers, the vendors, even my own mother happy. One little mistake and we don't make our numbers for the night, which means we're short for the week and the month too. Just once I want to have a weekend. A social life. I worked eighteen hours last Wednesday. Eighteen hours. A random fucking Wednesday, and we barely broke even."

I looked down; I was now standing where he had been earlier, his mise en place laid out to one side, the knife, the cutting board, the mortar and pestle arranged so neatly.

"She was trying to take what's ours," he said, a flinty resolution in his eyes.

He had always believed he deserved more; the wound of his father's abandonment still festered. I should have known this life was never going to be enough for him. While I didn't blame him for holding on to the dogged hope that he should be exceptional, I knew the grim, ruinous place where that kind of thinking led.

"Sara, think about it. We can fix the ceiling and sell this place.

determined they are. Dina or Wesley will show up with the other two."

This was the man I had married, whom I admired and adored. We were both children of immigrants, borne of parents who didn't stick around, so we'd learned to fight for our futures. But when had our understandings of how the world worked and what we deserved diverged so dramatically? I thought of his family's saying that no matter where I turned, I'd always end up back at home. It had struck me as warm and lovely before, but it now took on a sinister tone.

I had to warn Dina.

He came at me then, and before I could react, he had me on the ground. We struggled, the knife torn away from me, and while I fought mightily, he was overpowering me, twisting my wrist until I felt an arcing pain race up through my shoulder. I screamed, and the piercing noise gave me a split-second reprieve. Enough to reach up to the counter and grab the stone mortar. He didn't even see the blow coming.

Coulter lay motionless on the kitchen tile. I hurried to the closet for a fleece blanket and rolled him onto it, then dragged him with everything I had out of the kitchen and down the hallway to the bathroom. Once he was inside, I yanked the bathroom door closed as hard as I could, the knob wobbly in my hand. The door would hold, but not for long.

I worked methodically from room to room, turning over the contents of Coulter's drawers, feeling around the back of our closet, searching every inch of our kitchen cupboards. I rifled through the shelves and cabinets in our living room. I was stumped. Had I badly miscalculated? Were the three medallions in the bathroom with Coulter? Picking up the first thing I saw, I hurled the silver cup that held Coulter's precious bar tools against the wall.

Strainers, juicers, and stirrers littered the floor. Among them lay three medallions engraved with Bee's, Allie's, and my initials on the backs, hidden in a place he never thought I'd look. As I scooped them up, I felt as if I was seeing myself from above: a woman standing among the scattered ruins of her marriage, her life.

Slipping on my jacket, I took in the long hallway I'd walked a thousand times, past the kitchen and living room that had been the locus of so much laughter and good food, and ending in the bedroom we shared. I wondered if I had deluded myself, purposefully ignoring the telltale signs in order to prove I could make this relationship a success. To experience the closeness that had eluded me when I was younger. And to show the world I was worthy of love.

My gaze snagged on the blue-and-white ashtray sitting on the hallway table. Our prize pilfered from a grand Paris hotel, where we'd vowed to come back as guests someday. The sight of it—a talisman of dreams—cratered me. For a moment, I was stuck between this life and the next, between the husband I'd thought I knew, and Dina, anxiously awaiting my arrival. Between a love that flew too close to the sun and one that always brought me back down to Earth.

Cognizant of the mistakes I'd made, of failing to tell people what they meant to me, I had no intention of repeating a terrible history.

It was twenty to nine. I grabbed the ashtray and started to run.

25

THREE weeks later, I stepped inside Hugo's diner to find that while my life had been upended, the place was the same. It still reeked of buttery onions and burnt coffee. The waitress punched receipts on a metal spike, and Hugo barked orders through the kitchen window.

Wesley loved the diner's obstinate refusal to change. A younger me would have disagreed, painting its stubbornness as a betrayal. In the wake of my mother's death, I was exasperated by friends who cycled through English classes and soccer games, haircuts and check-ups, going about their lives as usual. The adults were the worst—their small talk at the carpool circle betrayed how oblivious they were to my upside-down world. The mere sight of them laughing on the sidewalk outside our little brick school made me want to scream.

With the benefit of time and perspective, I was coming around to Wesley's point of view. Maybe the years had made me calloused, or just pragmatic, but I was making peace with the way that life marches on despite us. There was comfort to be found in consistency.

After the Circus ended, I changed the locks to the apartment and hid myself inside. The feelings I'd sewn up for so long seeped through in unexpected waves, swinging me from wrenching guilt to paralyzing shame, from uncontrollable rage to nothingness. I kept returning to something a famous biographer once said about reconciling contradictions in his subjects, how once you really got into the psyche of a person, apparent incongruities weren't inconsistent at all. I didn't know how Coulter could be so loving and supportive of me, of his mother, of the restaurant his family treasured—and also so unhinged.

In the fleeting moments when clarity chased away the dull-edged haze of regret and despair, I could see that both of these things were true.

I scanned the counter and the tables lining the window. Allie gave a lukewarm wave from the corner, the same table where I'd sat with Wesley a few weeks ago.

"Didn't think you'd come," Allie said when I wound my way over. She looked like she'd been washed and hung to dry.

"Neither did I," I said.

I had ignored Bee's text the day before suggesting the five of us meet up. I was wrestling with enough of my own guilt that I wasn't sure if I could shoulder their blame, too, without falling apart. But I understood that if I didn't show myself today, the shame I felt now would be twice as daunting later. And in my gut, I knew I needed to be here to make amends.

We ordered coffee that we finished quickly and a piece of cheesecake neither of us touched. Allie checked the time, suggesting we give the others a few more minutes, but I was grateful for this time alone with her. We both had questions, and we were feeling our way through unfamiliar terrain, so I started simply.

"How are you doing?" I asked.

"Taking it day by day."

"Things okay with Brad?"

She raised a hand and signaled to the waitress for more water.

"Better now. He suspected something was up. He didn't know where I was going every day, but he knew I wasn't going in to work. Chloe put it together first."

Allie sat back as the waitress brought her a glass of water and refilled her coffee. I begged off on the coffee, already feeling a little disoriented.

"I guess I was afraid," Allie said. "I didn't want to let him down. He understood why I wasn't straight with him, but the thing he couldn't get over was why I thought he needed a certain lifestyle. I assumed he didn't want to move to South Orange because it would be a step down, and that really set him off. He doesn't care about money or status. Never has. I should've known that about him."

"And what about you?" I asked.

"I think I'm gonna be okay," she said with real effort.

I bit my lip to stifle the churning emotions I was feeling.

"And Chloe?" I asked.

"She's good," Allie said, a faint note of wariness in her voice.

"Tell me about her."

"Apps are in, so we're waiting to hear back from colleges. Hard to believe she'll be gone in the fall. She devours sci-fi novels. The more squalor, disease, and oppression, the better. An expert on how to survive when the world ends. For Halloween, she and her friends were rock-and-roll zombies, whatever that is. Still wants to believe in Santa Claus, though."

"She's a good kid," I said.

"The best," Allie said with a proud smile.

I pictured Chloe on the sidewalk in front of her music school, shoulders thrown back, fiercely protective of her mother.

"What's she doing tomorrow?" I asked. "Mind if I come see her?"

Allie downed her water and chewed on the ice.

"Pretty sure she's got school."

"After school, then," I said, warming to the idea. "I could take her for ice cream."

Allie hesitated.

"What?"

"I'm sorry for swapping you out for Bee, but you didn't seem all that committed," Allie said.

"That's fair," I said.

"Don't get me wrong. Brad and I would be thrilled to have you in her life, but only if you're gonna follow through."

Allie was right. I had no business asking anything of her. But of all the mistakes I'd made—most of which I couldn't undo—this one, at least, I could fix. I made a silent promise to invite Chloe to a concert, dinner, or even an ice cream run before the week's end. This time I would make it happen.

"I haven't been there for Chloe. Or for you. I'm sorry, Allie."

"Well," she said, "we're here now."

I wanted to leap over the table and squeeze her tight, but I could tell by the way her face lit up that the others had arrived. Allie was pushing out of her seat.

Bee hobbled toward us, trailed by Wesley, who shouted a greeting to Hugo. Allie and I were on our feet, eager to help, but Bee waved us away as she pulled off her black fedora. The bandage around her head was smaller, but her hair was cropped close, and she winced with every step. Allie helped Bee pull the cast on her left arm through her coat sleeve.

"God, I love this place," Bee said, falling into the chair next to me as Allie hung her coat and retook her seat. Bee grimaced, trying to put on a brave face. I could see how hard the adjustment might be when you were used to being the strong one, the golden one.

"Best Taylor ham and egg in the tristate area," Wesley said, dragging a chair over and settling in at the end of the table. I smiled, knowing it was true.

"How are you feeling?" I asked Bee gingerly, and she turned the whole of her torso toward me like her neck was stiff. She struggled to find the right words, which was disconcerting to those of us who had always envied her command of language.

"It'll take some time," Bee said, and we rushed to reassure her. If the doctors said six months, Bee would get there in three, though it was obvious the road ahead would be long.

We sat together in a pregnant silence; the moment felt significant. Bee bowed her head and put her good hand on my shoulder, letting it rest there. From this small act, a wave of gratitude rose up, threatening to wash me away. I was relieved when Allie beckoned to someone behind me, so I could dry my eyes without being too obvious.

Dina slipped in quietly next to Allie, and I could tell every muscle in her body was tense. We hadn't spoken since that last night of the Circus, when I barreled into the diner at two minutes before nine, but felt so overwhelmed by everything that had happened that I ran out a few minutes later without a word. I owed Dina an apology for thinking she had betrayed us. Her distrust of Coulter wasn't misplaced after all.

Wesley asked the question on everyone's mind.

"Should we talk about Coulter?"

They turned to me for answers. Their scrutiny was enough to render the neat script I'd rehearsed into a tangled alphabet soup, but maybe it was better this way. My roommates deserved the unvarnished truth.

"He's out on bail. Staying with his mom in Cohasset." I was surprised to find myself swerving to avoid his name. I wasn't sure why I still needed to keep up some kind of facade. We'd seen beauty and ugliness in each other, and still we were here together.

"For pushing you?" Wesley asked, unsure if she should be directing her question to me instead of Bee. Bee gestured at me as if to say this was my story, that it would be good medicine for me to tell it.

"Bee recused herself from the investigation," I said, "so it sounds like that piece will take more time. They know he tried to grab Bee's medallion, but they're still looking at what happened after that. Whether the push was intentional." Speaking the words aloud made me acutely aware of the damage Coulter had done. "But on the other thing, Bee charged him—"

"My office," Bee corrected me.

"Bee's office charged him for what happened to Clementine."

"What's the charge?" Allie asked.

"Attempted murder," I said, and the words settled over us like a wet blanket. Though I knew it was the right way forward, I needed to gather my courage for the trial, which reminded me. "I know you can't talk about the case, Bee, but your associate has been amazing.

She thinks they'll get a conviction. Thank you for everything you've done."

"It's my job," Bee said, "but you're welcome."

Allie started to say something, but Bee cut her off with a reproachful look. Hugo sidled up and slid a platter of cinnamon buns on the table, pushing the untouched cheesecake toward the window. Dina shifted uncomfortably in her seat.

"On the house," Hugo said, and then pointing at me, "as long as this one doesn't start turning the place upside down again." He beamed at me, then at all of us, and Wesley jumped up to hug him before he headed back to the kitchen. Allie, Bee, and Dina shot me quizzical looks, but Wesley and I just burst into laughter. The others waved us off and helped themselves to freshly baked buns, tearing into them with a gnashing of teeth that made me think they hadn't eaten a square meal in weeks. Probably none of us had.

"And what about you, Sara?" Wesley asked between bites. "What will you do now?"

"I don't know," I said, and it was the truth. My accounts were zeroed out. Selling our old car would cover day-to-day expenses for a while, but it wouldn't be long before I lost the apartment, which had moved to the next stage in the foreclosure process since Coulter was six months delinquent on the payments. I would file for divorce when I could come up with the money to hire a lawyer—I'd already put what I had toward engaging a defense attorney, who charged a staggering hourly rate. The commercial job was long gone, but I'd applied to a few portrait studios. Working with kids and families was work I could enjoy—far more than shooting razors and shaving cream.

Still, there had to be a reason why I'd ended up here. A reckoning, and also an opportunity. I still hoped to work on the matriarchal societies project, but the international version felt too bound up with Coulter's dream of dashing off clever dispatches from far corners of the world. I would instead try to put together a series with the matriarchs who ruled the communities a few blocks from where I lived—the mothers and grandmothers who had overcome unimaginable obstacles to make their way here, fighting on behalf of their kids and grandkids for the right to live in relative peace.

"I may be shooting school portraits for a while."

"What about your series on invisible women?" Allie asked.

"I'll figure out how to get back there when the time is right," I said. "I have an idea for a new series. Fabby thinks there's potential. When I have a few decent photos, she said she'll put in a good word around town."

Wesley nodded, and Allie clapped quietly. Dina hadn't said a word, but I caught a softening in her eyes and I could tell she was pleased.

The waitress squeezed in behind Wesley, shot glasses dangling from one hand. She dropped the glasses on the table, and before Allie could tell her we hadn't ordered drinks, she rushed off to serve a couple at the other end of the counter. Hugo ambled over, clutching a stout, dusty bottle.

"Heard your friend almost died," he said, as he filled each little glass to the rim.

Dina's curious expression told me we were wondering the same thing: Had Clementine been our friend? Yes, I supposed she was. In a way, she'd been chasing what we had been after for years: making sure Claudine's life had meaning.

"Don't know if you heard. We're getting run out of here in June," Hugo said, shaking his head to a chorus of moans and protests. "Thirty-five years this place has been in my family."

"That's fucking awful," Wesley said, and he gave a solemn nod.

"All good things come to an end," he said and rapped on the table as he took his leave. "You girls take your time."

"Speaking of endings," Bee started in as she dragged one of the glasses toward her, careful not to spill. "The Middlesex County DA is dropping our case."

Wesley raised her hands above her head in victory. Allie cupped a hand over her mouth. I felt numb.

"Why?" Dina asked.

"They wouldn't say," Bee said. "But it surprised me too."

My roommates donned accusatory looks and took turns protesting their innocence, but I had a feeling this was Clementine's doing.

Wesley raised a glass.

"Good fucking riddance," she said, and this was something I could toast.

The others tossed their shots back enthusiastically, but I had little desire to drink. I wanted to hold on to this moment, when an upside-down world was beginning to right itself, though I had amends to make. Wesley, surprisingly superstitious for a woman of science, said an untouched drink was an insult to our host, so I flipped the liqueur back and couldn't help wincing at the flaming trail of licorice that blazed down my throat.

When I looked up, Dina was whispering urgently in Wesley's ear, their expressions deadly serious. I was grateful they had put aside their usual bickering to avoid making an uncomfortable day worse, but when Wesley nodded with surprising deference, my curiosity was piqued. Dina burrowed into her bag and came up with a thick stack of manila envelopes.

"This is what we should've done from the start," Dina said as she handed each of us an envelope.

Allie didn't wait; she rifled through hers, eyes lighting up at its contents. Bee, who wasn't often caught unaware, regarded hers with curiosity; she knew what was inside, but she was more interested in how these envelopes had made their way to us, since Dina and Wesley had a pretty consistent record of lining up on opposite sides. Wesley sat back in her chair, taking us in with the wide-eyed look of a kid waiting to blow out the candles on her birthday cake. Dina was watching me.

This wasn't what I had envisioned when I handed Dina three

medallions. My hope was that she'd keep the money for herself. I wanted a different future for her—one that took her far from the narrow, unyielding path she'd walked her whole life. A new beginning. Room to breathe.

"Say something, you ingrates," Wesley said.

"Thank you," Allie said, her voice wobbling. She bowed her head, clutching the envelope to her chest. I imagined she was thinking about her girls, their futures, college tuition. She might start sleeping through the night.

"I think what Wesley means," Dina said, "is that the money belongs to all of us."

I pushed my untouched envelope toward the center of the table.

"Each of you should keep yours, but I can't take this," I said. "Wesley, donate mine to the clinic."

I started to get up, worried I'd embarrass myself if I stayed any longer, but Bee pointed at my chair. I lowered myself back down.

"No," Dina said, pushing the envelope back at me. "If you hadn't given me your medallions and gotten Bee's, too, we'd be writing a fat check to Harvard right now. Per the damn contract."

Bee laughed, and we joined in.

"What's this clinic we're donating to?" Bee asked when the laughter died down.

Wesley sat back in her chair, her expression turning serious.

"I quit," Wesley said, but no one had any idea what she meant. "Orthopedics."

I was stunned. I understood why she could no longer inhabit the same universe as her father, but congratulations didn't feel right, either, not when she was walking away from a career she'd chased her whole life.

"That's not all—I forwarded my father the photo," she said, and we understood immediately what she had done.

"Wes—" I said. She could be impulsive, but her tranquil expression suggested I didn't need to worry.

"You reminded me of the promise we made that night in Montauk," Wesley said, and I realized she was talking to me. "We were such babies then. We had no clue what real life would be like, how much of it is out of our control. So I sent my father the photo and told him I don't want his money. I'm done living by his rules."

"Wesley," I said, but my voice failed me. I wanted to tell her how excited I was about this new direction, how proud I was of her, but all I could do was wipe my eyes with the back of my hand.

"Good for you, Wesley," Bee said.

"When will you go?" Allie asked.

"To Santa Fe?" Wesley asked. "As soon as possible." The light I'd seen at the kickoff dinner resurfaced in her eyes. "I'll do primary care for a few months, see if I remember anything from med school. Get the clinic up and running."

I put my envelope in the middle of the table and Wesley laid her envelope on top of mine. This time, Dina didn't protest.

"I guess I'll go next," Bee said hesitantly. "You've probably heard the campaign is off. I'll finish my term, but after that I'm planning to spend more time with Doye and the kids."

Allie rushed in to say something—probably an assurance this wasn't the end, just a break from politics—but Bee held up a hand, signaling she was okay with where things had landed.

"I don't regret being ambitious," Bee said. "I'm proud of what I've done at the DA's office, but I haven't always been there when Doye and the kids needed me. I want to work on that."

She held up her envelope.

"Can you give this to the clinic in Claudine's name?"

Wesley nodded, and Bee placed her envelope on the pile. After a long pause, Dina did the same. Wesley grabbed Dina's envelope and threw it at her.

"What?" Dina asked. "My money's not good enough?"

"It's got nothing to do with that," Wesley said, and I stiffened, fearing what Wesley was about to reveal.

Wesley and I were the only ones who knew about the anonymous letter accusing Dina of plagiarism, which likely sank her bid for tenure. I had no proof, but I knew Coulter had sent it.

"Then what's the problem?" Dina asked.

I tried to catch Wesley's eye, but she was staring down into her lap, mulling something over. Dina had a right to know about the letter. Our friendship might not recover, but perhaps knowing the truth would prevent Dina from blaming herself.

"You chose to share the pot with us when you could've taken it all for yourself," Wesley said. "I appreciate that."

"Thank you, Wesley," Dina said, and she meant it.

Wesley caught my eye and gave me a quick nod, as if to say everything was going to be okay. She was right that this wasn't the time or place to share what we knew, but I resolved to tell Dina before too long. Once we had put the Circus behind us.

Allie was still clutching her envelope, but when she realized she was the last one, she started to lay her envelope on the pile. Dina pushed her hand away.

"Don't even think about it," Dina said. "Keep it for your girls."

Allie looked unsure, but we didn't back down.

"I put in for a teaching program," Allie said. "Aimed at getting midcareers to teach in New Jersey public schools. We'll see if they take me."

"Allie, you gotta be kidding," I said. "Having you as a teacher would be like winning the lottery."

Allie beamed.

"Watch out for those high school boys," Bee said. "They can be wily."

"Actually, I want to work with younger kids. Third or fourth grade. Still moldable in my image."

"Still wily," Bee said with a laugh.

"Never thought at my age I'd be starting over," Allie said. "But hey, plans change."

We voiced our hearty agreement. It felt right that Allie should finally have a chance to do the thing she'd always wanted. Freed from her father's shadow, Wesley was putting her own mark on the world. Bee seemed much less heartbroken about her break from public life than I would've expected, and maybe time with family would be a gift she didn't anticipate. But I still worried about Dina.

I remembered one of the last times the five of us were together before school let out, that spring of senior year. Claudine had been dead only a few months and the run-up to graduation—the parties, the pomp, the pageantry—felt bittersweet. A senior Bee had been infatuated with all year invited her to his graduation party in Montauk. We knew she had to go, and if she was going, we were all road-tripping south. On a Friday in mid-May, we drove down the coast in Allie's old beater. Allie took the wheel, Bee mapped out our course, Wesley recited the entirety of Ovid's *Metamorphoses*, and Dina and I took turns nodding off on each other's shoulders in the back seat. It still impresses me that we hopped in the car and drove eight hours on our friend's faint hope. Our peers might've been living this kind of peripatetic, windblown existence, but we were accustomed to following rules, trying to control every aspect of our lives. This was our golden opportunity to let go.

We got a flat tire in Connecticut, lost our way in a dicey part of the Bronx, and ate the best pancakes of our lives in a diner off the Long Island Expressway. Our adventure felt exhilarating and wild. We were undeterred when we rolled up to the party house and found a little cabin nestled in the dunes, a far cry from the grand manse that had taken root in our imaginations.

We pumped up Bee and she marched to the door, only to discover the party had been the night before—a real blowout. The host was nice enough—what a coincidence she'd been in the neighborhood, what were the chances that she was staying with a friend down the street, and did she want to come in and play poker with the guys—but she burst into tears the second she crawled back into the car. I expected we'd turn around and stay at Wesley's in the city before driving back to Cambridge, but Wesley wouldn't have it. We'd driven all this way. We were going to the beach.

We tromped across the dunes on a moonlit night, the sand damp and cold on our bare feet. Spring in Cambridge had been fickle, and thankfully we were still wearing wool sweaters and down puffers. We piled on our layers, and after we crested the last grassy dune to find the empty beach yawning before us, Wesley lifted her arms and threw herself down that hill, cartwheeling with all the furor she could muster. Soon we were all hurling ourselves toward the water, rolling, tumbling, until our hair and our underwear were full of sand.

I don't remember who suggested a fire, but Wesley was still smoking then, and soon we had a pile of driftwood that Dina kindled with the efficiency of an Eagle Scout. Clothes came off, Wesley liberated her emergency bottle of whiskey, and when we pooled our road-trip stashes of cookies and chips, we feasted like queens. The stories began to flow—what we thought of one another the first time we met in Harvard Yard, Wesley's reenactment of Bee's thwarted romance, the best and worst memories of the Circus. We paused only when the first light peeked above the horizon, spreading golden wings across the dunes. Dina stood up, proposing a toast to life. Wesley threw an arm around Dina and insisted we could do better than that. "To living unconditionally," Wesley shouted, and we howled with glee as we downed the whiskey in our water bottles. When we settled back around the fire, I made a point of soaking up as much of these women as I could—the shake of their heads, the peal of their laughter, the timbre of their voices—and where we'd come from, what we had done or achieved, melted away. I knew everything I felt in that moment was because of what we had shared.

"Sorry, guys," Allie was saying as she pushed up from the table. "My day to pick up Chloe."

Dina leapt up to give Bee a hand. Wesley gathered the coats from the rack.

"The reunion in June," Allie said, remembering. "Hotels are booking up. I found a house on the Cape we can rent for the week after. Plenty of room for spouses, kids, everyone. Are we in? Should I lock it down?"

Bee and Dina both nodded.

"Okay if I come too?" I asked, sliding out from the table.

I'd never been to a reunion before—they'd given up on me ever going. I was happy for classmates who were running companies and effecting good changes in the world, but I was always intimidated by the steady wave of success they had ridden since leaving Cambridge. And maybe I was running from Claudine's ghost. I could see now that I didn't need to spin a story about who I was or what I'd done with the last twenty years. It was enough to go as myself. Better, even, to go with my closest friends.

"That would be great," Allie said, unable to mask her surprise.

I was yanking on my coat when Bee put a hand on my shoulder. Without thinking, I rested my hand on top of hers.

"I feel the same, by the way," Bee said.

"About?"

"We should've cut the bullshit out earlier."

My eyes widened. Allie glanced from me to Bee. Dina looked amused by my embarrassment.

"You heard that?" I asked, then for the benefit of Allie and Dina: "Something I said to Bee when she was in the hospital. Didn't think she could hear me."

Bee grinned.

"Damn," I said, and Bee laughed, opening her arms for an affectionate hug.

The five of us moved outside. The wind had died down, and the snow had tapered to thick, soft flakes. We took turns embracing one more time. When a cab pulled up, Wesley, Allie, and Bee piled inside. Dina insisted she'd walk, and I fell in beside her. As we watched the cab pull away, I thought of the time we had spent together in Cambridge, when some fundamental part of our selves was forged, the crucible of our adulthood. I thought of the scars we carried, still visible yet fading with age. Mostly, I thought of the six of us, laughing together in our common room, feeling like the world was opening itself, like all the good luck we needed to make it out there lay within our shared walls.

"Dina, I should never have doubted you."

There was so much more to say, but Dina gestured toward the road, and we began to walk.

"Ever heard of the Grant study?" Dina asked.

I shook my head. I wanted to explain, to make things right, to know that we'd come through this. But this was how Dina made sense of the world. Dina and her stories.

"Longest-running longitudinal study in history. Started following so-called normal Harvard sophomores in the forties. Tracking everything in their lives, including—I'm not making this up—the length of their scrotums."

I laughed. Dina adjusted her glasses.

"The subjects are in their eighties now, half still alive. The goal was to figure out what made them successful. Able to paddle their own canoes, as they called it. Know what they found?"

I shook my head.

"Turns out these shining stars had darker sides. Government officials, novelists, professionals. Even JFK was a subject. By the time they hit fifty, a third of them showed some kind of mental illness."

This was Dina's way of saying that even the best of us had shortcomings. Her way of acknowledging our failings, forgiving one another and ourselves for being a little less—no, a little different—than what we thought we'd be at this point in our lives. I felt a wave of gratitude and affection.

"There were mountains of data locked up in file cabinets in an office near Fenway," Dina continued. "For years, the press hounded the author of the study to distill all that data into a kernel of insight. Know what he said?"

I shrugged.

"The only thing that made a difference was their relationships."

It wasn't where I'd expected Dina to land, not when we both struggled with expressing what we felt and articulating what we needed. We trudged on in silence. When I looked up, Dina had pulled away, her hands jammed deep into her pockets, shoulders folded in. She interpreted my silence as the same dismissal she had felt in the early hours of graduation day on Weeks Bridge, when Dina professed a bond of kenzoku between us. I was a coward then—I wouldn't make the same mistake again.

I rushed to pull a book from inside my jacket. The last of my mother's gifts, a 1960 first edition of *To Kill a Mockingbird*, given to me when I was thirteen and a half. While it wasn't easy to let it go, I knew Dina would appreciate it as much as I did, perhaps even more.

Dina traced the letters on the cover's aging cloth, flipped it open. Her face lit up at the signature inside. Then her expression wobbled, her composure on the verge of crumbling. She knew what this particular book meant to me, but apart from that I wasn't sure what it evoked for her. She had plucked an old copy from my bookshelf a few weeks after she arrived at school our junior year, claiming she'd read it dozens of times, and I was thrilled to find we had this in common. I'd assumed she shared my secret adoration of Atticus, the father neither of us had, but she pointed out the book's shortcomings, criticizing Atticus for being a flawed hero. I swelled with embarrassment. How naive and unquestioning my view of the world had been. How blind I'd been to the nuance and complexity she saw so clearly.

She bowed her head and clutched the book to her chest. I let her take her time.

"We become aware of the void as we fill it," Dina said when we started walking again. I held the thought, refusing to run from it.

"An Argentine poet wrote that," Dina explained. "Worked as a printer and a basket weaver, shirtless most of the time. He knew nothing about the popular philosophers. Didn't subscribe to any doctrine or dogma. Published one little volume. Some think he was the greatest poet of all time."

Dina tucked the book under her arm and stuffed her hands back into her pockets. I knew this was Dina's idea of a hero: a humble man achieving unexpected greatness.

"So what happens next?" I asked as we started to walk again, shoulder to shoulder.

"The tenure committee will make an exception. They'll reconsider next year, if I can get my book published."

"Dina, that's great news. And I know you'll do it. Publish, I mean."

She look unconvinced, but not bothered.

"I've been talking to a guy I know at Berkeley. They might be looking to add a tenure-track position to their department next year. In the meantime, they're open to a new lecturer if the budget gets approved."

"You'd go to California?"

"I know," she said with an incredulous laugh. "The whole idea is terrifying. But exciting too. I'll have to dye my hair pink or get a nose ring or whatever it is they do out there."

"Or you could go as yourself," I said, and she seemed to like the sound of that.

A westward migration felt right. The distance and the chance to reinvent herself would be good for Dina. I didn't know when we'd see each other again, but I knew we wouldn't call. We wouldn't write. The things we wanted to say couldn't be squeezed into a few otherwise wasted minutes. Short notes took thought and effort, but even rambling ones required a certain intimacy that had never come easily to us. We'd think of each other at unexpected moments. We would wonder what the other was reading, who she was spending time with, what she thought about where the world was going. Most of all, I'd wonder if time was being good to Dina. If she'd found contentment.

The more I thought about it, the more I loved the idea of California for Dina. It was the perfect next chapter, even if we never imagined it. Berkeley would challenge not only Dina's understanding of who she was, but how narrowly she defined success. She might realize she wasn't stepping down, but out into a field of possibility.

Dina and I stood together in a comfortable silence, neither needing to fill the space between us. When she disappeared through a curtain of falling snow, I felt awash in a strange peace. An expansiveness I remembered from childhood, when life was full of warmth and our futures seemed infinite. A sense that Dina and I had walked this same path in a previous life, and we were feeling the aftereffects in this one, which Dina had once described on a spring day in Cambridge as kenzoku.

As I turned away that afternoon, I thought of Dina, of Bee and Allie, of Wesley, and of Claudine, of the ways in which our lives were braided together, and I felt lucky to be on this journey with them. Each of us saw a better version of one another than she saw in herself. And we all felt like we'd gotten the better end of this deal we called friendship. We shared an unfettered desire that the other find only happiness. And this, it occurred to me, was what it meant to matter.

ACKNOWLEDGMENTS

I'M profoundly grateful to Michelle Brower, who continues to impress me as one of the kindest, most warmhearted people I know while also being an amazing advocate, and to Danya Kukafka, who read a very early draft of this novel ages ago and still signed up to coagent this project. Thank you, Danya, for lending your deep understanding of character and story to help make this book the best version of itself. I'm also grateful to the amazing team at Trellis, including Elizabeth Pratt, Allison Malecha, and Tori Clayton, as well as Carolina Beltran and Hilary Zaitz Michael at WME.

I feel so lucky that this book landed with my editor, Lara Jones, whose superb editorial eye and great sense of humor have made this process such a joyful one. My deep gratitude also goes to the team at Atria/Emily Bestler Books for their support, especially Libby McGuire, Emily Bestler, Dana Trocker, Karlyn Hixson, Abby Velasco, Falon Kirby, Aleaha Reneé, Paige Lytle, Shelby Pumphrey, James Iacobelli, Danielle Mazzella di Bosco, and Janet Robbins Rosenberg, whose close reading and thoughtful copyediting fill me with awe.

I could never have written this book, nor would this story have become a book, without the incredible Carinn Jade. Thank you also to Kate Hope Day, Janice Y. K. Lee, Aran Shetterly, and Christie Tate for so generously sharing their wisdom, and to the Northern California Writers' Retreat, Page Street Writers, Aspen Words, GrubStreet, and Community of Writers for showing me the beautiful power of supportive writing communities. I owe so much to Heather Lazare for giving me the last spot at her retreat and for introducing me to Michelle.

A big hug to Alexandra Lawani, Eric Lee, Wynee Sade, Janine

ACKNOWLEDGMENTS

Shiota, and Kimberly Twombly for listening and encouraging. And to my college roommates Eliza Parker, Rhian Thompson, and Lina Yoo, I carry you with me always. Your lifelong friendship is a gift.

I'm grateful to my father for the many tales he told me as a kid, some of which maybe weren't entirely true, but sparked something nonetheless, and to my mother, whose story merits a book of its own. Skylar, your insight and wit make me marvel, and, Theo, your compassion and humor brighten my day. To Erik, the extrovert in the family, I appreciate your optimism and love, as well as your dogged refusal to let me hide for too long when there is so much we still want to do.

And to you, my reader, thank you for spending your valuable time with me.